MW01042174

H E Λ I O Γ P A Π H I

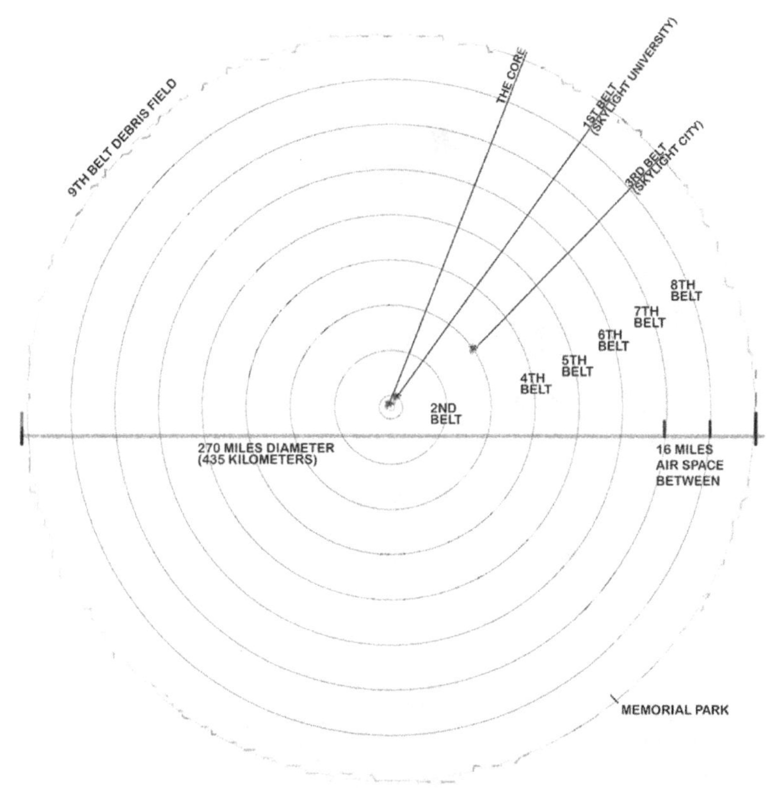
9TH BELT DEBRIS FIELD
THE CORE
1ST BELT
(SKYLIGHT UNIVERSITY)
3RD BELT
(SKYLIGHT CITY)
8TH
BELT
7TH
BELT
6TH
BELT
5TH
BELT
4TH
BELT
2ND
BELT
270 MILES DIAMETER
(435 KILOMETERS)
16 MILES
AIR SPACE
BETWEEN
MEMORIAL PARK

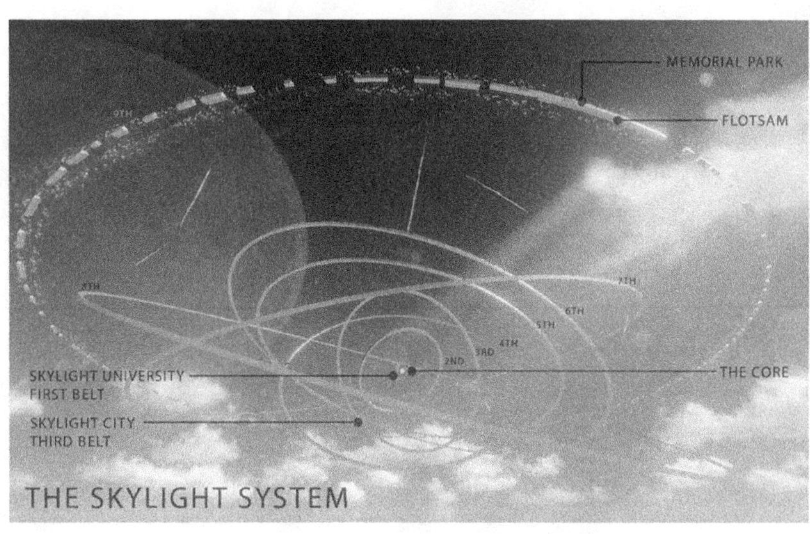
MEMORIAL PARK
FLOTSAM
9TH
8TH
7TH
6TH
5TH
4TH
3RD
2ND
SKYLIGHT UNIVERSITY
FIRST BELT
THE CORE
SKYLIGHT CITY
THIRD BELT
THE SKYLIGHT SYSTEM

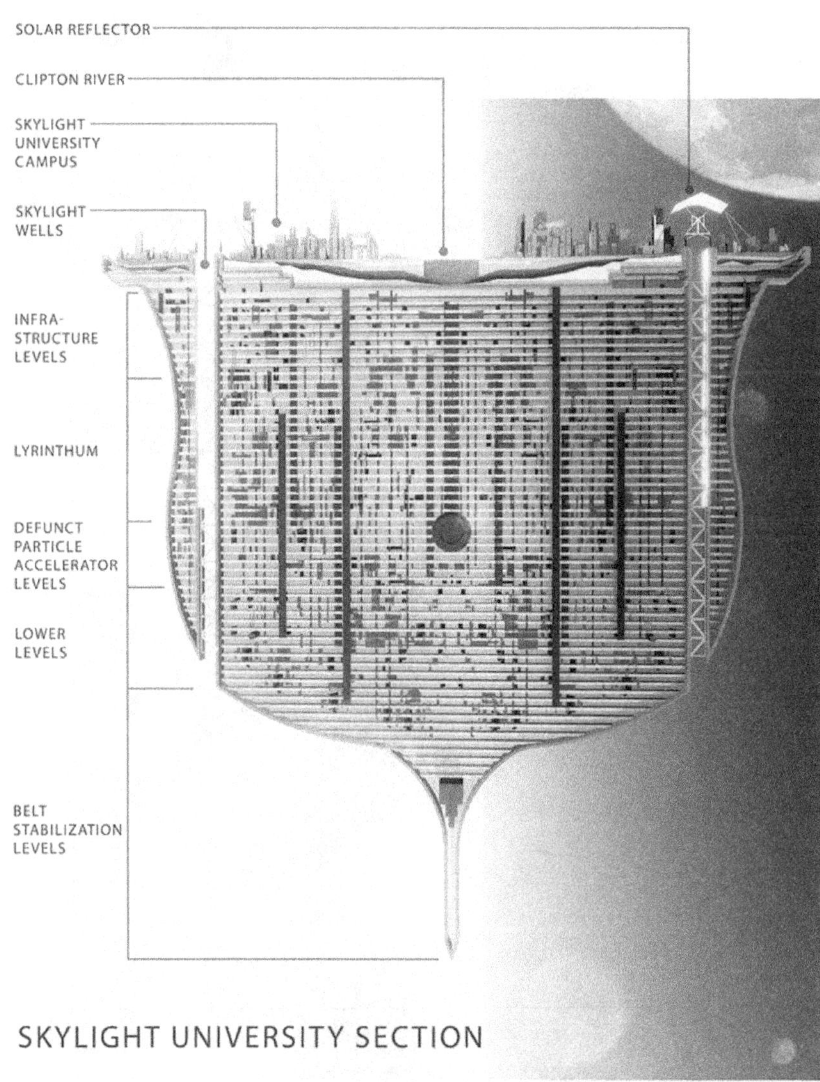

SKYLIGHT UNIVERSITY SECTION

THE PRISM AFFECT

THE PRISM AFFECT

J WINT

"If you want to find the secrets of the Universe, think in terms of energy, frequency, and vibration."

-Nikola Tesla

For Allen

CONTENTS

CHAPTER

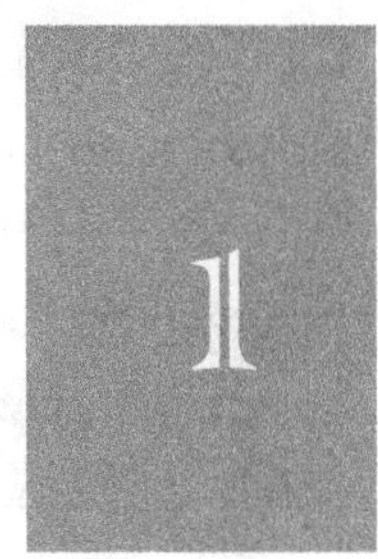

Skylight University

ΑΒΓΔΕΖΗΘΙΚΛ**M**
ΝΞΟΠΡΣΤΥ**Φ**ΧΨΩ

MYRANDA MASON WATCHED the blood-red moon drift in and out of the thickening cloud cover.

She wiped sweat from her brow with her sleeve and cursed at the humidity. The balmy evening signaled the onset of a storm, thanks to the early autumn heat. Looming thunderheads stood at attention along the horizon and threatened to choke out the moon's garish luminance. Having lived her entire life in the Skylight System, she knew storms were rare events and shouldn't be taken lightly. Tonight would be a bumpy night.

Thunder rolled in the distance as she kicked off her cleats and stretched her long legs. She leaned back on her elbows to get a better view of the moon, letting its reddish light wash over the chiseled features of her face. The moon was so close that she could see its features with the clarity of a telescope. Its pitted craters and mare seas grinned at her menacingly as a scud cloud scurried by. It blotted out the moonlight momentarily, leaving only her bright glowing eyes in the darkness.

She winced as she bent her legs, her quadriceps and calves

still sore from running all week. The cursed timed trials, coupled with her insistent anxiety, made her feel mentally and physically drained. Competing for a spot on the varsity squad was a challenge she enjoyed, but one she doubted she'd win. No matter how hard she ran or how many records she set, she was still a *prep* student, which was one grade below a freshman. The odds weren't in her favor, but she would do her best anyway. Being a *prep* student hurt her chances, but it still wasn't her biggest problem. She was also known as a *euph*.

She kicked the bleacher in front of her. Anger coursed through her when she heard that word. It was offensive, though no one else seemed to think so. Since she'd never met another person like herself, she knew very little about her condition. However, her eyes had just started glowing with more intensity since last night, and it frightened her.

I'm eighteen... and so alone.

If the legend of ephebus mortem held true, she had perhaps six years—maybe less. The one thing she desired more than anything else was to graduate from Skylight University before she died. She didn't want to go down labeled as a skylight fallout, someone who couldn't finish the difficult curriculum. The semester hadn't even started, and she was already thinking about graduation. But, if she could just test out of a few classes, she could walk in less than four years. That was more important than making the varsity squad.

She kicked her legs out and sprawled across the bleachers, lost in thought. She loved the solitude of the track facility in the evenings. The vacant stadium, the stillness after a long day of practice. It was her favorite place to hang out—away from the constant stares and name calling. Here she could relax, recoup, and gather her thoughts. Here... she felt at peace.

Prepare.

The voice echoed in her head and made her sit up and look around.

"Hello?" she called out.

A thunderclap answered. The sound rolled across the silent stadium, accompanied by a flash of lightning.

The storm was gathering.

She glanced nervously at her watch and quickly decided it was time to take shelter. Besides, she would need a good night's rest if she wanted to compete tomorrow, even if there was little hope of making the team.

With a last look around the quiet stadium, she grabbed her cleats and hopped down the bleachers two at a time. When she neared the bottom, she sensed something out of place.

The wind kicked up in a brief gust. She reached up to brush her red hair back when a sudden pain shot through her head. She gasped and clamped her eyes shut, waiting for it to pass. The storm front swept in around her, and the energy from the lightning intensified as thunder shook the ground. She thought her head might explode as the pressure inside continued to build.

Her hands trembled.

She could feel a presence nearby, something unnatural and angry. A surge of panic hit her and she charged blindly across the field with her eyes still shut. The wind buffeted her from side to side as she tried to maintain her balance. But with her eyes closed and the nauseous feeling in her stomach, she slipped and tumbled to the moist turf. She felt lethargic, and her senses grew hazy. She struggled to her hands and knees.

Look at me!

The voice boomed inside her head, sending chills through her body. She tried desperately to keep her eyes shut now, afraid to see what was standing in front of her. But as much as she tried, she could not disobey the voice's command.

She opened her eyes and let out a piercing scream.

A black mass floated less than a meter in front of her. It was difficult to see, like a mirage on a hot day, and it shimmered malevolently in the clash of lightning.

She tried to stand and run, but her legs wouldn't respond, despite the adrenaline pumping through her veins. All of her will was focused on the apparition that held her captive with its gaze. Her eyes grew wide with terror as it slid a small needle-like cylinder out of thin air. It lifted a wisp of smoke where its arm should have been, and her left hand mimicked its motion. Lightning outlined the shadow like a distorted mirror as it slipped the sharp device through the middle of her outstretched palm. The nail-like tube punctured her skin effortlessly, exiting through the back. The apparition jerked the needle away, leaving a gaping hole in her hand. Blood spewed down her arm and onto the glistening turf, covering her clothes and shoes. She felt her body changing, burning from the inside with an intensity she'd never known before. A purple glow filled the void in her palm. The light pulsed in rhythm with her rapid heartbeat. The supernatural light emitted a symbol that floated just inches above the gaping wound. Warmth filled her chest and seemed to set her soul ablaze. Her scream rose to match the howling wind, equaling the storm's fury around her.

Her last thought was the realization that she wasn't going to make the track team and she wasn't going to graduate. She was going to die.

As her memory faded, the last thing Myranda saw was the smoldering glow of the monstrosity's eyes, a glow so similar to her own.

. • • • • ● • • • • .

Two glowing pinpoints of light stared back at Jet Stroud from the window's reflection. Like two disembodied apparitions hovering amidst the dark clouds beyond, they taunted him—just like everyone else had throughout his life.

He hated those lights.

His shoulder-length black hair glistened in contrast with his pale complexion. Hints of stress lines caressed his mouth and eyes, not typical for someone his age. He was average height and slim, but not skinny. Thick black eyebrows and lashes matched his hair, something common in most ARC citizens. Numerous scars adorned his face and knuckles, and his nose had been broken on more than one occasion from fighting, thanks to his peculiar condition. He pulled his gaze from the window.

Peculiar?

Or cursed?

If it were only that simple. Other kids back home weren't so polite. He was a freak, a mutant, and too many other names to recall. He tried not to dwell on his condition—or disease, as some called it—since there was no explanation for it. Thanks to the neon-like illumination of his eyes, he'd been ostracized. Few people talked to him or offered to help, leaving him to fend for himself, even as a toddler. This lifelong struggle had taken a toll on him in more ways than one. The only person who had ever treated him fairly was snoozing next to him.

Jet looked at Curtis Jade, or Cutter, as the kids had called him back home. His massive, tattooed arms rested tightly across his barrel chest. His dark curly hair matched his dark skin and lay matted awkwardly against his broad forehead. Along his brow glistened numerous piercings that matched his silver tattoos. His choice of clothing personified his attitude, old blue jeans with ragged hems and a plain t-shirt in bright red, sure to attract attention. Cutter wanted to be left alone and had made that abundantly clear that morning. Still, he'd chosen to sit next to Jet, proclaiming it had been the only seat left. Though Cutter had never taunted or fought him, Jet knew very little about him. Cutter was somewhat of a loner, like Jet. He'd never approached Jet or tried to talk to him, though, and Jet was perfectly fine with that.

They'd been aboard the spacecraft, or skiff, for most of the day. Jet had napped off-and-on throughout the trip but was wide awake now as they approached their destination. The display in front of him lit up and read, *Arriving at Skylight University, innermost belt of the Skylight System.*

The college sat nestled on the outer portion of a huge metal belt. Even though it was the smallest belt in the system, it was completely encompassed by the massive school. Its buildings sat at odd angles, jammed tightly in between one another. Lush vegetation covered the campus like a silky ribbon, deftly woven between the structures. Constructed of stark white stone, the buildings contrasted vibrantly with the green hues of the landscape. Even though each building was unique, they all shared a featherlike characteristic. The low-lying mist opened to emit a burst of sunlight, causing thousands of tiny rainbows to dance on the air in a spectacular array of colors. The momentary display lasted only seconds before the mist engulfed the sun again.

Their skiff started to descend, and Jet buckled into his seat as they dropped rapidly through the clouds. He felt a soft bump, followed by a slight hissing sound, and the other students onboard stirred and stood from their seats. Jet stepped into line behind Cutter. Everyone moved onto a large platform that floated high above the campus below. Once they were safely on the platform, a protective stasis field surrounded them.

"What's this thing?" Jet asked, trying to steady himself.

"I think it's called a vector accelerator, like an elevator but really fast," Cutter said but didn't offer anything more.

The platform began to drop rapidly. Oddly, Jet's feet stayed rooted in place, like gravity had glued his boots to the metal grate. Within seconds it slowed to a stop with a gentle thump.

Jet stepped off the vector accelerator, and a faculty member directed him toward another one not far away. The herd of boisterous students jostled for position as they made the short trek across the plush campus grounds. Jet took in quick glimpses of stone buildings towering majestically into the mist. Surprisingly, the curvature of the belt was barely noticeable. Only the horizon gave any hint that the belt wasn't flat.

Soon they were aboard a much larger vector accelerator that took them up to an odd-looking building. The huge globe-like structure was made of glass and steel; its facets shimmered like a mirrored ball. The surface resembled a fish's scales, translucent, and stretched taut over a steel ribcage of catwalks. Faculty members directed them onto the surrounding catwalks leading into the building.

Jet stepped into the vast inner globe and let his eyes adjust. The lower end of it housed a dimly lit stage, and only the windows at the top and bottom of the amphitheater emitted any sunlight. Thousands of chattering students buzzed excitedly as Jet and Cutter found an aisle near the bottom and settled in. He took a deep breath to relax himself amongst the crowd of people.

The stage in front of them floated about a meter off the floor. Cutter struck up a conversation with a girl behind them as Jet read a plaque about the scientist who'd invented the antigravitational technology.

"So, you're both trying out for the team?" Jet heard the girl ask and turned to face her.

She immediately pushed back in her seat when she met his gaze. "What's wrong with your eyes?" Then her expression changed, and she placed a hand to her mouth in shock.

Jet realized instantly that she knew about his condition. "If you have something to say, I'm listening."

"Seriously, you're asking me?" She raised her eyebrows in disbelief. "Listen, I'm not getting involved. Besides, I'm not going to be the one who breaks the news to you."

Jet held her gaze, trying to decide if he should press her further. He'd spent his entire life trying to find out more information about his condition. He knew he'd learn more once he arrived at Skylight but hadn't expected it so soon. He decided not to push her, though. It was only a matter of time before he found out exactly what was going on.

"Cutter says you're a good point-blazer," she said. "You thinkin' about trying out for the team?"

"Yeah, that's the goal anyway," Jet said.

"I hear Skylight has one of the best athletic programs around," Cutter said.

"And the toughest," she added.

Jet took in discrete glances of her as she talked. She was tall, lithe, and athletic. Her dark hair was straight and cropped inward towards her long neck.

"I didn't catch your name," Jet said. "Are you a blaze player, too?"

"I'm Plexus," she said, not bothering to clarify if it was her first or last name. "And yes, I'm trying out for the blaze-out position. So, you two played in a cave league?"

"The ARC district, actually," Cutter interjected. "It's a hell of a league."

"Really? That's odd because I've never heard of it. You boys aren't in a cave league anymore," she smirked, more-or-less directing it at Jet. "If you want one of the point-blazer positions, you're going to have to earn it. Most upper classmen hate preps on the varsity squad. They'll make your life hell. And I hear the head coach is a real ball-buster. Don't look for any favors."

"That's what they always say about head coaches." Cutter shrugged his massive shoulders.

"What's a prep?" Jet asked.

"Academy students," she said. "First year kids…like us. Didn't they tell you anything in those caves?"

"I guess not," Jet said. He didn't know if he would make the team at a demanding position like point-blazer. But if he did, he hoped Plexus wasn't on his squad.

A lady made her way up to the podium, and Jet turned his attention to the stage.

"Welcome students," she said. "My name is Professor Bhiner, and I am honored to be standing here in Orientation Station once again." She paused and stepped from behind the podium, walking gracefully along the edge of the floating stage.

"It's always a joy to welcome students to this prestigious academy and college. Since I cannot possibly tell you everything there is to know about our system in the allotted time, we will use the following three-dimensional presentation. But before we start, we must go back nearly one hundred years to a very special man by the name of Christian Albright. He was the visionary responsible for everything you see here." She raised her hands and motioned to their surroundings. Jet caught a brief flash of light from her ring but dismissed it as stray sunlight.

"This entire system was his creation," Bhiner continued, "but the Core is what makes it all possible. I won't go into detail about how it works; just know that without it, the Skylight System could not exist. Skylight University was the first college ever built in Earth's atmosphere, and this very belt was the first of nine constructed around the Core."

Jet noticed the strange flash of light from her ring several more times. But he was so intrigued by the presentation that he soon ignored it.

"Knowledge was Albright's desire," she continued. "And he felt that it should pave the way for our future. With it, we can learn to appreciate what we have and educate future generations. Nature, as we once knew it, no longer exists on Earth. But thanks to Albright, we have regained some hope. The holographic presentation you're about to see is a summary of the history of Skylight. So, sit back and enjoy." She touched the pad on the podium, and the presentation filled the entire amphitheater.

Jet felt suddenly immersed as if he were living out the events inside the hologram. The first scenes showed the Unbalance that had ravaged the Earth in the past century. Because of the storm, life in the underworld became the norm. People fled the surface and burrowed out vast cave-like systems like the ARC district where he and Cutter had lived. Life was bleak until Christian Albright came along. In his early years, he worked alongside well-known scientists to create his breakthrough called the Core. Mankind assembled a team of scientists, engineers, architects, and contractors to build it. Two decades later, nine orbiting belts were slipped into place around the Core, and the Skylight System was complete. Much of mankind left behind the desolation of the earth to live amongst the stars.

The system's designers looked to past city planners for inspiration. Inner belts of the system were designated as placeholders for humanity—living and working, study and leisure. The middle belts were reserved for industry, factory, and manufacturing. The outer belts held the resources necessary to support the system. Wood, sand, water, and rock, for building materials as well as designated areas for livestock and crops. Skylight City on the third belt was a bustling melting pot of activity. A great meteor storm had torn apart the ninth belt, and a place called Memorial Park now occupied its largest surviving portion. For day lighting, the designers had developed large light wells, or Skylights, carved into the belt at equally spaced intervals. Huge sails redirected sunlight evenly across the belt's surface, regardless of the sun's angle. And at the center of it all was Skylight University.

Professor Bhiner returned to the pulpit. "As you can see, our system is quite diverse, with its lakes and forests. Nature is at the center of Skylight, as Albright felt it should be."

She paused as the holographic presentation ended. "Your journey begins here. If you pass the academy, you're allowed to skip a year at the University. But understand that the academy is much more than a steppingstone. Succeed here, and nothing can stop you."

CHAPTER

2

Ephebus mortem

ΑΒΓΔΕΖΗΘΙΚΛ**M**
ΝΞΟΠΡΣΤΥΦΧΨΩ

SOMEONE HANDED JET a backpack and the same pad-like device Professor Bhiner had used. It was called a holopad and was slightly larger than his hand and lightweight. When he touched it, a three-dimensional display projected in front of his face.

"Crux Field is open to the public today, so we're going," Plexus said as she and Cutter stepped onto the vector accelerator. It didn't sound like an invitation, but he was anxious to see the stadium too and stepped onto the accelerator. She let out a sigh and shifted over as the accelerator plummeted.

Plexus and Cutter stepped off as soon as the accelerator landed, leaving Jet to follow. They chatted about blaze as he checked out his new holopad and its various functions.

Cutter wiped mist from his pierced brow. "Does it always rain here?"

"It's annoying, but you'll get used to it," Plexus said. "Something about the heat from the belts and how they interact with the limited atmosphere. Clouds gather around the belts, not above them. That's why there's usually so much mist."

As if on cue, the mist dissipated, and the clouds opened to let sunlight flood through. Thousands of tiny rainbows surrounded them in a wash of color, like a bucket of paint spilled from the heavens.

"It's called the Prism Effect," Plexus said. "The sun's angle is constantly changing because the belts are never stationary. You just never know which direction it will come from."

They wandered the campus, having no idea where the stadium was. Eventually, Jet took out his holopad, wondering if it might help. He located a three-dimensional map that showed the entire campus with the different departments labeled into sectors. He scrolled until he found Crux Field and touched that area on the map. The holopad pinpointed the stadium and projected a yellow path in front of them.

Jet led the way, occasionally pointing his holopad toward random buildings. One particular building caught his attention when something fluttered across the display. It reminded him of a heat mirage of sorts. He stopped, and Cutter ran into him.

"I think this thing's broken," Jet said, inspecting the device before pointing it back at the building.

"That's Alpha Hall," Plexus said. "We're looking for Crux Field."

"I know," Jet said. He shook the holopad. "I… just thought I saw someone's name, but no one's there now."

"What was the name?" Plexus asked and inched away from Jet and toward Cutter.

"Solan Alexander, at least that's what it said."

A soft chiming filtered from above, breaking the awkward

silence. They all looked up to see a huge floating time dial. Inside its clear chrome-colored envelope, large bells whirled and clanged announcing the time.

"Come on, we'd better hurry before the stadium closes," Cutter said.

Soon they saw the gigantic arena, and Jet put his holopad away. Floating above the stadium and illuminating the clouds was the holographic image of the school's crest.

"Notice the logo," Plexus said to Cutter, picking up her pace. "The torch surrounded by the nine stars."

"What about it?" Cutter asked.

"Well, I heard another student say there's a lot of mystery surrounding it. The torch is very similar to a lower-case letter i. Something to do with the Heliographi Memoirs and Christian Albright. I think we'll hear more about it in class."

In front of the stadium were thousands of students waiting in line for season tickets. They hurried past the line, up the monolithic steps, and into the arena. Soon they were standing before one of the most incredible sights Jet had ever witnessed.

Being inside Crux Stadium was like standing inside a giant upside-down bowl. The stasis dome towered high above, its transparent surface allowed them to see through to the misty sky. The artificial lighting seemed odd, perhaps from the dome's pulsating stasis field. Bleachers lined the inside of the dome and cantilevered out in smaller rings towards the top.

Jet stepped onto the playing field and noticed a group of students near the middle where a tour appeared to be taking place. They walked over to join it.

"...this field is the first ever to utilize Dr. Harllow's

antigravitational technology, and it has revolutionized the way field sports are played today," the tour guide said.

Jet looked down at the turf and noticed for the first time that it was made of a spongy substance that felt similar to the playing fields back home. There, hardy plants known as Shale Ferns were used to cushion the solid rock.

"And, when the games are played under the special lighting..." the tour guide continued, holding up his holopad and pressing an area on the floating display. The arena lights dimmed and faded to iridescent.

Jet looked down again and felt his knees threaten to buckle. The entire field had disappeared. Amazingly, it held the weight of their tour group without any signs of stress. He could see seating far below him now, making up the bottom half of the stadium. This was the secret behind cramming a quarter of a million fans into the stadium on game days. Jet felt like he was standing on thin air. He took a wobbly step but didn't fall.

Their tour guide continued, giving the crowd some background information about the sport of blaze. "Blaze is based on another popular sport from a past era. It can be a rough game and involves running, passing, and blocking. Each team is comprised of three separate squads. The main squad in the middle gets more points than the two flanking squads if it scores. It also gets an additional mid-blazer and two blaze-blockers, which is necessary because it's more vulnerable. The two flanking defensive squads can blitz if ignored. And the game gets really exciting when the squads intermingle or team up. Without a good point-blazer, things can get confusing. Well, that's pretty much it. Any questions?" the guide asked.

Jet had heard enough and turned to leave. He stumbled into another group of students and tried to walk around them, but several blocked his path. Jet recognized them as upperclassmen, judging by their varsity blaze clothing.

"That's Korbin Daze," Plexus whispered. "Skylight's lead point-blazer."

Daze stood in the middle of the group. His hair was cropped close to his scalp in military fashion, and a hooked nose dominated his facial features. His t-shirt had his uniform number and the school crest on it, and was stretched tight across his muscled chest. Daze stood statue-like with his arms crossed and stared at Jet.

"Preps," one of the players whispered to Daze. He nodded without looking away from Jet.

"You're in the wrong place," he said. "Especially you, Stroud. Yeah, I know who you are."

Jet wasn't sure what to say. He wanted to give Daze the benefit of the doubt, but so far, Plexus appeared to be right. These upperclassmen seemed hell-bent on making things difficult.

Daze nodded to Plexus. "I've heard about you. They say you're one of the fastest blaze-outs around. So why are you hanging around this guy? You don't want to ruin your chances of making the team."

"I'm sure she can make up her own mind who she hangs out with," Cutter said calmly.

Daze looked at Cutter for the first time. Daze was large but still had to look up at Cutter. "You know you're going to have to go through me, right? I make the rules around here. This is my team."

At least eight upperclassmen surrounded Daze. Cutter looked at them and then back to Daze. "Seems doable."

Daze turned to Jet but directed his next question at the other two. "So, let me get this straight, neither of you are worried about the bad luck?"

"No such thing, in my opinion," Cutter said calmly.

Jet looked on, confused by Daze's comment. "What's that supposed to mean?"

Plexus stepped away. "I thought you were joking earlier, but you really don't have a clue?"

Jet felt a bit of concern seep in and shook his head. "What are you all talking about?"

Daze started to laugh, and Plexus joined in. Only Cutter remained silent and stared at the ground, hands in his pockets.

Jet felt like he was back in the caves. The familiar sense of rejection hit him and his hope of finding acceptance turned to ash. He clenched his jaw and struggled to contain his anger. Nervous anxiety shot through him as the laughter continued. Cutter glanced sidelong at Jet with a mix of sympathy and exasperation on his face.

Jet took a deep breath and relaxed, his anger dissipating. He didn't need to prove anything to Daze or Plexus or anyone else. He'd been through all this before, and he would do it again, if that's what it took. He felt more determined than ever to make the team.

He looked up at Daze, finally relaxing his jaw. He stepped forward, causing Daze to take a step back, and missed the grin on Cutter's face. "I'll see you on the field."

Daze took a moment, then shrugged. "Just don't get too close to him," he said to Plexus. He turned and left, followed by his teammates.

Jet, Cutter, and Plexus stood there for a long minute, staring after the group.

"Not the right foot to start on, especially with him," Plexus commented. Jet shook his head but didn't say anything.

Cutter started walking towards one of the exits. "That was fun. Hopefully, the semester is the same."

Plexus turned and walked in the opposite direction. "See ya at tryouts, Cutter."

"Nice girl," Jet said, noticing the way Cutter's eyes followed her.

"Yeah, I think she likes you," Cutter shot back.

"Look, Cutter. I don't want to get dragged into an argument. I just want to know what Mr. Hotshot meant by *bad luck.*"

Cutter shook his head and kept walking. "Library's just around the corner if you need answers."

Jet reached out and grabbed Cutter by the arm. "I want to hear it from you. Why are you running away?"

Cutter pried his arm free. "I'm not running from anything."

"Really? It sure looks that way to me. What are you so afraid to tell me?"

"Who said I was afraid?"

"There's a reason you're not talking. I'm not blind."

"It's not really my place. And besides, I need to go unpack." Cutter started to walk away again, and Jet took a few steps after him.

"Cutter, we're the only two that made it here from the entire ARC district. That's gotta count for something."

Cutter didn't slow and continued toward the exit.

"Wait," Jet persisted. "Just… do me this favor. After that, I'll leave you alone, I promise." Cutter was his last link to the ARC district. Perhaps this was the closure that would allow them both to move on from their old lives.

Cutter's expression softened. He stopped, and Jet could tell he was struggling with something internally. "I'll tell you what I know. Then we go our separate ways."

"Alright," Jet replied.

"Let's talk outside," Cutter said.

Both walked silently until they were a good distance outside the stadium.

"This is far enough." Jet leaned against a large tree and crossed his arms, waiting to hear what Cutter had to say.

Cutter gathered his thoughts. "I know what they call your disease, and I know what they say happens to those who have it."

"Go on."

Cutter shook his head. "You sure you want to hear this?"

"I'm going to find out sooner or later," Jet said. "Might as well be from someone I know."

Cutter shrugged. "You have a condition called ephebus mortem, or E.M. It's rare, and there's no cure. There can be side effects, like hallucinations, dementia, and insanity. Everyone who's been diagnosed with it has died before the age of twenty-four. There's a rumor that it can infect others with *bad luck*, but that's never been proven. That's it. That's all I know."

Jet stared at Cutter and then erupted in laughter.

Cutter stood, hands in his pockets, not smiling. "You can laugh all you want, but that's not gonna help."

Jet wiped tears from his eyes. "What, you're serious? You expect me to believe that?"

"Look, I'm just telling you what I know. But for your sake, I suggest you take it seriously because I don't think this is a joke."

Jet stopped laughing and tried to discern the look on Cutter's broad face. "You really are serious. And… is that concern I hear? I mean, just a moment ago you were—"

"Listen. I've told you what I know. Are we done here?" Cutter lifted his backpack.

Jet hesitated, startled by his sudden change in mood. "I guess so. Take it easy, Cutter."

Cutter slung his backpack over his massive shoulder and turned to leave but paused. "One more thing you should know. Ephebus mortem translates to *the youthful death*."

CHAPTER

3

Solan Alexander

ΑΒΓΔΕΖΗΘΙΚΛΜ
ΝΞΟΠΡΣΤΥΦΧΨΩ

JET FELT CERTAIN that Cutter was wrong, or maybe it was a parting joke. He knew his condition, or disease, was rare. But dead before the age of twenty-four was absurd. Cutter was often indifferent and sometimes unpredictable, but this type of hoax didn't fit his style, and that's what concerned him the most.

With classes beginning tomorrow, he decided to pay a visit to the library. Cutter was right—if he wanted answers, that was the logical place to start. But first, he needed to stop by his dorm room and unpack. He pulled out his holopad and found the location of his dorm. It was in the middle of a place called the Commons, a large open plaza a short walk from the library.

The Commons was packed with students relaxing and soaking up the periodic rays of sunlight. Restaurants and an arcade populated the ground floor, while the living quarters occupied the upper floors. A towering atrium spiraled up through the center with balconies surrounding it. He took the vector accelerator up to the thirty-second floor, walked down a wide corridor, and stopped in front of his room.

The door stood slightly ajar.

"Great," Jet muttered. "I've got a roommate." It was something he hadn't considered. Whoever it was wouldn't be happy.

He pushed through the doorway and paused. All was silent. Clothes and other odds and ends littered the floor of the living room, and Jet's bags sat piled along one side.

The dorm was airy with tall ceilings and lofty windows. The sunlight filtering in was mottled and gray from cloud cover. There was a restroom off to one side, along with two separate bedrooms and a small kitchen. Jet heard someone stirring in one of the rooms and nudged the door open with his foot to find Cutter lying on his bed.

"You've got to be kidding me," Jet said.

"Close the door," Cutter mumbled. He was lying on his back with the crook of his arm covering his eyes from the light.

Jet stood in the doorway, wondering how the semester would play out. Not only would he see Cutter at tryouts and practice, but here as well. He still hadn't checked his class schedule. What if they had the same classes too?

Cutter kicked his feet off his bed and walked into the living room. Jet followed him and sat down on the sofa.

Jet shrugged. "I had nothing to do with this, by the way. We can talk to the academy about it if you want."

"I already did just before you showed up. Once living arrangements are set, they can't be changed unless it's an emergency. Some faculty member probably assumed that since we're from the same place we'd be okay living together."

"Well," Jet said. "We can set our study schedules to alternate. We'd only need to see each other at tryouts. What's your schedule like?"

Cutter grabbed his holopad, and they both checked their schedules. They shared just one class, Skylight History.

"I'll take Tuesdays and Thursday mornings," Cutter said.

"Works for me," Jet said.

Cutter hesitated, started to say something, but picked up his holopad and walked into his room and shut the door.

Jet finished unpacking and found that his closet was stocked with clothing provided by the university. Sweaters, coats, gloves, all with the Skylight University Crest. He changed and headed straight to the library.

Like the stadium, the main library was breathtakingly large, and perhaps the biggest building on the entire campus. Its monumental steps seemed to climb for miles, up between massive entry pillars.

Jet strode through the front door and into a large atrium that stretched to the very top of the building. Brief flashes of sunlight poured in through its clear oculus overhead. Numerous balconies lined each level with students quietly studying. He made his way toward the front information desk and waited in line behind two girls. One kept glancing back at him, and he tried to ignore her by going over his class schedule.

"What's wrong with him?" the girl whispered to her friend.

"It's that thing, you know—euphoria moria, or something like that," her friend whispered back.

"It's called ephebus mortem, actually." Jet smiled and gave them a slight nod. "And I hear it's contagious."

Startled, the girls gathered their items and left. Jet shook his head and stepped to the front of the line.

"Can I help you?" the lady behind the counter asked curtly.

"I'm looking for information on—"

"The kiosks at the end of the atrium." The librarian pointed toward the far end. "Next please." She waved to the student behind Jet.

He shifted his backpack, used to being brushed off. He found the box-like structures called kiosks and stepped inside of one, noting its simplistic appearance. A thin backrest adorned one side with a blank console on the opposite side.

"What now?" he mumbled, setting his backpack down.

"Please repeat your request," a demure voice murmured from the console in front of him.

"Huh?" he asked, confused.

A holographic menu appeared, surrounding him with the definition and history of the word *huh*. It began to explain where the word had originated and how the slang version of it was used in every known language.

"Stop!" Jet said. The voice ceased, and the information stopped scrolling across the display. "What I meant to ask about was... ephebus mortem."

The information on the hologram changed as the voice spoke. "Ephebus mortem—a term coined in the late 21st century by the famous scientist, Madastur Renzie—is a rare condition with very few known cases over the last century. The telltale sign is a distinct glow from the subject's eyes. All known cases have perished before the age of twenty-four, mostly in unfortunate accidents. Most cases have suffered severe dementia and hallucinations. However, the body of a victim has never been recovered for an autopsy, which adds to the mystique. Many believe that ephebus mortem spreads bad luck, but there is no evidence to support this claim. As of today, no cure has been found. Currently, there are only six known cases, four of which attend Skylight University and

Academy. One case, Myranda Mason, was recently killed at the university."

It was odd to see his name included in the list of students attending Skylight. He read the list of names. Cord Ledbetter, Bo Blake, Vail Hart and himself, all currently attended Skylight University. Two other girls named Kamber Caster and Tetra Wride lived on Skylight City.

Shock settled in, and he slumped against the backrest, struggling to digest the news. It was true; Cutter hadn't been lying.

This machine could prove to be an important resource for him throughout the semester. It was a great way to get information without having to confront someone. He wondered how reliable it was, though. He assumed it provided correct information, even though he questioned what he'd just heard, and decided to test the kiosk and see if it was accurate.

"Show me the entrance exam score for Jet Stroud."

The kiosk hummed to life again. A holographic number floated in the center of the console: 1,782. He smiled, noting his name was near the top of the all-time high scores. However, another name among the entrance scores caught his attention—one he'd just seen. A girl named Solan Alexander, who had popped onto his holopad display earlier that day near Alpha Hall, had scored an amazing 1,785 out a possible 1,800—a nearly perfect score.

The holographic image of a stunning dark-skinned girl appeared on the console. Jet rubbed his forehead thoughtfully. He pulled out his holopad and looked at it. Perhaps its capabilities were limited, and it could only locate people within short distances? He could only assume that it had simply malfunctioned since he hadn't actually seen the girl, just her name.

"Tell me more about Solan Alexander." Jet poked his head out of the kiosk to make sure no one was eavesdropping. He felt like he was spying on someone he'd never met.

"Solan Alexander was a former President of the Heliographi Club and currently holds records in the javelin throw, high jump, and the 1,600-meter run. She originated from one of the few fishing communities located on North America's inundated eastern seaboard and graduated from Skylight University with honors. She died on May 5th, 2272 A.D., in a bizarre skiff accident shortly after graduation. Solan was nearly twenty-four years old and had been diagnosed with ephebus mortem at age seven."

Jet almost fell out of the kiosk.

Solan Alexander had been dead for nearly ten years!

Yet he had just seen her name, he was positive. Jet looked at his holopad again, examining it closely. It looked to be in perfect condition with no dents or scratches.

"Repeat the side effects of ephebus mortem," Jet whispered. A sudden feeling of anxiety shimmied down his spine.

"An unexplained glow in the eyes of the subject is the most discernable sign of ephebus mortem," the kiosk replied. "In all recorded cases, the victim has died before the age of twenty-four. Hallucinations, dementia, and insanity are often associated."

CHAPTER

The Heliographi

ΑΒΓΔΕΖΗΘΙΚΛ<u>Μ</u>
ΝΞΟΠΡΣΤΥΦΧΨΩ

JET SPRINTED ACROSS the campus grounds the next morning, late for his Social Science class. Using his holopad, he finally found the Science Department and slowed to gain his bearings. Something in the distance caught his attention. Intrigued, he walked over to a large plaza. Situated in the center stood an immense statue hovering above a steel pedestal. Nine metallic stars set into the paving surrounded the statue. Wind swirled gently around it, creating a subtle vortex that tugged at his clothes, urging him closer. High above, tethered to the plaza with large cables, was the huge clock called Chroma. Its intricate internal cogs churned softly and emitted a ticking sound that filtered down in a soothing sort of way. The translucent bubble surrounding it displayed the time, date, and news headlines like a digital ticker tape.

Jet read a plaque displayed on the pedestal.

Revelations Plaza

"For the Greater Unity of Humankind"
In Memory of Christian Albright, Founder of Skylight University
2121 — 2225 A.D.

The statue depicted Christian Albright with unkempt hair and a neatly trimmed beard. He held a set of drawings in one hand, perhaps the blueprints for Skylight University, and his other hand stretched skyward toward Chroma.

A loud crash from Chroma shattered the silence. Jet looked at his watch and cursed—his class was about to start. He shouldered his pack and sprinted off.

He stepped through the front door of Dorcher Hall and up the stairs two at a time, eventually slowing to a walk. Peering through the classroom doors, he saw no sign of his professor at the lectern. He walked in and bounded up the steps of the lecture hall to a seat near the middle and settled in.

Holographic images projected onto the walls, displaying a plethora of information about the Earth's history. A holographic timeline ran around the perimeter of the hall, charting every known civilization. Social Science was a required course, but one he knew very little about.

A thin young lady walked into the lecture hall and stepped onto the stage. She moved gracefully behind the lectern and laid out several holopads. Her shimmering blouse matched the hint of golden highlights on her dark skin and hair.

"Good morning, class," she said, digitizing her holopads. "I assume that you're ready to learn a bit about Earth's history, much of which can be attained through the study of our past civilizations. I am Professor Sterllar Sylvant."

The lecture hall remained silent as most of the students stared admiringly at her.

"Very well then, let's get started," she continued. "Can anyone tell me which of our former civilizations has been the most influential in today's society?"

Several students raised their hands.

"Yes, you in the front."

"What about the Romans?" the girl asked.

"And why the Romans?" Sylvant replied. An image of the Roman Coliseum floated over the stage.

"Sport?" the girl suggested as other students nodded in agreement.

Sylvant clapped. "Considering how important sports have become, I would agree." Images of blaze and track flashed around the lecture hall. "Who else?"

"What about the Greeks?" another student asked.

"Good, yes. The Greeks. They emerged as one of the first advanced civilizations in Europe, whose impact is still evident today," Sylvant stated. "In many ways, their philosophies paved the way for modern science, math, and architecture. The Greek alphabet was a major influence on later societies. Even though the Romans took control of Greece, the Greek culture and way of life eventually conquered Rome itself."

Sylvant walked across the stage as more images projected around the lecture hall. "But what about the Egyptians, the Mayans, or the Aztecs? And who would possibly argue that one was less important than the others? It won't be me," Sylvant said and stopped walking. "The fact is that all of our past civilizations were vital to our way of life. Our goal this semester will be to discover why and how. Now, please digitize your holopads for today's lesson."

Professor Sylvant finished the session and assigned them some reading for their next class. Jet stood to leave and made eye contact with her. Sylvant nodded and smiled at him. Surprised, he glanced around to see who she was looking at, but no one else was near him. He gathered his things and decided to risk a conversation with her.

"Jet Stroud… am I correct?" she asked as he approached the stage. Up close she seemed familiar as if he had seen her before.

"You know who I am?" he asked.

She shrugged. "I just noticed your name on the class roll, and… well, you are hard to miss."

Jet smiled at her. "At least you're honest."

Sylvant wasn't afraid to look him in the eye. She was one of the few people so far who didn't seem unsettled by his presence.

"Congratulations, by the way. I saw that you scored very high marks on your entrance exam," she said as she gathered her items.

"Luck, I guess," Jet said.

"I once knew a person who scored very high marks on her exam, too. Believe me, luck has nothing to do with it." Sylvant stepped off the stage and made her way to the exit, glancing at her watch a few times.

Jet was still at a loss for words. There was something familiar about the young professor that he couldn't quite put his finger on.

"I have an appointment in a few minutes. But, would you care to walk with me?" she asked.

"Sure," Jet replied, a bit shocked.

Outside, dark clouds crouched along the horizon, and the air was thick and humid. He was curious about what Sylvant wanted with him, so he started with some small talk. "I assumed that the weather here never changed."

Sylvant looked to the clouds. "We have storms, but not very often. The Core has a limited atmosphere, and heat usually builds around the belts, which in turn attracts moisture and clouds. But I'm not a meteorologist, just a humble sociologist."

"Well, you must be very good at your job."

"Are you assuming because I'm young, I have less knowledge than the older professors?"

"No… I didn't mean—"

Sylvant shook her head and smiled. "I'm just kidding. Most of the tenured professors don't like me much. So, I know what it's like to be an outsider, you see?"

Jet continued to stare at her and then looked at the sidewalk. "But I am an outsider, whether I like it or not," he said. "I'd hoped that Skylight would be different."

"In what way?"

He shrugged. "That people would be more accepting and less judgmental. So far, it's probably worse."

"Give it a chance. It's only the first day of class."

"I hope you're right, but I'm not holding my breath."

Sylvant nodded. "I'm somewhat familiar with ephebus mortem, actually."

Jet shook his head. "I thought you specialized in Social Science?"

"Well, yes, that's true. But my older sister had it, so I know more than most people when it comes to E.M."

Jet nearly tripped over his feet. "Your sister, you said? Was her name Solan Alexander?"

Sylvant gave him a suspicious look. "How did you know that?"

"When I was checking my entrance exam score today, I noticed that she beat me by three points. You look just like her."

Sylvant didn't look at him, and he could tell she was mulling something over. "It's hard to believe she's been dead for nearly ten years. Most people wrote off her skiff accident as just that; an accident." Sylvant paused and cleared her throat. "I'm sorry. I don't mean to be rude by talking about this in front of you. I know it's tough enough dealing with everything else."

"It's okay," Jet replied. "Please, I'd like to hear more if that's alright?"

Sylvant pursed her lips and nodded. "The authorities insisted that her skiff, and everything in it, was incinerated. She was a good pilot, though. I don't believe she crashed her skiff. But, they claimed there was no evidence… how convenient, right? I was furious at how quickly everything was dismissed. There was no body, no clues, no motive. And, no one would talk to me about it after that. Not the police, the Skylight commissioner, or any university officials."

Jet could tell that she was still emotional, even after a decade.

"I loved and admired my sister—she was my best friend," Sylvant continued. "I still think about her. She was one of the bravest people I've ever known. Having to deal with E.M. and everything that came with it took its toll on her. She fought it all the way, though. It really hurt to let her go."

"I'm sorry," Jet said, not sure what else to say.

Sylvant took a deep breath. "I tried to follow in her footsteps as a student here, but I could never match her accomplishments. After graduation, I decided to teach Social Science, and here I am. I'd hoped to learn more about my sister when I took the job…. so far I haven't."

Jet stopped to face her, and she returned his gaze. He sensed no fear or discrimination in her eyes. He considered telling her about seeing Solan's name yesterday. She struck him as someone he could trust, someone who might understand him. But he quickly reconsidered. Mentioning her sister's name probably wouldn't be a good start. He decided to save that for later.

"It must be difficult to talk about her," Jet said. "I hope I didn't upset you—"

"No, I wanted to talk with you about it. Otherwise, we wouldn't be standing here," she said. "It just seemed too coincidental… you, being in my class with over a million students on campus. Perhaps it's a sign? Maybe I was meant to help you?" She looked at her watch and gave it a tap. "I'm off to my next appointment. We'll talk later. Sound good?"

Jet watched her leave.

He'd always managed to care for himself, thanks in large part to his condition. But having a Skylight Professor offer to help him, who, strangely enough, happened to have a personal connection with ephebus mortem... well, that *would* be a blessing. Professor Sylvant was right about one thing; it did seem oddly coincidental that he'd ended up in her class.

· • • • ● ● ● • • • ·

LATER THAT AFTERNOON, he met Cutter at Crux Stadium for their first blaze tryout. They'd been inside the stadium for the tour, but it had been mostly empty. Now, it bustled with activity on and around the field. As they strode into the arena, he noted several floating skiffs above the field used for commentators or coaches to bark orders to players below. One skiff floated toward them.

"Preps?" the coach asked. Cutter nodded.

"Down the ramp and to your left. Hustle!" the man ordered.

They followed his directions down the ramp and through a labyrinth of corridors beneath the stadium, finally arriving at the locker room where most of the team was suiting up. The Skylight University logo was a mystic blue field with stars surrounding a flaming red torch. The locker room reflected this color scheme along with the uniforms.

Since the team's roster hadn't been determined, Cutter and Jet were issued training uniforms and assigned a temporary locker. The equipment was top-notch, and their practice uniforms fit perfectly. The helmet had a stasis field over the visor, along with a modified holopad built into the side. It was called a holocypher and allowed the players to view the plays and communicate with the sideline coaches. Jet had had to memorize all the plays back in the ARC league, but this device would make things easier, though it would take some getting used to.

"Listen up!" one of the assistant coaches shouted. Everyone fell silent. "Today is the first day of tryouts, which will last through the end of the week. You will be tested on your agility, speed, endurance, and decision making. You may try out for any position, which you will officially declare once we reach the field. The top players will be selected for the position in which they are best suited. By Monday, you'll know if you've made the team. Most of you will be cut or reassigned. Don't expect any favors!"

The players headed up to the field through a long, sloping tunnel. More players joined them from another locker room, which Jet assumed to be upperclassmen ready to defend their roster position. He spotted Daze among them, who presumably had the head point-blaze position. But there were two flanking point-blaze positions available, and he was determined to land one of them.

His attention settled on a man who could only be their head coach. Hemmond Plannar towered over the other coaches and an air of command surrounded him. A long scar adorned his left cheek from his lip to his ear, and his hair was turning gray at the temples.

There were nearly seven hundred players gathered around when he clapped his hands for everyone to quiet down.

Plannar looked at the sea of players, his gaze finally settling on Jet. "Everyone look at the player next to you. They probably won't make the team this year." Plannar had an odd accent that was difficult for Jet to understand.

"I'm determined to get your maximum effort. If that scares you, then off you go! I've great hopes for this season, an' you should too. This is the most prestigious athletic program, an' the sport of blaze is the heart an' soul of this university. You're all privileged to be standing on this field. If you disrespect that, off you go!"

No one spoke as Plannar walked through the crowd of players. "Let's get to it, then."

Plannar broke the team up by positions. Jet was grouped with several point-blazers, including Daze. The bulk of the players were positioned at mid-blazer or blaze-out, with the big guys at blaze-blocker.

Most of their practice consisted of speed and agility time trials. The point-blazers worked on throwing the blaze, timing, mechanics, and situational decision making.

Cutter had a fantastic first day, and so did Plexus. Because of Cutter's size and speed, he was placed at the mid-blazer position, though he had taken a few snaps on the defensive unit as well. Plexus led all players in speed with the quickest forty-yard dash time. Jet ended up with average results on all the speed and agility trials. He knew those weren't his strengths, though. He would need to rely on his decision making and throwing accuracy if he wanted to make the team.

Coach Plannar finally gathered everyone at midfield.

"Not bad for a first day," he hollered. He walked over to stand in front of Jet. "Strud, where'd you learn to thro' like that?"

"Excuse me, sir?" Jet asked, confused.

"Thro'!" Plannar made a passing motion like he was throwing a large rock.

"Oh, back in the caves, sir," Jet replied. The rest of the team erupted in laughter.

"Settle down," Plannar growled. He faced Jet, his hands behind his back. "You made some good decisions out there today. You keep your calm… I like that, Strud." He turned to face the team. "Returning players, I expect more out of you this season. You preps, pay attention to what's happening around you. Alright, that's it for now. Same time tomorrow."

Jet left the stadium, not bothering to shower or wait for Cutter. The dark clouds he'd noticed earlier were building along the horizon. It looked like a storm was brewing, and he didn't want to get caught in it. He walked briskly, using his holopad to guide him along the quickest route back to the dorms. A quiet flash of lightning illuminated the low-lying clouds in the distance, drawing his attention to the moon's red face. Students scurried by as light sprinkles covered his face. He heard Chroma toll seven o'clock as he passed through the Mathematics Department. Jet recognized Alpha Hall amidst the other buildings and stopped.

He turned his holopad toward the building, wondering if it might malfunction again. But he saw no name and the pad seemed to be working fine. Jet slipped it into his backpack as a muffled thunderclap rolled in the distance. He felt a sudden urge to explore the building and stepped through the massive bronze doors for a look inside.

Since it was after hours, the lights were dim, and the corridors were silent. He walked leisurely down the wide hallway and read the plaques and awards on the walls. Jet stopped and peered up at one plaque high on the wall. It projected a holographic image of a dark-haired girl. Her glowing eyes made the hologram stand out in the darkness.

"Solan Alexander, President of the Heliographi Club, 2272 A.D.," Jet whispered. Once again, he was shocked at how much she resembled her sister, Professor Sylvant. *What was it about Solan that intrigued him so much?*

Jet continued to walk and didn't stop until he reached the center of the building. Its large atrium extended upward to a clear oculus above that emitted flashes of lightning. Jet noticed a pattern set into the floor, but it was too large to make out. Intrigued, he decided to go higher for a better look.

Jet climbed one of the grand staircases and didn't stop until he reached the top. He leaned against the guardrail and gazed down at the strange pattern below, finally recognizing it as the Heliographi symbol he'd heard so much about.

While reading through his Social Science assignment, he had learned several interesting facts about the symbol. Christian Albright had fashioned it of the Greek theta symbol, divided it in half with a backward slash, and surrounded it with twenty-four stars. In classical Athens, the theta represented the Greek word thanatos, or death, because of its resemblance to the human skull. The theta was also the eighth number in the Greek alphabet, yet it had a value of nine—the Skylight System had nine orbiting belts. But, after half a century of debate, no one was certain what the Heliographi symbol really stood for.

A streak of lightning broke his train of thought. Jet looked up through the oculus and decided it was time to leave. He headed back down the staircase and across the atrium floor, the sound of his shoes echoed across the vacant space. With one last look at the Heliographi symbol, he pushed through the door and into the wind.

The storm was intensifying. Lightning grew closer, and thunder boomed overhead. It started sprinkling again, and he pulled out his holopad to light the quickest way back to the dorms. A sudden flutter of light caught his eye near the far corner of the building. He turned his holopad in its direction and a name popped into the display, accompanied by the heat mirage—*Solan Alexander.*

He leapt forward, sprinting through the rain and slowing when he reached the area. He scanned the building and found nothing. His hands shook as he thought about the side effects of E.M.

Am I starting to hallucinate already? This can't be happening to me... not this quickly!

He shook his head, then noticed footprints in the mud and knelt to look at them. He followed them into the flowerbed, stopping every so often for a flash of lightning to light his way. He continued to search the area as the storm gathered fury around him. A thunderclap shook the ground, and the rain grew heavier until he was drenched and shivering. Something on the building's wall caught his attention, and he crept closer for a look.

In the middle of a large stone block was a small engraving. He bent close and saw a glowing symbol that was quickly fading away. Jet rubbed his hand over it cautiously but felt no heat. He was so close to the building that his nose nearly touched the wet stone. Another bolt of lightning lit up the wall, finally revealing a

Heliographi symbol. In the middle of the symbol was a lowercase letter *i* instead of the typical backslash, though. The footprints in the mud stopped in the same spot.

CHAPTER

Cord Ledbetter

ΑΒΓΔΕΖΗΘΙΚΛ<u>Μ</u>
ΝΞΟΠΡΣΤΥΦΧΨΩ

A SLIVER OF LIGHT spilled from beneath a door at the end of the hallway. He inched forward, his fingertips brushing the cold stone walls. His shoes scraped softly along the dusty cobbled floor. The echo lingered.

A momentary chill caused his skin to prickle. He froze just as a dark mass drifted past him and toward the door. He bit his lip as his heart raced. The apparition seemed unaware of his presence, though, and eased around the door like smoke through a crack. He sensed that something bad was about to happen from the room beyond, and fear gripped him.

I should turn back... now.

The sound of muffled voices urged him ahead, though. He nudged the door open to see a young lady sitting behind an easel, her back to him. He sensed her fear. The paintbrush she held wavered mid-stroke near the center of the canvas. The painting in front of her resembled a color wheel, a circular spectrum that depicted a multi-colored eye. It was divided into twelve equal portions, which were further subdivided to create twenty-four total sections. But what was happening to her paintbrush drew Jet's attention. Nine droplets of red paint radiated out from the center of the eye, rolling across the rough canvas like an explosion. Each bead moved rapidly in different directions, eventually pooling into bloodlike splotches. Then the girl began to scream.

The shadow behind her was nearly invisible. It shifted in the candlelight, making it difficult to see. The thing stared into her eyes, holding her captive with its gaze. He felt a sudden pressure inside his head, and a voice spoke to him.

YOU!

He turned and fled, not waiting to see what happened to the young woman. As he neared the end of the hallway, something odd happened.

It began to snow.

The hallway faded as snow fell in heavy sheets. The moonlight flickered and went dark, like a candle being snuffed out. He lost his footing and fell face-first into the thick snow. Exhaustion enveloped him. He didn't care about the cold or pain in his head. He simply wanted to lay there and sleep, forgetting his struggles, disappointments, and misery.

A voice called to him, and he managed to raise his head. Something approached rapidly, gliding gracefully across the snow with pale, ghostly arms extended.

Prepare.

Jet lurched awake and his holopad clattered to the floor. He was sitting in a lecture hall as thousands of students filed out. Shocked, he realized he'd slept through his first day of history class.

Cutter slid his holopad into his backpack. "You missed the lecture, by the way."

"That's great. Thanks for waking me," Jet muttered. He stood and gathered his things, slinging his backpack over his shoulder.

"You talk in your sleep, too," Cutter said.

Jet walked out of the lecture hall with Cutter a few steps behind. Jet waited until they were a good distance outside and stopped to face him. "Something on your mind?"

"Just wondering why you haven't looked for the other kids like you," Cutter said. "It's the first thing I'd have done."

"The semester just started, and I've been pretty busy," Jet snipped.

"Or is it because you're trying to avoid them?" Cutter continued.

Jet shook his head. "I'm confused. Are you trying to help me now?"

"I saw what happened last night," Cutter said, crossing his arms.

Jet's eyes narrowed. "What about last night?"

"What made you react like that? What did you see at Alpha Hall?" Cutter asked.

"Wait. You followed me?" Jet said, growing irritated. "Listen, what I saw is my business, and if I catch you following me again—"

"You'll what?" Cutter said.

Jet sighed. "If what's happening to me upsets you, then mind your own business."

"I've told you about the side effects," Cutter said. "Hallucinations, delusions."

"I'm aware of what *they say* about the side effects," Jet replied. "So what?"

They continued to gather stares from passing students. Cutter lowered his voice. "All I'm saying is that some of these other kids are seniors, and they've dealt with it for longer than you. Go talk to them, what have you got to lose?"

Jet stared at Cutter without saying a word. After a moment, Cutter shook his head and left.

Jet watched him leave and wondered where Cutter's change of heart was coming from. He'd never shown any real concern before. Why now?

Jet found a vacant table at the commons and ate lunch. He continued to mull over Cutter's comments in his head. Once again, Cutter had a point. The other students here might be able to shed some light on things for him. But tracking them down, just as the semester was getting started, along with blaze, didn't leave much time for him to play detective.

He finished the last of his meal and was about to leave for his next class when a thin young man slipped deftly through the crowd and made eye contact with him. Jet could clearly see he was one of the students with E.M. by his glowing greenish-yellow eyes.

"You're Jet Stroud, am I correct?" the young man said, stopping in front of Jet. There was a smooth, silky drawl in the tone of his voice.

"That's me," Jet said.

"Name's Cord Ledbetter." Cord looked at him and waited expectantly with his hands behind his back. Jet guessed Cord was perhaps a bit younger. He had dark hair, thick eyelashes, and a neatly trimmed goatee that came to a point beneath his chin. He wore a black collared shirt, black slacks, and polished dress shoes.

"Have a seat," Jet said, nodding to the bench across from him. But Cord continued to stand and slicked his hair back with a tug. "We should talk."

"Okay. What's on your mind?" Jet asked.

"Perhaps we should take a walk. A little privacy would be nice." Cord nodded over his shoulder at a few students listening in.

Jet shouldered his pack and walked with Cord until they were a safe distance from the Commons.

"Of course, I don't mean to be rude," Cord said. "I just prefer a little breathing room when it comes to certain matters."

"How'd you know my name?" Jet asked.

"You're the new kid. There's not too many of us. I did the math."

"So, you were following me?" Jet asked.

Cord shrugged. "Perhaps. Regardless, I thought we should talk. I hope that's okay?"

"Look," Jet said. "I just found out about this ephebus mortem stuff. I'm not sure what to think about it, to be honest. Where I'm from, no one ever talked to me, and I had no idea what I had until I got here."

"You'll get used to it. Takes some time, once it sinks in," Cord offered.

Jet nodded. "Want to tell me a bit about yourself, since you already seem to know everything about me?"

"I'm into math, you might say. I'm on path to set a few academic records. But I realized none of that matters much, if I'm dead before I graduate."

"Are you always this blunt?"

"Pretty much," Cord said. "No time to waste, and I don't really care much what others think. No offense."

"None taken," Jet said. "So, how old were you when you found out, if you don't mind me asking?"

"It's a fair question," Cord said as he walked with his hands held behind his back. He thought for a second. "I've known for as long as I can remember. My parents decided to tell me when I was young, but I didn't understand until grade school. Then one day, I was thirteen, I suppose, it hit me—I would probably spend the rest of my life alone. Surprisingly, that didn't bother me."

"How did your family handle it?"

"My parents were always supportive," Cord said. "They were excited about me coming to Skylight, hopeful I might discover new opportunities. We still talk, but I've tried to distance myself from them."

"Why's that?"

"To spare them, of course," Cord answered. "They don't deserve the ridicule. I understand why I'm ostracized, but there's no reason they should be. They've earned a better life, and I can give that to them by keeping my distance. Plus, the more I'm away from them, the easier it will be to cope if and when it happens."

"You don't miss them?"

"Rarely, actually," Cord said. "I suppose I'm so used to being alone that it hasn't really fazed me. You don't feel the same for your parents?"

"Never knew them," Jet said.

"My apologies," Cord said, but with no real emotion in his voice.

"Let me ask another question, something that makes no sense to me," Jet said. "Why do you think we all die *before* we turn twenty-four?" Jet asked. "I mean, what kind of disease has a clock that accurate?"

Cord shrugged. “I don’t understand it either. Sounds like a hoax, but it isn’t. I’ve done loads of research, and it checks out with previous students who had it. In the past, it’s always some bizarre incident. At first, I refused to believe it. I’ve always relied on facts, and this seemed ridiculous to me. But… I can sense things. It’s some sort of premonition I sometimes get in my head.” Cord touched his forehead. “Maybe that sounds strange, but I feel like it’s all connected.”

“You feel it, too?” Jet lowered his voice.

“Yes. And it’s grown more prominent over the years I’ve been here. Skylight University is a brilliant place but spooky at times.” Cord stared at the ground as if trying to make an important decision. He cleared his throat. “Let’s be candid. There’s a lot we need to discuss and not a whole lot of time, I feel.”

“Well, here we are,” Jet said, looking around them. There was no one nearby. “Nothing to worry about, right?”

“I’m not so certain, actually.”

“Are you referring to eavesdropping students?” Jet asked. “Because I’m not concerned with what they think about me.”

“Me neither, but it’s not the students we should be concerned about.”

“Who are you referring to then?”

Cord rubbed his chin thoughtfully. “Have you seen something strange since you arrived here?”

Jet didn’t know Cord and wasn’t certain how much to trust him. He had an idea of what Cord was talking about but decided to play it safe. “Why do you ask?”

“I’ll assume from your response that you have witnessed… let’s just say, something peculiar.”

Jet shook his head. “Peculiar?” he asked. But he thought

immediately about Solan Alexander, the girl whose name he'd seen on his holopad twice now.

"I don't need to spell it out for you," Cord said and stopped walking long enough to watch Jet's expression. "You're smart, I've seen your entrance scores."

"Yeah, okay. I've seen something peculiar, as you say."

Cord nodded. "That's good. There's more proof with each documented occurrence."

"Proof, maybe. But it's coming from a euph, I hate to remind you," Jet said. "No one's going to believe you or me or anyone else. We might as well be seeing UFO's."

Cord started walking again and ignored the comment. "I've been trying to formulate plausible theories for quite some time, actually. It's been rather frustrating."

Jet shook his head and laughed. "I don't think math will solve our problems. Have you talked to the others yet?"

"I never got a chance to talk to Myranda Mason. But a few years ago, I talked to the other two. Let's just say it was a failure."

"Why do you say that?" Jet asked.

"Vail Hart is a woman with issues. All she wants is to be left alone and wait for the end to come. She's given up; her negativity is like a cancer. I don't think she's worth approaching again."

"And the other one?"

"I tried to speak with Bo Blake at a track meet once. He simply ignored me. He may have already lost it, I'm afraid. I'm not the best at convincing people anyway."

Jet looked at him. "What exactly do you want, Cord?"

"Obviously what we all want—a cure. And since you're new, I thought perhaps you'd be interested in doing something about it."

Jet thought for a second. "Maybe I was too optimistic. I guess I was expecting the cure would be available as soon as I arrived. I assumed Skylight had everything. I realize now how ridiculous that sounds. I'm starting to see this isn't going to be easy."

"It didn't take long for me to come to the same conclusion, don't feel bad."

"So, what are you proposing?" Jet asked.

"Well... I've heard rumors," Cord said, lowering his voice. "Not long ago, there was talk about a few former students with ephebus mortem and something about old paintings. Supposedly, these paintings had something to do with the famous artist named Shiloe Van Saint."

That got Jet's attention. In his dreams, there had been a young lady painting in her studio, but the rest was fuzzy. He wondered if this was somehow connected. "This artist, Shiloe Van Saint, do you know anything about her?"

"I've read plenty about her. She died a long time ago, murdered in her own home. Some say she was the first true case of E.M. Her paintings are rumored to hold secrets, though I've never seen one in real life."

Jet nodded. "What else do you know about these two students?"

"Their names were Solan Alexander and Joshia Kembler," Cord said. "I did some research and found out they were both former track stars."

"They were students here, about ten years ago," Jet said.

"So, you already know about all this?" Cord said.

"Not really. I just know the name Solan Alexander and that she was a student ten years ago. I don't know anything about the other girl."

"Well, I believe there's more to this, and I'd like to find out." Cord popped his collar straight. "I'm asking for your help. The others want nothing to do with it."

"Assuming I join you, I'd like to do this a certain way. Can you agree to that?" Jet said.

"Works for me," Cord said and stuck out his hand. "What are you thinking?"

"Even though you had no luck approaching the others, I might," Jet said and shook Cord's hand.

"They probably don't know any more than us," Cord said. "I imagine they'll say no."

Jet shrugged. "Then we've lost nothing by asking, right?"

Cord took a deep breath. "Perhaps I'm being overly skeptical, I apologize. Just be careful with Bo and Vail. You'll get a lot of resistance from both."

"Well, I'm always up for a challenge," Jet said and reached into his backpack to retrieve his holopad.

Cord pulled his out of a black satchel and held it next to Jet's. "We're connected now. Just call me when you're ready to get started. Don't wait too long."

"Hold on." Jet stopped him. "I never heard your opinion. Do you think ephebus mortem is real?"

"Why do you think I'm here?" Cord didn't blink as he stared at Jet. "I'm a rational person… I don't believe in nonsense. I need proof, numbers, facts. But whatever *this* is, it keeps happening over and over again. If we're going to save ourselves, we need to think outside of the box… the clock is ticking."

CHAPTER

The Stacks

ΑΒΓΔΕΖΗΘΙΚΛΜ
ΝΞΟΠΡΣΤΥΦΧΨΩ

LATER THAT DAY, Jet decided to visit the library. After his last conversation with Cutter, he'd changed his mind about studying at the dorm room. He wasn't sure how he felt about Cutter following him, so he needed a more private place to study and eventually found a spot on the eighth floor. A small table, tucked behind a large rack of holopads, away from prying eyes. Jet dropped his backpack, sat down, and began to study.

After an hour or so, he'd finished his Cosmology and Quantum Mechanics. But halfway through his Social Sciences, a group of students sat down nearby and began chatting. It didn't take long for them to notice him, and the finger-pointing began. Jet lost his focus and shut down his holopad.

He wandered down multiple levels and eventually found himself in the basement, one of the older portions of the library, at least that's what he assumed by the outdated look of the furniture. It had an antique feel to it, like images he'd seen in a history book. The smell of the air grew musty like rain on a dirty walkway.

He turned a corner and noticed a gate stretched across a hallway with a sign that read, "Off Limits." Beyond it was a peculiar looking bookcase built into a long wall.

Go to the bookcase, a voice said.

"Hello?" Jet said, and stopped to look around.

What is happening to me? he thought. *Were voices also part of the side effects?*

He stepped past the gate and walked over to the bookcase. It was well crafted in dark redwood with intricate scrollwork. A strange pattern rimmed the midsection of it. He reached out and traced the scrollwork with his fingertips, noting how out of place it seemed. His hand brushed over a loose panel, and he paused. He slid the panel open to reveal a worn brass handle inside. He contemplated what to do and wondered if he was breaking any school rules by being in the basement. But soon, his curiosity got the better of him, and he pulled the lever.

There was a groan as the old bookcase protested at being disturbed. A portion of it swung open to reveal a stone stairway. A dank breeze gushed from the opening and made him cough. He waved dust away and cupped his hand over his eyes, trying to peer into the darkness.

"Why not," he muttered and stepped onto the narrow stairway. He pulled the bookcase closed behind him and stood at the top landing, waiting for his eyes to adjust. Inch by inch, he felt his way down the stairs and stopped at the bottom to listen. Remembering his holopad, he pulled it out and used the display to light the room.

He stood inside a vast chamber, surrounded by thousands of metal racks containing perhaps millions of books. A barrel-vaulted ceiling above spanned the length of the room. He walked down the aisles, letting his fingers skim over the books' dusty spines.

In the middle of the chamber stood an antique table and chairs, surrounded by half-burned candles on bronze pedestals. Wax entrails clung to the dusty candles and lay in dried clumps on the floor. The claw-and-ball table seemed to fit perfectly amongst the archaic books. A draft hummed through the space and up the stairs, causing cobwebs to pulse in rhythm. Its barely audible howl tickled his ears with invisible fingertips. It all looked rather sad—and spooky.

He approached the table cautiously, noticing the disarray. On it was a box of matches, several of which had been used and discarded onto the floor. He opened the box and struck a match, then lit several candles.

It was then he noticed the crystal chandelier above the table, swaying gently in the breeze. The candlelight refracted into tiny prisms of light that danced around the room. The space was exactly what he'd been searching for. Finally, some privacy.

Jet continued to explore the aisles, walking as if in a trance.

The book.

He stopped suddenly, as if waking from a dream. His fingertips brushed over a book that sat halfway off the shelf, as if someone had recently handled it. There were footprints on the dusty floor below it. Jet pulled the book out and read the inside cover. According to the index card, it had last been checked out almost ninety years ago. It was about the young female artist named Shiloe Van Saint. Jet guessed that there were millions of books in the chamber. It seemed more than a coincidence he'd stumbled upon this one in particular.

He sat down at the table and opened the book. The pages depicted Van Saint's artwork, which was mostly horrific images of the Unbalance. The depressing recount of the death and destruction mankind had caused was difficult to look at. Though there was no picture of her, he knew she was the young woman in his dreams.

He flipped to the center page, and a holopad clattered to the floor. He picked it up and placed it on the table. A breeze hummed through the space, sending a chill down his spine as he powered up the holopad. A holographic index floated into view. Jet scanned through it and noted the last entry was dated 2272 A.D., ten years ago. In the background of the hologram something materialized, and he caught his breath. It was Solan Alexander, her glowing eyes unmistakable.

"This must be her journal," he whispered. Her expression seemed vacant, and her face was gaunt like a sweater stretched thin from too much use. She glanced around skittishly, and dark circles clung beneath her eyes. The background behind her continued to solidify, and he noticed she sat in the same wing-backed chair he was in. Solan had been in the stacks when this particular holographic recording was made.

He glanced through the index of entries again. Some of them only had dates, but others had titles like *First day of time trials, Coach Minnett,* and *End of term finals.* One entry, labeled *Tyberius Alexander*, caught his attention. That name struck a chord in his head, and he tried to access it, but it was passcode protected. He tried random words, but after several attempts, he crossed his arms and sat back.

Another breeze howled through the stacks. Jet shivered and snapped the book closed in frustration. He slipped Solan's journal into his backpack and took the book back over to the stack where he'd found it. Just as he was sliding it onto the shelf, he paused.

Behind the empty slot was an old masonry wall. Engraved into one of the bricks was a Heliographi symbol.

In the distance, Chroma tolled eight o'clock, and his stomach grumbled. Reluctantly, Jet slipped the book back into the empty slot, covering the symbol, and left the stacks.

The library was all but vacant as he made his way toward the front rotunda. He decided to stop at the information kiosk on his way out. He set his backpack down and stepped into the box.

"Tyberius Alexander," Jet said, getting comfortable.

The kiosk hummed for a second, and then it shut down. Jet stood patiently, waiting for a response. But the display remained blank. Just as he stepped out to try a different kiosk, it suddenly came back online. "No entry found for Tyberius Alexander," the automated voice said. "Please revise your request."

"Revise my request?" he asked, puzzled. "Does Tyberius Alexander exist?"

The kiosk remained silent.

"I'll take that as a no," he replied. "What about Shiloe Van Saint?"

"Shiloe Van Saint was born in 2136 A.D.," the voice began. "Her paintings were infamous for depicting what some considered to be the apocalypse during a time when Earth was experiencing natural disasters never before seen. After her death, Van Saint's work gained popularity, and her unique style inspired a new generation of artists. In 2265 A.D. rumors of hidden messages led to an investigation. Professor Klifford Keoff was commissioned to head up the research, but no evidence has been found to support these rumors. Van Saint was murdered on her twenty-fourth birthday in her subterranean studio, prematurely ending her career. Some historians believe she was the first true case of ephebus mortem."

The voice grew silent as Jet leaned back, flabbergasted. He stepped out of the kiosk, trying to get a grip on what he'd just heard. So, there *was* a connection between Van Saint and E.M. However, the only name on his mind at that moment was Tyberius Alexander.

CHAPTER

Cutter's Pact

ΑΒΓΔΕΖΗΘΙΚΛΜ
ΝΞΟΠΡΣΤΥΦΧΨΩ

Jet arrived early to practice the next day. Starting positions would be assigned after that day's tryouts, and this was his last chance to impress the coaching staff. When he got to his locker, his practice uniform was clean and neatly folded. He changed and anxiously made his way up to the field.

Coach Plannar surprised the team by announcing there would be no practice that weekend. However, he was quick to note that they'd only have Sundays off for the remainder of the season. "At this level, practice is the bread an' butter of a good team," he reminded them.

Several more players were cut or shifted to different positions, leaving the total number of point-blazers at seven. Of these seven, the competition would be fierce. The remaining point-blazers were top-notch, culled from the best districts around the Skylight System. Skylight University had its pick of the litter when it came to athletes, and Jet was thankful for his hard work over the years in the ARC district. Although there would be a need for backup point-blazers throughout the season, no one relished the thought of sitting the bench. All the remaining point-blazers were guaranteed a position on the team. Now it was simply a question of *who* would make the starting squad.

The point-blazers ran through numerous plays that day. It was difficult keeping up with the jumble of players moving around the field simultaneously. With the season opener rapidly approaching, he had a lot of formations to memorize. The holocypher attached to his helmet's visor was a lifesaver, though, and he finally felt comfortable using it.

Coach Plannar called practice for the day and requested everyone view their announcements after they'd left the stadium. He also reminded them about the celebration at a restaurant called *Blazers* later that evening. Everyone was invited, and Jet assumed that included him.

He went to his locker and sat in front of it, staring at the metal door. It had never been easy when it came to blaze. He'd had to scrap and claw his way onto every team because of ephebus mortem. But he clung to the hope that Plannar could see beyond E.M. and judge him based on his ability. Most of his professors hadn't shown prejudice so far, so maybe Plannar would treat him the same way.

A holopad sat on the upper shelf of his locker. It blinked, indicating there was an announcement on it. Jet found himself halfway hoping he would be cut from the team. *The semester would be so much easier*, he thought.

But, life without blaze would be like going through withdrawals from an addiction. He stared at the tiny holopad as the other players changed and left. After what seemed like hours, he changed, stuffed the holopad into his backpack, and left.

He returned to his dorm room around 7:30 that evening. Cutter wasn't there, and it looked like he hadn't been there all day. Jet tossed his backpack onto the sofa and placed the announcement on the counter. He took a deep breath as a hologram of Coach Plannar appeared.

"Congratulations, Strud. You are a talented player, an' we welcome you to the team. Though your physical skills are above average, we will work to improve your speed, agility, and strength. You show great decision making and leadership, which are extremely important at the point-blaze position. Most importantly, your drive to win is key to your success. We've great hopes for this season, an' you'll play a big part in our starting offense at right flank point-blazer. Numbers'll be assigned on Monday."

The hologram faded, and Jet slumped back on the sofa. He felt exhausted and exuberant at the same time. He sat forward and watched the announcement again. That's when he noticed a tiny symbol floating over one of Plannar's rings, which was barely detectable in the hologram. Adrenaline surged through him as he watched it a third time. He grabbed his jacket, stuffed the announcement into his backpack, and left for Blazers. He had proof now, and maybe Cutter would see it as well.

The ride on the commuter skiff was annoying. Other students, faculty, and citizens stared blatantly as he sat alone. Several kids pointed in his direction, like he was some rare and bizarre animal.

The commuter docked at a busy terminal on Skylight City with thousands of other skiffs landing and taking off. He followed the signage, getting lost several times, and eventually found the right vector accelerator. It took him to street level where he tried to hail a cab without luck. He used his holopad to get directions and walked to something called the T-Spine. The mass transit system hovered from an overhead track several stories above street level. He paid the fee from his student account, found a seat in the back, and zoned out.

It was less crowded on the T-Spine, and each compartment

had its own privacy screen. Jet relaxed and enjoyed the rush of exhilaration as the people-mover shot forward. He took in the city's spectacular skyline from the comfort of his cabin. The streets below buzzed with activity as the citizens hurried home from work. Color lit the tall buildings' glassy facades even through the mist. Blues, greens, and reds reflected off the buildings and filtered along the dense streets.

Several minutes later, the T-Spine slowed to a halt. Jet funneled out with the other passengers and walked casually along the busy sidewalk. Blazers was easy to find. Hundreds of people crowded around the front door, waiting in line to get in. Jet showed his varsity clothing and was granted immediate access. The interior of the restaurant displayed holographic statues of famous athletes, sports memorabilia, and holovision sets tuned to every imaginable sport. Jet found the team situated in the center of the restaurant in a space called *The Team Huddle*. Fans and news crews cluttered around the players and coaches, interviewing them. He looked on in shock; he hadn't anticipated all the hubbub. The immense popularity of blaze finally hit him.

Jet made eye contact with Cutter, who was slouched in a corner booth with Plexus and another blaze-out named Traser. Plannar stood in the center of the space, surrounded by the media crews. As soon as he looked at Jet, several cameras turned his way, placing his image on every holovision set in the restaurant. The din and clamor died down to a light hum. Jet's hope of a stealthy entrance was ruined. His quiet evening was gone, and most likely, the rest of the semester as well. The brief pause of silence was followed by a rush of cameras flooding his way. He braced himself for the onslaught.

"Jet Stroud, you've made the team. Do you think you can survive the semester?" a female reporter asked, holding a mic in his face. The rest of the reporters did likewise. The camera lights blinded him as the restaurant went silent again. Jet shielded his face with his hands, but the glow from his eyes shone through.

"He doesn't think he'll survive," the lady said when he didn't respond and jotted it down on her holopad.

"That's not what I said." Jet tried to force his way through the thicket of cameras. They backed away cautiously, only to reform the line. More ridiculous questions were flung at him, which he ignored. Every time he tried to get past, the media crews followed and blocked his path. He was about to give up and leave when Coach Plannar stepped in.

"Alright… that's enough for tonight. Let him go through." Plannar tried to speak pleasantly, but it sounded like a growl. The reporters stood their ground for a brief second, then the camera lights shut off. The patrons around the restaurant returned to their conversations and meals.

"Strud," Plannar acknowledged him with a heavy clap on his shoulder. "You're gonna have to get used to it. Cutter's over yonder. Go on an' eat." Plannar made his way back to his seat.

Jet glanced tentatively at Cutter. Traser and Plexus looked away, but Korbin Daze stared him down the entire time with a smirk on his long face. Jet headed toward the corner booth and slid in next to Cutter.

Cutter was wearing his favorite pair of ripped jeans, a simple pair of white sneakers, and a SLU blaze t-shirt already torn at the waist. It was at least two sizes too small and showed his tattooed biceps, which glittered silver in the light. Plexus sported a jaw-dropping pair of business slacks and blouse that looked painted on. Traser's fiery red hair was pinned in ponytails, and she wore slacks and a matching blazer.

The four of them sat silently as a waitress took Jet's order from the next booth. Traser finished a plate of fries, mopping the final bit of ketchup with the last one, and promptly excused herself. Plexus slid out right behind her without a word, leaving him and Cutter alone in the booth.

Cutter looked at Jet. "You mind shifting over? Or better yet, move to the other side."

Jet realized how odd it looked but stayed put. "Didn't mean to run your friends off."

"What makes you think they're my friends?" Cutter asked.

The waitress returned and placed Jet's drink at the end of the table. "Why else would they be sitting at the table with you?" Jet said. "In fact, why are you still here?"

Cutter had finished his meal, and both plates were pushed to the side. He sat slouched with one arm on the back of the booth, frowning at Jet. "I didn't ask them to sit with me—they sat here because they wanted to. And I'm sitting here now because I can't get out." But he was making little effort to leave. "I'm guessing you made the team?" he asked.

"That's right," Jet said. He took the holopad out of his pocket and tossed it onto the table. It clattered around on the tabletop like a coin, coming to rest directly in front of Cutter.

"What's this for?" Cutter asked.

"It's evidence. Go ahead, play it."

Cutter turned the holopad on, and an image of Plannar expanded over the display. Jet paused the message about halfway through. "Look… right there." He pointed at the ring on Plannar's hand. "See that?"

"What, the ring?" Cutter hunched forward and looked closer. "What about it?"

"Not the ring, the symbol above it."

Cutter shook his head. "I don't see anything."

"You can't see that?" Jet pointed at the hologram hovering just above Plannar's ring with both hands.

Cutter shook his head again. "No, I don't. Why did you come here tonight? To show me this? To prove something?"

Jet considered it. Was he trying to prove that he *wasn't* seeing things to Cutter, or to himself? Either way, Cutter didn't seem to care… or did he? "If you don't care, then why did you follow me that night?"

Cutter shrugged and crossed his arms. "Maybe because you can't seem to figure it out."

"Are you serious?" Jet asked, feeling his frustration grow. "You think that I need your help after all I've been through? But, since we're on speaking terms now, there's something I've been meaning to ask you. Why don't you have any friends… real friends?"

"Friends?" Cutter asked, his eyebrows coming together in confusion. "I can't believe you're going to lecture me on that."

"Why not?" Jet said.

Cutter shrugged again, but didn't say anything.

"And here's another one," Jet continued. "Why do you try so hard to be different?"

Their waitress returned, dropped his food near the end of the table, and left. Jet sighed and reached for it.

"What are you getting at?" Cutter fixed him with a glare.

"You could have as many friends as you want. You could be as popular as you want. Instead, you push it all away. Why? To be different?" Jet pointed at Cutter's tattoos and piercings. "The ripped jeans… always a worn-out t-shirt."

"So, my choice of clothing and appearance would suddenly make me a different person?" Cutter mused.

"You've got everything you need to live a normal life, and yet you don't take advantage of it." Jet shook his head. "I just don't get it."

"What's so special about being normal?" Cutter said, an edge of irritation in his voice. "Jet, you were born different, I get that. But why would you ever wish to be normal? Why is it so important to be accepted by these people?"

"So, if I got a few tattoos and wore ripped jeans, that would fix everything?" Jet asked.

"You get my point," Cutter said. "Forget these people. Just live your life."

Jet heaved a sigh. "I don't care if these people like me, Cutter. That's not the point. It's just… what's it like to be accepted? What's it like to wake up one day and know people won't talk behind your back or call you names? What's it like to know you're not going to die before you turn twenty-four? I'd give anything to live just one normal day, which is something you get to do every day. I don't have a choice. I never did."

"So, I guess you've accepted the fact that this isn't a joke?" Cutter asked.

"I accept the fact that *some* of it isn't. But, you're right. It's time to do something about it, I've made up my mind. I'm going to find a cure, and I don't care what anyone says, including you. This may be the biggest challenge of my life, but I'm going to see it through."

Cutter suddenly grinned and clapped him on the back. "That's more like it!" he said, giving Jet a playful shove.

Jet sat back, confused and a bit suspicious. "Is this a joke?"

"I knew you wouldn't quit, Stroud," Cutter said. "I knew you wouldn't disappoint me."

Jet stared at him. “What would you know about me, or anything that I’ve been through?”

“Look, maybe you didn’t realize it, but I’ve been watching you for a long time. I saw you get into so many situations on the blaze pitch and thought to myself, how the hell is Stroud gonna get out of this one? And I’ll be damned if you didn’t always manage a way out.”

“So you’re a fan?” Jet asked. “After all this time and you’re just now telling me this? You could have said something years ago.”

“You didn’t seem to need any help then and you probably wouldn’t have wanted it anyway.”

Jet thought about it. “I don’t know, maybe.”

“You never quit, you always found a way to win,” Cutter continued. “You’ve motivated so many others along the way. The players listen to you… think about that for a minute. Even with your condition, they still follow your lead. If you can take what you do on the field and make it happen off the field, I have no doubt you’ll find what you’re looking for. What you think is a weakness is actually your strength, and maybe that’s why I stayed out of it. Dealing with E.M. has forced you into situations others will never experience or understand. The struggles you’ve endured are a gift.”

The unexpected compliment caught Jet off guard. He had been so busy dealing with everything else that he’d never paid attention to how he chose to address his own problems. Now, he felt guilty about judging Cutter the way he had.

“Well, I don’t know what to say. Thanks, I guess.”

“Just… be yourself,” Cutter said. “Use what you’ve learned to your advantage and you’ll be fine.”

“I don’t know about that,” Jet said. “I’ll be honest with you,

Cutter. I did see something that night at Alpha Hall, and it scares me. Turns out I'm not the only one, though. I just met a kid who also has E.M. He's seen some strange things, too."

"You realize what the experts say," Cutter reminded him. "The first signs are hallucinations—"

"Of course," Jet interrupted. "But none of them have ephebus mortem either!"

"Easy… I'm just saying," Cutter said and held up a hand. "Look. Can you at least sit over there?" Cutter nodded to the bench across the table. "This looks a bit awkward."

Jet sat down opposite him and settled in, studying his roommate. Cutter seemed different now that they were acting like civilized adults. "So, is that why you never picked a fight with me?" Jet asked. "Was it out of pity?"

"Why would I want to fight you?"

"I don't know. Maybe because I'd fought every kid in the ARC district at least once," Jet said. "I just assumed we would one day, after a game or something. They called you "Cutter the Terrible". But you never even approached me."

"In all the years you've known me, have you ever seen me get into a fight?" Cutter asked.

Jet thought for a moment and realized that it was true; he'd never seen Cutter in a fight.

"Are you really that surprised?" Cutter asked. "No one messed with me, and I had no desire to fight anyone. I'm sure my appearance had something to do with it."

"Is that why all the tattoos?" Jet asked.

Cutter hunched forward and tugged at his frayed t-shirt sleeve. He pointed at one of the tattoos on his massive bicep. "See this one?"

Jet looked at the silver tattoo. Leaves and vines intertwined around his arm, delicate and wispy. It was the first time he'd really paid attention to it, but it was the last thing he'd expected to see on a person like Cutter. "It's a shale fern, isn't it?" Jet said.

"That's right. You know these plants grow all over the ARC district. They've adapted to the dark environment, don't need sunlight, and grow right through the brittle shale. They're drought-resistant and draw moisture from the air like a succulent. They're survivors. But they're also fragile and have no natural defense."

"So, why a tattoo of a shale fern?" Jet asked.

"It's the first tattoo I ever got… two weeks after my father murdered my younger brother."

Jet sat back in shock.

Cutter watched him for a second. "Yeah, bet you didn't know that about me, huh?"

Jet shook his head.

"My parents didn't dump me like yours did," Cutter continued. "I lived in a halfway home because I ran away, one down at the very end of the district. Didn't live there too long, but long enough. Ran away for obvious reasons, guess I was about thirteen. My younger brother, Kedrick, was only eight. He was handicapped. Couldn't walk, and it took a lot of our resources. My father came home angry one night, a tough day at work, I suppose. I didn't see it happen, only heard it. Pretty sickening sound, though. Father used something heavy, probably a pipe. Two heavy thumps, and that was it. There wasn't even a scream, but I knew it was over as soon as it happened. I climbed out the window and ran… just ran like hell. It felt like days later when I ended up at the halfway home. We were just kids, fragile, like this shale fern, too small and frightened to defend ourselves. Especially him, with his handicap. Two weeks later, I swore I'd never run from anything again. I swore I'd never be responsible for anyone else's suffering. So, I got this tattoo. I wanted something I'd see every day, to remind me. But it wasn't enough." Cutter sat back, stone faced and emotionless.

"What do you mean?" Jet asked.

"It was like I couldn't remind myself enough. I worked odd jobs, and eventually I met a guy who owned a tattoo parlor. I started working for him when I was eleven and soon I'd saved up enough to get my next tattoo." He pointed at a larger one on his right forearm. It was the same delicate detailing, silver and leafy, intertwining up his arm. "Then came more—I couldn't seem to stop. I'll never forget my brother. I see him in my dreams, when I'm awake, when I practice. He's with me all the time. These tattoos stand for more than just Kedrick, they represent the weaknesses that I've overcome. You've lived through similar pain; I know you have."

"Are you saying that I need your protection now?" Jet said.

"No, not at all. You've found your own way to cope, just like I found mine. We're not that different."

He looked at Cutter. The kid he'd spent almost his entire life with yet known so little about. Cutter had had his fair share of tough breaks, too, it seemed. He felt guilt at how he'd judged Cutter. He had done the same thing that everyone else had done to him. It suddenly dawned on him why Cutter avoided friends—he was afraid of losing them.

"Are you turning over a new leaf?" Jet asked.

"Maybe it's time for both of us to turn over a new leaf," Cutter said.

"This isn't pity, is it?" Jet asked.

"Hey, I don't know a damn thing about that."

"What about the others with E.M.?" Jet asked. "Do they deserve pity?"

"I don't know. Is it really up to us to decide?"

Jet considered. "I watched the old news report on Myranda Mason. She was the prep student with E.M. who died the day before the semester started."

"Yeah, I saw that report," Cutter said. "It was all over the news."

"She was like us, just getting started," Jet said. "I didn't know her, but I don't want people to feel that way about me when I'm gone. I don't want to be pitied."

"I think you're doing the right thing by talking to the other kids with E.M.," Cutter said. "You're doing something about it and that's what's important. That deserves respect, and if you need my help, I'm right here." Cutter held out his large hand.

"Well, I guess it's a good thing we're on the same team this time," Jet said and shook Cutter's hand. He couldn't remember ever feeling so thankful for a little help.

CHAPTER

The Hydra 7

ΑΒΓΔΕΖΗΘΙΚΛ<u>Μ</u>
ΝΞΟΠΡΣΤΥΦΧΨΩ

On Wednesday morning, Jet waited patiently outside of Dorcher Hall for Professor Sylvant. He wasn't scheduled for her class until Thursday but decided he couldn't wait to talk to her.

His goal was simple. He would try to gather as many willing people as possible and search for information. Beyond that, he didn't have much of a plan… yet. His gut told him it would take all of them to do this, and Sylvant's resources would be a key factor. She had offered her help, but he wanted more from her. He wanted her to join their group. Cord was committed, and Cutter had volunteered. He was uncertain about Vail's whereabouts, and Bo was still a question mark. His vision of a union might consist of only three people, but it was better than one. And if he could get Sylvant onboard, their chances looked much better. But today, he had something else to ask her.

Ten minutes later, Professor Sylvant walked out of Dorcher Hall with a few students following her. Jet approached and fell in beside her. The other students glanced at him and hurried off.

"Oh, Jet," Sylvant said. "I thought it was another student." Her demeanor softened. "Aren't you in my Thursday class?"

"Right, but I was wondering if we could talk," Jet said.

Sylvant hesitated and looked at her watch. "Sure, if you care to walk with me."

"That's fine," Jet said.

"What's on your mind?" Sylvant said but didn't slow her pace along the busy sidewalk.

Jet kept up and wondered how to begin. The name Tyberius Alexander had been stuck in his head for the last several days, and he decided to start there. "Do you know a man by the name of Tyberius Alexander?" It was a straightforward question, but her response caught him off-guard.

Sylvant stopped abruptly in the middle of the crowded walkway. Jet had to take a few steps back. "Is everything okay?" he asked.

Sylvant clamped her satchel to her chest and stared at the ground. "Where did you hear that name?"

"I... stumbled across it in an article," Jet said, which was a half-truth.

"That's impossible," she whispered.

Students continued to buffet them as they stood in the middle of the sidewalk. Her dark skin seemed a shade lighter, and she tapped her satchel nervously. Jet wondered how a name could make her react in such a way. Apparently, it meant more to her than he'd thought it would.

Sylvant started to speak several times but stopped to reconsider. She looked at her watch again, pulled out her holopad, and typed in an address. "Meet me here tomorrow. It's a café outside of Skylight City called *The Hydra 7*. Don't talk to *anyone* about this, Jet. I mean it."

. • • • • ● • • • • .

AFTER PRACTICE THAT evening, Jet browsed through the school directory again, trying to find more information on Vail Hart. Every time he dropped by one of her classes, she was never there. He set his sights on Bo Blake instead. After Myranda Mason's so-called murder, along with Cutter's continued urging, he decided to pick up the pace.

He'd heard rumors that Bo ran up to twenty kilometers a day, which made him an easier target to locate. He assumed Bo would still be running after blaze practice. He just needed to find him somewhere along the cross-country course, which wove its way through the campus and into the Clipton Woods. Jet made his way to the forest's edge, found a large oak tree, and sat down next to it.

Runners flitted by like wisps of smoke in the setting sun. He listened to the soft pattering of shoes on the dirt path as crickets hummed in the background. Jet pulled out his holopad and surfed the system's network as he waited.

He read an article about attaining a skiff license, which was something he'd been considering, despite the cost. The university provided student athletes with an allowance, and the online exam would drain his account for the month. Cutter didn't want to spend his money on a license because he didn't mind taking the commuter skiff. But Jet hated the crowds, and a license would help him avoid all the harassment. He made the arrangements, transferring most of his school allowance credits to the proper authorities, and took a study course. Then he settled in and took the exam, which he passed in less than twenty minutes. Now all he had to do was swing by the university hangers and join the flight club. He'd have unlimited access to the university's skiffs any time he needed one.

The tangerine sun dipped lower on the horizon, and nearby lamps flickered to life. Jet stood and stretched his legs, stowing his holopad in his backpack. He assumed he had missed Bo and cinched up his backpack to leave, then paused.

Peering at him from the purple shadows of the forest's edge was a pair of glowing eyes. They hovered, then blinked.

"Bo?" Jet asked. "Is that you?"

The eyes blinked again. "Why are you here?"

"Just want to talk. That's all," Jet said.

"About what?"

"I have a proposition you might be interested in."

Bo stepped from the shadowy forest. He was tall and lanky, like most runners, with legs built for churning out long distances. His sandy blonde hair was feathered back to one side, windblown and unkempt. A rugged beard barely hid the stress lines on his face and reminded Jet of a moth-eaten quilt over distressed leather. But like the rest of them with E.M., Bo's glowing eyes dominated his facial features.

"I already know what you want," Bo said. "I hope you have a better excuse than the last kid."

"You mean Cord," Jet said. "He has a name, you know."

Bo nodded and mopped sweat from his brow. "Whatever."

"All I want is to find a cure," Jet said. "Just like you."

"Good luck with that, prep." Bo turned to leave.

"So, you've already given up?" Jet asked. "I didn't expect a great track star like you to quit so easily. I'm disappointed."

Bo clenched his jaw. "Watch it…"

"Or what?" Jet said. He felt no more intimidated by Bo than Cutter, and Cutter was much larger. "If everyone's right about E.M., then it doesn't matter, right?"

Bo lingered. Jet could see he wanted to leave, though. His plan of goading Bo to listen to him was working. "Whatever you have to say, do it quickly," Bo said.

"I want you to join us. I've found some evidence that I believe will help."

"Show me," Bo said.

"I will if you agree to meet with us. If you're still not convinced after that, then you're free to go. It's that simple."

"Sounds like you've got it all figured out," Bo muttered. He considered Jet in the fading sunlight. "You're Jet Stroud, the new point blazer. Saw you on the news the other day."

"Then you know how annoying it is," Jet replied. "Wouldn't it be nice to not deal with that anymore?"

"It won't ever happen. You'll figure that out sooner or later."

"That's a matter of opinion, Bo."

"That *is* my opinion, though, and I know a little more about it than you. But tell you what. I'll humor you."

"Good." Jet held out his hand, but Bo didn't bother to shake it.

"Tell me when and where. This better be worth it."

"I'll call you. I'm still waiting for one more."

Bo shook his head and chuckled. "You must be talking about Vail. You're making a mistake, pal. But, hey, good luck with that."

Blake took Jet's holopad, punched in his personal number, and handed it back. Jet watched him sprint off into the mist. He breathed a sigh of relief. Three out of five were now committed, at least to hearing what he had to say. The plan was coming together, but there were still two very important people left to convince.

· • • • • ● • • • • ·

JET BOLTED OUT of his ten o'clock class the next day and thought about dropping by the university hangers to register his skiff license. He decided he didn't want to be late for his lunch date and instead took the commuter skiff for what he hoped was the last time.

The flight to Skylight City took less than twenty minutes but felt like an eternity with everyone staring at him. Once the skiff landed, he made his way down to street level and hurried over to the T-Spine. He climbed into a private cabin and finally relaxed.

The other passengers disembarked at stops along the way. Before long, he was the last one on board. The T-Spine stopped at the last station.

Jet stepped onto an elevated platform and watched as the transit reversed itself in a blur of mechanical gadgets and gears, reassembling on to the rail line directly above. It hissed, sputtered, and shot back down the charged rail with a thunderclap, leaving him all alone.

The elevated platform gave a commanding view of his surroundings. Across from him was a roundabout with a towering stone fountain that appeared to be broken. Its once white stone was stained and discolored, and stagnant water lingered in the basin. Jet counted six streets that fed into the roundabout with a seventh road dead-ending into a gloomy looking café. A backlit sign hung from an awning that read *H7,* with the 7 flickering. The façade's deep setbacks gave the café a foreboding appearance. Other odd-shaped buildings filled the surrounding areas. A few shops lit the storefronts, but most businesses had closed long ago. Jet walked across the empty roundabout and stepped into the lonely café.

There were a handful of people inside, sipping tea and browsing the network on their holopads. Sitting near a corner window was Professor Sylvant. She lowered her sunglasses and motioned to him. Jet took a deep breath and walked over to her table.

"I was starting to wonder if you had changed your mind," Sylvant said, pushing her sunglasses on top of her head. "Have a seat."

Jet sat down, shifting in his seat to get comfortable. He waited quietly for her to talk.

Sylvant looked out the window towards the old fountain in the center of the roundabout. She ran her finger along the bridge of her nose, lost in thought. "Being here brings back memories," she said with a hint of sentiment in her voice. "This was once a popular part of Skylight City. That fountain was called The Hydra and used to be one of the most famous landmarks around. I came here every day after class when I was a student, just to get away from campus." She shook her head. "How quickly things change, and not always for the better."

Jet remained silent until their waitress appeared.

"Two cups of tea," Sylvant said, and the waitress hurried off.

Jet was beginning to feel tense as he sat across the small table from her. If someone recognized them sitting at the secluded café, word would spread quickly. She was taking a risk to meet him off campus like this.

"Sylvant—"

"It's alright, Jet," she interrupted him. "I know you're concerned, but this is important. You mentioned a name to me yesterday."

"I remember," Jet said.

Sylvant crossed her arms and pursed her lips to one side. "I'd really like to know how you got that name."

Jet shook his head. "If I told you, you'd laugh and walk out the door." Jet knew she wouldn't take no for an answer, though, and he wanted something from her as well. It was a gamble, and he'd just played his first card.

Sylvant stared at him and took a deep breath. "So, we're playing this game, are we? You want to know more about Tyberius, I assume? Fine, I'll go first then." She sat back, crossed her arms, and cleared her throat. "My sister and I were best friends, though sometimes you wouldn't know it. We were competitive and fought constantly. Still, she would have given her life for me without a second thought. We were raised in a small fishing community where our father was a captain on one of the vessels. One day, when I was very young, a storm blew in and capsized his ship. It was something that happened often, I just never thought it would happen to him. His name was Riddoux Sylvant… he drowned that day. Solan and I were both young and took the news hard."

Their waitress returned with two steaming cups of tea and set them on the table, eyeing Jet openly as if trying to place his face. Sylvant waited for her to leave and lowered her voice. "The day of my father's funeral, Solan told me something and made me swear never to repeat it." Sylvant paused, holding his gaze. "She told me that Riddoux wasn't our real father, yet we were both led to believe that he was. Why she believed this, she never said. Solan just had a knack for finding these things out."

"So that's the connection… Tyberius Alexander," Jet muttered, finally putting it all together. "Solan thought he was your real father."

Sylvant nodded. "She believed he was still alive but didn't know where he was. In fact, she felt so strongly about it that she even changed her last name. A few years later, she was accepted into Skylight University, and she continued to search for information about him. We kept in touch over the years, but she never mentioned his name again until the day before her graduation. She sent me a holographic message about him and was excited to share some news but wouldn't say what it was over an open channel. Then, before we spoke again, she was gone. And all I had was the name of a man who apparently didn't exist."

She paused again and looked out the window at the fountain. "Solan discovered something that I still haven't been able to verify. I thought when I came to the university as a professor, doors would open, and I would find answers. That hasn't happened. I thought I'd reached a dead-end… that is until you unexpectedly showed up in my class." Sylvant set her tea down and lowered her eyes at him, ready to hear his side of the story.

Jet didn't consider very long. He needed her help and now was the time to trust his instincts. Sylvant would either choose to believe him or dismiss his story as a foolish delusion of ephebus mortem. He sat forward and locked eyes with her. "I believe that your sister is still alive."

Her gaze didn't waver as she probed his glowing eyes, as if trying to detect a lie. "How?" she asked in an unsteady whisper.

"It's a long story," Jet replied. He glanced around the room again. Despite the lack of people, he felt like a spotlight was on him. People were starting to recognize him, thanks to the media and blaze.

"Jet, we aren't leaving here until you tell me," she said.

Jet nodded. He owed her an explanation. "The night of the storm, I saw Solan's name on my holopad. Maybe it was the lightning or something else, but I don't think so. It's the second time I've seen her name."

"Is that it?" Sylvant asked.

"No, there's more. One day, when I was in the library, I found a journal."

"And?"

"I think it belonged to your sister."

"Where... how?" she asked, leaning forward.

Jet shook his head. "Doesn't matter. What's important is that it mentions Tyberius Alexander in one of the entries. I could use your help figuring a few things out."

"So, you… have her journal? Is it with you?" Sylvant asked.

"I *assume* it's hers," Jet replied. "I also think it's been tampered with, so there's no telling. And no, I don't have it on me right now."

Sylvant was quiet for a moment. "My sister died ten years ago. I've put that behind me… I don't believe in ghosts, Jet."

Jet felt his chance slipping away. He'd hoped she would believe him but had apparently been wrong. Without Sylvant's help, it would be difficult, maybe impossible. But he wasn't giving up yet. He had a backup plan. Sylvant wanted the journal badly. As much as he hated to, he decided to use it as leverage.

Jet grabbed his backpack and stood to leave.

"Hold on." Sylvant reached across the table but pulled her hand back. "I didn't say I wouldn't help you."

"You don't believe me, you just said it. How can you help me if you don't believe me?"

"You have my sister's journal. I need to see it. So, what can we work out?"

"Sylvant, this seems to involve you somehow, and I don't know why. I didn't just stumble across that journal out of pure luck. I didn't just end up in your class coincidentally. Don't you think there's something more going on here?"

"What is it you want me to do?"

"I've been talking to the others with E.M. We're planning to meet and talk about our options. Look, I'm a student with limited resources. We could use a professor who has connections. Otherwise, this isn't going very far."

Sylvant tapped her nose. "This is getting risky. I could lose my job."

"If you need more time to consider, I understand. But I need an answer soon."

"You're good," she said with a smile. "Okay, Jet. Count me in. It's what my sister would have wanted anyway. But I can't guarantee for how long. And I don't know how much help I can give. There are limitations, you understand?"

Jet nodded. "Thank you."

"But first, I'll need to see that journal," she said and held out her hand. "You're a horrible liar."

"How'd you know I had it with me?"

"I'm around students all day," she said. "I can read people like a book."

"It's password protected." Jet took the journal out of his backpack and placed it on her palm. She quickly put it in her purse.

Sylvant's watch beeped, and she glanced at it in frustration. "I've got to get back to the university."

"Are you always this busy?"

"I'm on call around the clock. This is exactly what I'm talking about. It will get worse near the end of the semester, too." She dropped a few credits on the table.

They walked out the front door and stood on the vacant sidewalk. "I'll call you when we're ready," Jet said. "Hopefully, sooner rather than later."

"What are you waiting for?" Sylvant asked, donning her scarf and shades.

"A girl named Vail Hart. I've been trying to find her, but it's almost like she doesn't exist, except in the student directory."

"I've heard of her," Sylvant said. "She'll be tough to convince. You sure about her?"

"I think we'll need everyone we can get. Hopefully, I can find her soon, though."

"I suppose that's your call. Good luck." Sylvant hailed a cab and sped off.

Jet watched her leave and tried to ignore the feeling of uncertainty. He kept telling himself Professor Sylvant was someone he could trust. She wasn't involved in this by accident, he just wasn't sure why, yet.

He grappled with his thoughts as he crossed the desolate intersection to the T-Spine. He climbed up to the elevated platform, found a bench, and waited. He thought about Vail and wondered if he should just forget about her. Everything he'd heard so far seemed to be negative and locating her was proving to be a pain. But in reality, it made him want to find her even more. He needed to meet this girl, he was beyond intrigued by her now.

Minutes later, he boarded the T-Spine, unaware of the dark mass hovering in the shadows near the fountain.

CHAPTER

The Cauldron

ΑΒΓΔΕΖΗΘΙΚΛ<u>Μ</u>
ΝΞΟΠΡΣΤΥΦΧΨΩ

OVER THE NEXT several weeks, Jet searched relentlessly for Vail. He even asked one of her professors where she might be but got no response. He had very little contact with anyone during that time, including Cutter, although Cord had called a few times requesting an update. He reminded Jet that time was of the essence. Still, Jet refused to set a date for their meeting without first speaking to Vail.

To make matters worse, the blaze season-opener loomed just around the corner. With just a few days left, practice sessions had grown frantic, and the intensity level quadrupled. Plannar pushed their practice sessions late into the evenings, sometimes finishing with the stadium lights on.

Jet left practice late on Friday feeling exhausted. His normal routine was a trip to the library stacks for some solitude and study time, followed by a thorough search of the network for any sign of Vail. But instead, he'd agreed to meet Sylvant at the *Hydra 7* that evening. She had viewed Solan's journal and was ready to talk.

This time he reserved a skiff from the university flight club. Even though it was late, university skiffs were available twenty-four hours a day. There was no one on duty when he arrived, so he used his holopad to enter one of the hanger bays.

The hovering skiff was glossy black with a tail fin that looped up and over the back of the hull. Twin engines sat discreetly beneath the swept-back wings, and the university crest was emblazed beneath the cockpit. The aircraft utilized the latest anti-gravity thrusters, which hummed softly inside the hanger and bathed everything in a greenish glow.

After a quick inspection, he climbed into the cockpit and fired up the engines. He guided the skiff out of the hanger and waited. When he was cleared, he jammed the thrusters into overdrive and shot skyward.

Soon he was circling over the *Hydra 7*. From his vantage, he could see the surrounding area better. The alleyways behind the shops emitted jetties of steam. Off in the distance stretched a pitted field and beyond was an abandoned factory. The setting sun turned the air around the factory to a deep shade of red.

Jet piloted the skiff to a designated landing area, which was mostly vacant, and walked down an empty alleyway towards the café. He recognized the confident strides of Professor Sylvant and waved at her. But something caught his attention in the shadows of the fountain. He stopped in the middle of the roundabout, mesmerized by the shape he saw. Sylvant walked over to him.

"Jet?" she asked. "Everything okay?"

He didn't respond, still gazing in the direction of the fountain. She snapped her fingers in front of his face to gain his attention.

He blinked and looked at her. "Sylvant, over there next to the fountain... do you see it?"

It was the heat mirage again. It shifted around the base of the fountain, blurry and transparent. But it was too cool for a heat mirage, though it looked exactly like the ones he'd seen on hot and humid days.

She glanced in the fountain's direction while pulling him out of the street. She shook her head. "No, I don't see anything. Are you sure you're okay?"

Jet looked at her defensively. "I'm fine, thanks." He walked towards the fountain with the mirage in his sight. Sylvant followed, the heels of her shoes clicking across the vacant intersection. Jet stepped up to the fountain's basin for a look around, but the mirage was gone.

"I swear… it was here," he said.

"What was here? What are you talking about?" she asked.

"There was a… a shape, or something like a mirage here, just now."

Sylvant cleared her throat. "Why don't we go inside. We need to talk about this." She flashed her sister's journal in front of his face.

Jet hesitated. He wanted to understand what he'd just seen as much as he wanted to hear about the journal.

The shape suddenly reemerged near one of the alleyways, steam momentarily cloaking it. Then, the sunlight dimmed and turned everything a shade of rust.

"There. It's there!" he hissed at her. "You can't see that?"

She peered toward the alleyway. "Jet. You're starting to worry me."

"You don't believe me, do you?"

"Jet, I'm trying to understand, but I don't know what to say."

"I'm going after it," Jet said. "I want to prove to you—"

"Whatever it is, let it go!" Sylvant looked down the dark alley and back at him. "We can talk about it inside the café, alright? My first concern is your safety."

Jet could see the uneasiness in her expression. "Sylvant, I'm asking for your help, not your protection."

It was growing darker, and an unsettling stillness seemed to descend around them. Sylvant recovered her composure. "As a professor to a student, it's my responsibility to look after you. You need to come with me."

Jet watched the mirage move down the alleyway and vanish into the steam. "I can take care of myself. I'll call you later, Sylvant. I promise." He sprinted down the alleyway, leaving her behind.

Plumes of steam gushed from the buildings lining the alley and hid the fleeing mirage. The sunlight was nearly gone, making it difficult to see. Jet had to stop a few times to see where he was.

The chase came to an abrupt halt when the alley ended at a brick wall. The mirage was gone. Jet backtracked, looking for signs of it. He noticed a ladder on one building and climbed up three stories and onto the rooftop. He skirted the parapet and stopped to regain his bearings.

The sunlight flickered and dimmed, like someone sliding a gossamer drape in front of it. Jet looked at his watch, surprised to see there should still be half an hour of daylight left. What happened next made the hair on his arms stand up. One of the system's outer belts crossed slowly in front of the sun, casting a long shadow over the cityscape beyond. The eclipse's shadow inched eerily across each building, engulfing the city in darkness. Jet had read an article about the event, something called a skylight eclipse.

His skin grew cold as the eclipse overtook him. From the rooftop, he watched the leading edge of it creep doggedly across the pitted field and towards the dimly lit factory in the distance. Fleeing just ahead of the eclipse was the shimmering mirage.

Jet leapt over the building's parapet and onto an adjacent rooftop. He scrambled across a metal bridge spanning the alleyway and sprinted across the field.

He entered the abandoned factory minutes later and slowed to a halt, kneeling against a storage tank to catch his breath. He could hear equipment running in the distance, which seemed odd since the factory appeared to be vacant. A rust-colored smog from old chemicals still lingered in the air. Rogue weeds grew up through cracked concrete, and above him, a maze of catwalks and pipes cast a kaleidoscope of patterns onto the pavement.

He crept further into the factory, searching for the mirage. The ground below his feet quivered, and the sound of equipment grew louder. Tremors accompanied a dull scraping noise that sounded like metal grinding on metal. Something big moved below the surface. He placed his hand on a storage tank and felt it vibrating rapidly.

Jet followed the thrumming for several minutes before stumbling upon a vast clearing. Rusted sheet metal walls rose up to create a circular pit. Sand and dirt covered the ground, and tumbleweeds piled along one end like skeletal remains. In the center stood an oddly shaped contraption that resembled the smokestack of a ship. Its bow pointed skyward like a steel chimney with steam spewing from it.

An uneasy feeling settled over him as he hid in the shadows. He was in the middle of nowhere and chasing a mirage. It was getting late, and the eclipse had him on edge.

How was he going to explain all of this to Sylvant?

He'd have to worry about that later. At the moment, he had a decision to make... continue or turn back?

He made up his mind to turn back. He stood to leave, took one last look at the smokestack, and froze.

The mirage had reappeared.

This thing is leading me on! Jet thought as goosebumps erupted on his flesh.

He sprinted straight at it, covering the thirty yards in seconds, and slid to a halt next to the smokestack. He searched frantically for signs of the mirage. The smokestack appeared to be a control device, and it was littered with valves and conduits. He turned the valves, hoping to open a hidden doorway or some panel perhaps. After several minutes, he stopped. The thing had vanished.

"What now?" he muttered and took a deep breath. He walked cautiously around the equipment a second time and delved between two large pressure valves he hadn't noticed before. He wedged himself between them, pushing conduit out of his way, and finally popped through and into a dark corridor beyond.

For several seconds all he could see were spots dancing in his vision. He reached out to feel his surroundings and his hand brushed across a large conduit. He struggled to his feet and followed it. He walked, crawled, and stumbled in a downward direction, eventually noticing a reddish light ahead.

Jet stopped at the edge of a large compartment. Below were dozens of iron cauldrons, clustered tightly together. A foul smell emanated from them, and the air was hot and sticky. He mopped sweat from his brow and covered his nose from the stench. All was silent except for the sound of dripping water. Whatever had been making the grinding noise was gone for the moment.

He was about to step onto a rusted catwalk when something shimmered from the corner of his eye. The mirage materialized on the opposite side of the space, perched on the catwalk. Jet stared at it, finally getting his first good look.

No matter which way he tilted his head, light seemed to bend around the thing, manipulating its form. Its outline flowed like the folds of a long cloak, and it moved in quick, random motions. The shimmering cloak hovered, darted, and disappeared in a burst of speed. Jet thought again how this thing seemed to be playing a game and wondered if it was a trap. But if the mysterious cloak had wanted him dead, it would've already done it.

He removed his left hand from his nose to help keep his balance, and his stomach lurched from the stench. He ignored the sensation and concentrated on his footing. Once he reached the other side, he hurried down the stair to ground level and walked cautiously around the large iron cauldrons. The sound of electronic beeps drew his attention, and he stepped into a control room.

The computers were old and outdated. They whizzed and hummed, sending off a bit of heat. Jet assumed the control room was responsible for running the factory complex. But why it was still operating with no one around was a mystery.

He stayed close to the back wall to survey the space, then moved in closer to one of the computers and looked at the monitor. The faded screen flickered, and the command prompt required a password. In the monitor's background was a symbol of a Heliographi and the current date and time. He'd seen the symbol so often lately that it no longer surprised him, though. He turned to browse the holopads on the shelves behind him. He picked up one titled *Skylight Eclipse Patterns*, examined it, and slipped it into his backpack, not sure why.

The computer behind him beeped. He wheeled around to see that the password had been entered, granting him access. He looked around the room, but only the computers were there, chirping softly at him. He walked over and sat down behind the screen. He was now looking at a live feed of a group of people standing around a large conference table. Jet leaned in closer, trying to make out who they were, and shook his head in disbelief.

"I must be losing my mind…" he whispered.

Several Skylight University department heads and professors filled the room. Coach Plannar pointed at Janet Bhiner like they were having a heated argument. President Starr and Professor Keoff stood in each other's face having their own disagreement. Several officials and members of the authorities stood to one side and yelled accusations at the professors. It looked like a fist fight might break out at any minute. Jet couldn't hear anything they said, but he read one word from Coach Plannar's lips.

Myranda.

A heavy thud shook the control room, and the computers around him whirred to life. The sound of scraping metal he'd heard earlier had returned. He had seen enough and decided it was time to leave.

When he stepped out of the control room, the door shut and locked behind him. Above, he saw the source of the grinding noise. A huge steel door was sliding shut over the cauldrons. It rattled the floor like an earthquake and stirred the stench inside the cauldrons to life. The fumes burned his eyes, and he could barely breathe. He needed to get out of the compartment and away from the cauldrons. He sprinted up the metal stairs two steps at a time. When he reached the top, the sliding door was nearly shut.

At the last second, he dove beneath the door and rolled out of the way. It shut behind him with a resounding thud that echoed down the dark corridor and diminished into silence.

Jet lay on his back, breathing heavily and listening. What little light there had been was gone now. He checked himself for injuries and stood, feeling around for the large conduit. After several minutes he located it and made his way up the ramp. Before long, he was squeezing between the pressure valves and into the cool night.

He rested just long enough to get his bearings and plunged across the large clearing to the safety of the shadows. Jet ran, trying to fight off the panic he felt in his gut. He couldn't remember the way out and kept running into dead ends. He was lost in the factory.

After nearly an hour of running, he stopped to clear his head. He sat down to focus his mind and calm himself. A thought filled his head, almost like a voice. He could hear it speaking to him, not with words, but emotions. He listened to it, stood, and walked calmly.

Minutes later, he stood at the edge of the complex. In the distance, city lights twinkled at him through the heavy mist. He began trudging across the rugged field and back to his skiff, fully aware that he was being followed.

CHAPTER

Apex

ΑΒΓΔΕΖΗΘΙΚΛ<u>Μ</u>
ΝΞΟΠΡΣΤΥΦΧΨΩ

By the time Jet made it back to the university, it was past eleven o'clock. Still, he had promised to call Sylvant. Even though it was late, he was certain she'd be worried about him. Just outside the hangar bay, he checked to make sure no one was around and called her from his holopad.

"Jet!" Her expression hardened. "What were you thinking?" She snapped up in her seat, barely visible behind stacks of holopads. Holographic images of the homework she was grading made her difficult to see.

"I'm fine," Jet said. "I'm back at the university now. It's okay."

Sylvant eased back and crossed her arms. She glared at him. "You should have listened to me—"

Jet held up his hands. "Wait, Sylvant. I need to say something. I understand your concern. But I'm fully capable of taking care of myself."

"And you're also my student," she reminded him. "Which makes you my responsibility."

"True, I am your student. But I've also been watching after

myself my entire life. I appreciate your concern for my safety. But if I wanted your protection, I would have asked for it."

She sighed and paused for a few seconds. "I apologize... I'm overreacting. I thought of my sister, especially when you started acting strange tonight. I couldn't stop thinking about her, and... I just want to make sure you're safe, that's all. I know you're going through some issues you don't understand. Can you tell me about it?"

Jet scratched his forehead. "I wish I knew where to start..."

"Why don't you start from the alleyway," Sylvant said.

He tried his best to recall all the details but felt like he was rushing his story and paused when he reached the part about the control room. "Sylvant, before you say anything, just listen because I know this is going to sound crazy."

She continued to look at him. "I'm listening."

"I saw several Skylight professors tonight. They were in a conference room at this abandoned factory complex, arguing about something. I thought I heard one of them mention Myranda's name—"

Sylvant's brow furrowed, and she quickly held up a hand. "That's enough, Jet. This isn't a secure connection."

He stopped and nodded. "What did you find in Solan's journal?"

She sat back. "You were right; someone's hacked into it. Bits and pieces of it are definitely missing."

He considered, then looked at her. "I think it's time. I've decided to have the meeting on Monday."

She shook her head. "Not at the café, I hope. People are beginning to notice you, especially with the season about to start. Blaze draws a lot of attention to you."

"I have another place in mind," Jet said.

"Where?"

"Inside the main library."

"The library?" she said, shocked. "That's probably the *worst* place we could meet!"

He shook his head. "Not the area I'm thinking of. Just meet me at the front, let's say eight o'clock."

She looked at him doubtfully but nodded. "I hope you're right about this." Sylvant leaned forward to close the connection.

"Hold on," Jet said.

She rubbed the back of her neck. "It's late, Jet, and I've got a ton of work to do."

"I just need to know one thing." He could tell that she was nervous about talking over the open line, but he pressed her anyway. "Are you certain you didn't see anything in that alleyway tonight?" He held his breath.

Sylvant stared back at him through the static-laden hologram and shook her head. "No. I'm sorry, Jet. I wish I could say yes." After a brief pause, she broke the connection.

He sat on the cool stone bench and tried to relax. Staring at the blank hologram, he felt suddenly alone. His one consolation at that moment was that he'd made up his mind. The meeting would take place on Monday, and the union created after that would determine the course of the semester—not only for him, but for the others as well. The biggest downside was having it without the final student, Vail Hart. But he could wait no longer.

. • • • ● ● ● • • • .

Saturday morning was a big day for Jet. It was the first game of the season and the start of his college career in blaze. When he walked into the locker room at Crux Field, the team was already suiting up. The locker room looked like a war room with players reviewing last-minute strategies with their respective coaches. Holopads suspended from the ceiling displayed footage of their opponent, Ogden University. Nervous chatter and tension filled the room. It had been a busy week with full scrimmages and late-night practices. Jet's entire body ached, but he felt prepared.

Just before game time, the team gathered in the tunnel and waited. he stood next to Cutter and the hulking form of Rand Blixer, one of the starting blaze-blockers in his squad. Plannar went over some last-minute details, reminding the defense to focus on Ogden University's All-System point-blazer, Thadson Marc.

"If we can contain him, then we've got a chance to win," Plannar growled.

"You ready for this?" Cutter asked.

Jet took a deep breath and nodded. "I hear this is one of the most exciting traditions in blaze. The charge onto the field."

"Don't fall down," Cutter joked, looking around the crowd of players.

"Who are you looking for?" Jet asked.

"Plexus. I think she's near the front..."

Jet was about to ask why when the announcer's voice boomed from outside. The team surged forward, forcing him up the tunnel. The sound of cleats filled his ears as he ran to keep from getting trampled. With a blast of smoke, they sprinted onto the field. The roar of the crowd was deafening inside the massive stadium. His heart hammered in his chest as the quarter of a million fans cheered them on. A sea of blue and red filled the stadium above and below them with banners waving wildly in the bleachers.

It was a perfect day for blaze. The stasis dome was open, which made the field glisten iridescently over the clear turf. The Ogden University Holospears were gathered near the far end zone, stretching and getting loose. Their bright gold uniforms were similar to Skylight's, except in color, their gold emblems dazzling in the autumn sunlight. The team captains met at midfield for the coin toss. Skylight won and chose to defer the blaze, which meant they would defend first.

Jet stood on the sideline and watched in awe. The noise level inside the stadium grew to a fevered pitch as the first drive got underway. It was the Holospear's star point-blazer, Thadson Marc, that delivered the first score of the game, though. He connected on the second play with a flanking blaze-out who sprinted sixty-five yards for six points. Once the main squad scored, they left the field along with that particular defensive squad. Gameplay became less complicated after that since there were fewer players on the field. But despite giving up the first score of the game, Skylight's two flanking defensive squads held, and he was now ready for his chance.

The three Skylight receivers returned their separate kickoffs for good starting field position. The three Skylight squads took the field and were greeted by an earsplitting roar. Butterflies fluttered briefly in his stomach as he listened to the chanting fans. He glanced across the field at Cutter, who was now in the left side offensive squad as the starting mid-blazer.

Jet's holocypher crackled and delivered the first play call, which also lit up on the inside of his visor. Only he could see it as he faced his squad. They huddled around him, waiting for the call. Traser and Plexus, his speedy blaze-outs, stood tall and lanky on one side. Haltz, the squad's stout mid-blazer, hopped up and down in anticipation while the blaze-blockers stared back at him patiently, led by Rand Blixer. Jet relayed the first play of his college career, and they clapped in tandem before breaking the huddle. It was an interference route across the middle to free up Daze's receivers. After that, Traser and Plexus would have to get open for a pass.

Daze's snap count sounded in their helmets and lit up on their visors so they could hear over the roaring fans. Jet felt the rough texture of the blaze on his fingertips and dropped back into the pocket that formed around him. The thrill of the game took control, and he felt more at home than he'd felt since he arrived at the university. Plexus and Traser rolled out across the middle, and Haltz rushed up to the front line to help block. Plexus managed to dash out of the tangle of players and waved her hand. Jet released the blaze just before taking a hit squarely under his extended arm. He hit the clear turf and never saw his first completed pass.

At the same time Daze connected with one of his blaze-outs on a slant route. On the opposite side of the field, Cutter found a hole and galloped down the field and into the defense's secondary. The three plays developing in tandem had the crowd bellowing in excitement. Just as Plexus dove into the end zone for three points, Cutter crossed the line seconds later and tied the game at 6-6. Daze's blaze-out made it to the twenty-five-yard marker before being tackled.

Having scored, Jet and Cutter's squad left the field while Daze's squad tried to add another six points. But the Holospear's defense held, and Daze's squad was eventually forced to kick a field goal for three points. Skylight held the lead, 9-6, after just one series, and it looked to be a high scoring game.

But the pace settled down after that, and Skylight only

managed to score six more points before halftime. Meanwhile, Marc's squad tacked on nine additional points, making the score 15-15. Jet took several more vicious hits and felt a bruise developing on his right side. But he wasn't about to complain, afraid that Plannar might bench him as a precaution.

Plannar gave a calm, but intense, halftime speech down in the locker room. He pointed out several mistakes and decided to change his original plan. "Well, I guess we'll be moving the defense around some. Gotta pressure Marc, otherwise he'll shred us to bits!"

The Skylight kick return unit took the field for the second-half kickoff. Jet's receiver muffed the blaze and barely recovered, giving his squad horrible field position. The first drive of the game belonged to Cutter, who broke free and sprinted down the field to the ten-yard line. On the next play, Jet decided to use this to his advantage. He sent Traser and Plexus on a pattern near Cutter's squad, using them as cover but careful to maintain the required ten-yard limit.

Blixer hiked the blaze, and Jet dropped back, trying to buy enough time for Traser and Plexus to make it across the field. Two defenders broke through and forced him out of the pocket. He scrambled and released the blaze at the last second before being tackled. Plexus caught the blaze and weaved into the end zone for three points.

Cutter's squad scored on the next play, leaving Daze's squad on the field. This time, Daze's mid-blazer carried the blaze across the line for six points, making the score 27-15, Skylight.

The Skylight defense held the two flanking squads to their own territory. But Skylight's main defensive squad couldn't contain Marc, and his squad eventually scored six points, bringing the total to 27-21. And, on the very next series, Marc scored again to tie the game, 27-27.

In the waning moments of the fourth quarter, Jet's was the only squad on the field, and he led them into scoring position. Only eight seconds remained, and it was up to them. A score could end the game now. Otherwise, it would go into overtime, and Marc would have another opportunity.

The play call filtered into his holocypher. He reviewed it and turned to face his squad. "Play action to you, Haltz. Plexus, slant pattern. Traser, you're the interference…" Jet trailed off.

The team looked at each other, confused.

"Is he okay?" Traser whispered, snapping her fingers at him.

Something shimmered in the far endzone, drawing his attention. The cloak was there, hovering in the seventh row up. In his holocypher, a name appeared: *Solan Alexander*. Jet stood there, dumbfounded as the game clock ticked down. *Not now*, he thought to himself. *Not now!*

Haltz clapped his hands in front of Jet's face, trying to get his attention. "Hey! Time's running out."

He finally broke the huddle. They settled in at the line-of-scrimmage as he barked out the snap count. He took the blaze and dropped back several steps. He turned to fake a handoff to Haltz and hid the blaze behind his back as he rolled out of the pocket. Plexus stumbled just enough to allow her defender to gain a step. Jet needed to make a perfect throw now. Two more defenders blitzed him. Jet focused, blocking out the crowd noise, and released the blaze. It soared through the air and dropped just inches over the Holospear defender and into the reliable hands of Plexus. She dove into the end zone with the blaze held tight to her chest pads. The three points made the score 30-27, just as time expired. The stadium erupted as the entire team charged into the endzone and raised Plexus up. Jet laid on the ground, completely ignored by everyone except Cutter, who pulled him to his feet and clapped his back hard enough to rattle his teeth.

· • • • ● ● ● • • • ·

JET SKIPPED THE celebration that evening at Blazer's and went straight to bed. He awoke early the next morning and called everyone to tell them about his decision to have the meeting on Monday. Cord reacted calmly, Cutter didn't seem to care, and Bo hung up before their conversation had ended. Professor Sylvant seemed indifferent, and he wondered if she was having second thoughts. In short, no one seemed too excited.

He didn't feel like spending his day off in the stacks, even though Sunday was normally his day to catch up on homework. Cutter had mentioned that the auditorium at Orientation Station was usually empty, which surprised Jet since it was so large. He assumed it was always full of students, but decided to see if Cutter was right.

After a brisk fifteen-minute jaunt, he stood at the threshold of the auditorium and let his eyes adjust to the dim light inside. It appeared Cutter had been right—he always seemed to be right. Jet found a seat and started working on some of his studies.

A few hours later, he stifled a yawn and decided to have a look around. Perhaps he could catch a glimpse of the sunset before nightfall.

As he left the auditorium, he noticed a stairway spiraling up and around the top of the auditorium's dome. The stair narrowed until it reached the top and ended at a pair of doors. A sign embedded into the floor read, *Welcome to Apex. The Top of Skylight University.*

He stepped through the doors and experienced a rush of wind. Extending out about fifty meters was an elliptical-shaped observation deck. Sprinkled around its perimeter were information kiosks and telescopes, along with a few couples. A clear stasis guardrail encircled the oval platform, and beyond, a few puffy clouds passed silently by. The stillness was breathtaking.

No one made eye contact with him as he strolled around the deck. The only structure was the tower-like vestibule he'd entered from, which protruded skyward like a needle. Above, several balconies jutted out from it and cantilevered over the platform's edge.

He paused when he spied a pair of black boots swinging from one of the highest balconies. A ship's ladder, bolted to the tower's side with a locked gate, led up to the balcony.

Climb.

He felt the voice overtake him, and he hopped over the gate and climbed up the ladder. When he reached the top balcony, he stopped to steady himself from the wind, shook his head and stumbled out of his trance.

Standing in front of him with arms crossed was a girl. Her glowing eyes blinked, and a mischievous scowl lit across her face.

CHAPTER

The Union

ΑΒΓΔΕΖΗΘΙΚΛ<u>Μ</u>
ΝΞΟΠΡΣΤΥΦΧΨΩ

JET STARED OPENLY at the girl standing in front of him. He knew who she was even before asking. She stared back at him with glowing, turquoise eyes as if she already knew what he wanted.

"Hello," Jet said and held out his hand.

"How did you find me?" the girl said, not bothering to shake his hand.

He shrugged. "Luck, I guess."

There was an awkward moment as they each stood their ground.

Jet finally broke the silence. "You don't seem surprised to see me."

"Should I be? Are you someone famous?"

Jet shook his head. "No. I just wonder why you're not shocked like the others?"

"Shocked at seeing another *euph*?" she asked.

"Not exactly how I'd say it, but yeah."

"Well, how would you say it?" she said.

Her sarcastic tone, mixed with spite, bit right through to the core. The others appeared to have been right—this girl didn't want to be bothered. Still, he pressed on. "I would've said someone like *us*."

The look on her face turned to frustration, then disgust, and he thought she might take a swing at him. But her expression was quickly replaced by a smirk of indifference. She turned away from him and began tapping the metal guardrail impatiently.

He noticed her matted hair for the first time, which had been dyed blue and green to match her glowing eyes. Her nose and facial features were dainty, and her skin was pale and radiant in the waning sunlight. Vail's clothes looked like they'd been plucked from a dumpster. Her black jacket was riddled with holes, like her jeans, and her worn boots were one size too large. Despite her disheveled appearance, Jet found her strangely attractive, but in an unruly sort of way, of course.

"You're a tough person to find," he said. "How do you get out of class so often?"

"Why do you think?" she said. "We're a disruption. If you were a professor, wouldn't you want us out too?"

Jet shrugged. "I don't know, some of the professors don't seem to mind—"

"Why don't you just quit while you're ahead?" Vail interrupted. "You're wasting your time."

He hesitated. "What's that supposed to mean?"

"Let me guess," she continued. "You think you can pull a group together, find a cure, and save us all. Does that sound about right? It's going to take more than the five of us."

"Four of us," he corrected her. "Myranda Mason is dead, according to the authorities, anyway."

There was a split second of shock on her face, but it faded quickly. "See what I mean? This isn't a game of blaze, *Stroud*. You can't win at this. The sooner you accept that fact, the better off you'll be. But I imagine someone like you won't quit until *it* happens."

"What do you know?" he asked.

"Probably as much as you, or has becoming a superstar blaze player given you more insight?"

He took a step back. He'd just met this girl, and she was already mocking him. "You think because I play blaze that I'm treated any better than you?"

"Well, aren't you?"

"If you call being bullied and ignored by your teammates better treatment, then sure."

"That's exactly why I won't join you and the others. Do yourself a favor and just... go jump off a balcony," she said.

"Sounds like you have nothing to lose. Why are you so against joining us?"

"Do you know how many students like us have tried and failed already?" she asked. "If there's a cure out there, we'd know."

"What if I said I have information they didn't?" Jet said.

Throughout their conversation, Vail had been tapping the guardrail impatiently, but she suddenly stopped when he said this.

"Tell you what," Jet said, "If you agree to meet with us, I'll share this information with you. What do you say?"

She smirked. "Nice try, but I don't think so. You're wasting your time and everyone else's, trust me." With one final slap on the metal rail, she turned to leave.

If he let her leave now, he might never find her again. He thought frantically about what to say that might change her mind. Then it hit him… this place was her sanctuary, just like the stacks were to him. She had managed to remain hidden, thanks to this place. He was betting she'd hate to lose it and have to find another.

"Wait!" Jet said, raising his voice. The handful of couples below stopped kissing long enough to see what the commotion was.

"Lower your voice!" she hissed.

"How important is this little hideout to you?"

Vail clenched her jaw. "I'll… find another place."

"Will you? Come on. You're a senior, and I bet it took a while just to find this place. I know it's important to you. I'll leave you alone and I won't come here again. Just agree to meet with us… that's all I ask. Otherwise, I'll be here every day and—"

"Okay!" she said, throwing up her hands. "If it will get you out of my hair, fine! Just tell me when and where."

"Tomorrow, at the library, eight o'clock sharp," Jet said. "And don't even think about skipping."

· • • • • ● • • • • ·

MONDAY EVENING AFTER practice, Jet waited patiently near the front of the library for the others to show up. He was learning to read his roommate's behavior as the semester unfolded and could tell Cutter was curious to see the ragtag group he'd assembled. "This should be interesting," Cutter had said after practice. And true to his word, he was the first to arrive. He spotted Jet near the information kiosk and sauntered over, setting his backpack down.

They waited in silence as Jet tried to work on a few of his assignments.

Cutter nudged him. "Is that Cord?"

Jet looked up to see Cord walk through the front and stand directly in the center of the atrium. He was dressed in pressed black slacks, and a black oxford shirt with the top button unslung. He slicked his hair back and looked around confidently.

"You couldn't tell by his eyes?" Jet asked.

"I was joking," Cutter said. "Look, there's another."

Bo walked in, tall and lanky, and stood next to Cord amidst the throng of students milling about. Cutter stood to join them, but Jet held him back.

"Wait, I want to see how they react," he said. Cutter sat down again and crossed his massive arms. A few minutes later, Professor Sylvant walked in and looked at her watch impatiently. She saw Cord and Bo and stood near them but didn't speak. Jet had told Sylvant who would be in the meeting, but he hadn't told the others about her. "Alright, let's go see what I've gotten us into," Jet said.

Jet and Cutter walked over to the middle of the atrium and stopped in front of them. Cord nodded to Jet and eyed Cutter suspiciously. Bo stood with his hands in his pockets, trying to appear calm. His long blonde hair was pulled back into a top knot and still wet from taking a shower after practice. He fidgeted with a strap on his backpack while Sylvant whistled to Jet and tapped her watch.

"Where's the girl?" Cutter asked.

"Who the hell's this?" Bo asked.

"This is Cutter. He's my roommate," Jet said.

"How's he supposed to help us?" Bo said. They were the

same height, but Bo looked like a pole standing next to Cutter's enormous frame.

"He wants to be a part of this," Jet said. "And we're going to need all the help we can get, Bo."

"It's fine, let's just get on with it," Sylvant said.

Bo and Cord noticed her for the first time. "Professor Sylvant?" Cord asked.

"Cord," she acknowledged. "I hope it's alright if I'm involved as well?" she said, eyeing Bo.

Cord nodded. "Of course. But I think we should continue this conversation elsewhere," Cord reminded them in his slow drawl. "We're gathering quite a crowd."

"He's right," Sylvant said. "We need to move on. So, where is this place you spoke of?"

"We're not leaving until Vail shows up," Jet said.

"You actually found her?" Cord asked. "I'm not sure that's a good idea, Jet."

"Why not? We've got everyone else involved, it seems," Bo said. "Might as well add another."

"Jet, I'm warning you now about Vail," Cord said. "She's a bit unpredictable—"

"Oh, shut up, Ledbetter."

Everyone whirled around and stared at Vail, who seemed to appear from thin air. She ignored them and looked directly at Jet. "This had better be worth it, Stroud."

"All of you, follow me and keep up," Jet said.

He led the motley group across the rotunda. They trekked up several levels and around the perimeter of the massive facility. Jet wanted to make sure they weren't being followed for a few reasons. First, he had Sylvant's career to consider. If she were seen holding a private meeting with them, it could cause problems for her. And secondly, he liked the solitude of the stacks and wanted to keep it a secret. The group remained spread out, and after fifteen minutes, along with several complaints, they finally stood in front of the old bookshelf.

"This is it," Jet said.

"It is?" Bo asked skeptically.

"It's a bookcase, Jet," Cutter added. "And that gate says this area is off-limits."

"This has gone on long enough," Sylvant said. "Where is this place?"

"It's right here," Jet said.

Sylvant crossed her arms. "I'm serious."

Jet slid the false panel sideways to reveal the brass handle. He pulled it, and the wooden section of the bookshelf swung open to reveal the stairs.

No one said a word.

Jet quickly ushered the stunned group down the stair, closing the panel behind them.

At the bottom, everyone paused, disoriented. Jet hurried over to light the candles. The space lit up, and cobwebs swayed in the breeze. The dank air greeted them in a low, rhythmic thrum. The prismatic spray from the chandelier drew a few awes.

"Well?" Jet asked.

"Guess you weren't kidding," Bo said.

Each of them wandered off, curious what lay beyond. Jet let them explore and sat down at the table to wait. After what seemed like an hour, they began to return and sit down at the table. Jet waited patiently for them. Sylvant was the last to return.

"I… don't know what to say," she said.

"Neither did I, at first," Jet replied.

"This place is like a time capsule," Bo muttered. "It's like no one's been here for a century."

Jet nodded. "A few things I noticed, though. Come look at this." He walked over to the main shelf and pulled a few books down. Cutter and Bo stood behind Jet, while Sylvant and Vail peered into the slot. Cord was the first to notice the Heliographi symbol.

"But why here?" Cord asked.

"I don't know," Jet replied. "I do have a theory, though."

"This should be interesting," Vail said.

Jet ignored her. "I think it's a doorway."

Bo shook his head. "Doesn't look like one."

"It's not the first symbol I've seen. Bo, Vail, Cord… you've all been here for almost four years. Don't tell me you haven't seen at least a few of these around campus."

Bo clenched his jaw. "I may have seen one or two, prep. But I don't believe for a second it's a door."

Sylvant frowned and examined the shelf. "I don't see how, Jet. This entire shelf is bolted to the wall."

"I don't know how it works, yet," Jet sighed.

"Is this another conspiracy theory? Because I'm sick and tired of hearing about those," Vail said, leaning against the shelf and crossing her arms.

"I didn't say that," Jet said. "I'm just telling you what I think. I'll leave the conspiracy theories for later."

"Let's focus on why we're here, shall we?" Sylvant said.

Cord nodded. "She's right, Jet. Let's get to the point."

"Fine. We'd better sit down because this might take a while." Jet took down one of the books and led them back to the table. Everyone took a seat, except for Cutter and Bo. The group waited silently as Jet paused to gather his thoughts. He considered the importance of the meeting. It had been nothing short of a miracle that he'd managed to get them all together in the same room; he needed to make this count.

Sylvant cleared her throat.

Jet looked up and took a deep breath. "First things first. Everyone here has to swear that what we discuss stays down here. I don't want to compromise Sylvant's career, and I don't want to give away this location. Besides, none of us need to draw any more attention to ourselves. That means coming and going from the stacks. Do we have a deal?"

Everyone nodded but remained silent.

"Good," Jet continued. "We don't need introductions. I think we all know each other, except for Cutter. He's my roommate and has agreed to help. Professor Sylvant will help, for as long as she possibly can. As you've all probably heard, Myranda Mason is gone. This was supposed to be her first year in the Academy. It should be a reminder that we don't have much time. I hope what I have to share tonight will help give us some new insight."

Jet looked around the table, the glow from their different colored eyes shone eerily in the flickering candlelight. Even though he knew he looked the same to them, it still gave him chills.

"What makes you think you've found something special?" Bo asked. "Other students like us have come and gone. Seems to me they would've found something by now if there was a cure."

"I tend to agree," Cord said. "I'm not trying to be a pessimist, but there have been numerous cases of E.M. over the last century. All have met with the same conclusion."

"Get to the point, Stroud," Vail said. She leaned back in her chair with her tattered boots propped on the edge of the table, partially blocking her face.

"Sylvant," Jet said, holding out his hand. "Can I have the journal?"

She hesitated, then reached into her bag and pulled out the holopad and handed it to Jet. He held it in the candlelight, letting them all get a good look at it. "The owner of this journal was a girl by the name of Solan Alexander," Jet began. "She attended Skylight about ten years ago, but unfortunately died in a skiff accident just after graduation. There are a few things I'd like to point out about her. She served on several school boards, set about half a dozen track records, obtained one of the highest entry exam scores in school history, and she also had ephebus mortem. She was Professor Sylvant's older sister."

Jet stared at each of them in turn before continuing. "At the beginning of the semester, I was wandering around the library and stumbled upon this place, where I found this book." Jet flopped the book about Van Saint onto the table, scattering dust and causing the candles to flicker. "Inside of it, I found Solan's journal." He gently laid the holopad on top of the book.

"I've heard about Solan," Vail said. "She's somewhat of a legend around campus. I didn't realize she was your sister."

"Yeah, that sucks," Bo blurted out.

"I appreciate your concerns, but that was a long time ago," Sylvant said with an edge of irritation. "Let's just move on." She nodded for Jet to continue.

"Notice the artist's name on the book," Jet said.

"Shiloe Van Saint," Cutter muttered and lifted the book. "What about her?"

"She was rumored to be the first true case of ephebus mortem. Turn to the middle," Jet said. Cutter did so and laid the book onto the table for everyone to see.

"This painting is called *The Plan*," Jet said. "I found Solan's journal on this page."

"What's significant about that?" Vail asked.

"This is the same painting I've seen in my dreams. I just never realized who the artist was. Don't you think it's odd that I found the journal on this particular page, in this particular book, in this particular restricted area?"

They were all silent before Cord spoke up. "I've actually had a similar dream, only it was a different painting. I wonder…" He leaned forward and began leafing through the pages. "This one. This is the one I've dreamt about."

Everyone looked at the painting in the book. "*The Realization*?" Cutter read aloud.

"Mine's called *The Verification*," Bo said. He turned the pages again and stopped on one of the paintings.

"Wait. You already knew the name of the painting?" Vail asked.

Bo shrugged. "I've been here long enough to do some of my own research. I kinda think Jet's on to something."

"I don't mean to change subjects, but during the first week of the semester, I saw Solan's name appear on my holopad twice," Jet said, closing the book. "It was like a mirage of sorts."

Bo and Vail cast uncertain glances at Sylvant. She noticed their concern and spoke up. "What we discuss down here will stay down here, you have my word."

"Okay, fine. But I want to hear what you think," Vail said, making no effort to hide her distrust. "Do you think we're crazy?"

Sylvant returned her gaze with arms crossed. "I'm uncertain what to believe."

Vail kicked back in her chair, waiting for more.

"Growing up with my sister, I watched her endure more abuse than anyone should have to deal with, thanks to E.M.," Sylvant said. "I witnessed her wither away each week she called; her transformation was heartbreaking. By the time she graduated, I almost didn't recognize her—I could only imagine what she was suffering through. Was she delusional because of E.M.? Was she really seeing things? I suppose to her mind the answer was yes. To this day, I'm still uncertain what to believe, although I admit there is some mystique surrounding it."

Cord spoke up, breaking the tension in the room. "I believe I know what Jet is speaking of."

"Are you talking about the paintings?" Cutter asked.

"No, I'm referring to the mirage. I would say it resembles an apparition, if I had to describe it, though I don't believe in ghosts. I know that sounds ludicrous, but it's the closest description I can think of."

Sylvant nodded. "And what about you two?"

Bo and Vail looked at each other. "Similar to that, yes," Bo said.

"So, back to the journal," Jet said. "Sylvant, I think it's time."

Sylvant picked the holopad up and held it. "Before we watch anything, I want you all to understand something. I intend to help as much as I can, but my duties as a professor come first. As long as everyone is clear on this, I promise to do all I can."

Everyone waited expectantly as she held the holopad gingerly in her fingertips, reluctant to press play.

"Professor," Jet whispered, "We need to see what's in the journal."

Sylvant nodded as if finally committing. "Some of this is difficult to watch," she said and placed the holopad on the table and pressed play.

CHAPTER

Solan's Journal

ΑΒΓΔΕΖΗΘΙΚΛΜ
ΝΞΟΠΡΣΤΥΦΧΨΩ

THE HOLOPAD FLICKERED to life like an old fashion reel-to-reel projector. An image of the former student, Solan Alexander, appeared magically over the table, her three-dimensional figure sitting in one of the old wing-backed chairs, speaking the phrase, "Say the magic word…".

Sylvant leaned forward and typed in a word. Jet read it aloud. "Fishplumb?"

"Her favorite curse word," Sylvant whispered, then held up a finger for silence.

Solan's voice came to life and filled the room as she reached forward to adjust her holopad, causing the three-dimensional hologram to flicker momentarily. Jet could tell the entry had been recorded near the beginning of her school career. She looked young and spry with an expression of excitement. Jet held his breath as Solan's account began.

"Autumnal Equinox. Semester one, day one," Solan said. "We just finished orientation. It was amazing! I'm so excited to finally be here. This place is like a dream come true. I'm sure I'll miss home and especially Sterllar, but the sea can wait. Hopefully, the people here will accept me, and I can make new friends. I have Cosmology later today with Professor Keoff, who must have pre-selected me, since I didn't get to pick any of my own classes—oh, except for track! It's going to be a challenge to squeeze all of it in this semester, but I'm excited about it all the same..."

The hologram faded suddenly as if the entry had been spliced. Then the next entry began.

"Autumnal Equinox. Semester one, day seven," Solan said, as the next entry floated into focus. "I had my first timed trial today. Coach Minnett suggested I tryout with the sprinters, which I was nervous about at first. According to her, I'm a natural, and she placed me in the 400-meter and the 800-meter. I hope I don't disappoint her. I thought for sure she'd be as rude as the other people I've met so far. Instead, she was happy to have me on the team..."

Once again, the hologram faded out mid-sentence just as the next one began.

"Autumnal Equinox. Semester one, day thirty-five. Today when I was exploring the library, I stumbled upon an area in the basement filled with thousands, maybe millions, of books. It was that strange premonition I sometimes get, guiding me like a voice..." She paused momentarily, and a brief look of panic crossed her face. "I don't think anyone has been down there for ages. It's a lonely, but quiet place. It's just what I've been looking for. I think I'll go back again tomorrow." The hologram flickered as she shifted in her chair. "I also found a book. It's about one of my favorite artists named Shiloe Van Saint. There were several of her paintings in the book that I've never seen before. A few of them stood out, but I'm not sure why..."

In the next entry, Solan was sitting in the basement stacks.

"Autumnal Equinox. Semester one, day sixty-seven. I spoke with Sterllar today. It's difficult to contact her over the network because of the storms. Sis says that mother seems sad, but I know she'll keep an eye on her. I miss home already. I know that sounds bad. Despite the beauty of this place, it feels cold now, not like it did when I first got here. The students can be cruel, but the professors, most of them anyway, seem sympathetic…"

"Vernal Equinox. Semester two, day one. Today is the beginning of a new semester, and I'm hoping that I can find some answers. Most of the students went home for the winter break, but I decided to stay here. It wasn't bad at all. In fact, it was peaceful and quiet without all of them around. I did some more research on ephebus mortem but haven't found much. I won't let it rule my life, no matter what happens. Somehow, I'll prove them all wrong. I just need time to find the right answers…"

"Vernal Equinox. Semester two, day fifteen. I witnessed something at today's track meet that I don't understand. There was… something near the top row of bleachers. If I turned my head in a certain direction, I could see a shape, like a cloak. I don't know… maybe it was a mirage, I'm not sure, but it frightened me. I've decided not to talk about it, at least until I know more." Solan paused and straightened in her seat. "I also had another nightmare. This time I actually fell asleep during class, which has never happened to me before. All I can remember are brief flashes of paintings and the feeling that I was actually there. I asked Joshia Kembler about it… she has E.M., too. She's had similar dreams and was eager to talk about them with me. Of the three paintings in our dreams, only two still exist, though. *The Realization* and *The Plan*." Solan held up Shiloe's book and pointed the paintings out. "The third one, *The Verification*, was destroyed in a fire long ago. I don't know why we're having these dreams, but Joshia and

I agree on one thing—it's time to go see the paintings in person. Maybe then we can get some answers…"

"Vernal Equinox. Semester two, day forty-two. After Cosmology this afternoon, I caught Professor Keoff following me. I feel like he's been watching me. The voice inside my head has become so strong lately that it's difficult to think at times. I wish it would go away and…just leave me alone!" Solan looked frazzled and slightly thinner as she tried to straighten her matted hair before continuing. "It's just one more thing to deal with. I only wish Sterllar was here. I miss her…"

"Vernal Equinox. Semester two, day sixty-four. I found another strange symbol today on the outer portion of the track facility. It's the same as the others, a Heliographi symbol with a lower case *i* in the middle. I asked Coach Minnett, and she says she's never seen it before, but I think she's lying. Are the side effects happening already?" Solan paused and leaned forward, pressing the palms of her hands to her eye sockets before regaining her composure. "Last night, I saw the mirage again. I followed it, but as usual, it disappeared. I feel a sense of urgency pounding inside my head. Something is happening, or about to happen. I can feel it…"

The journal paused suddenly and skipped forward to her final semester. When Solan came into focus, her skin was pale, and the dark circles around her cheekbones made her haggard appearance even more shocking. The greenish-yellow glow of her eyes glistened with tears. Jet heard Sylvant choke back a whimper.

"Vernal Equinox, Semester eight, day eighty-nine. Graduation is this week, and then I'm going home for two weeks before I move to Skylight City. Next week is my twenty-fourth birthday, and I'm scared. Ephebus mortem… it took Joshia Kembler last week. She was one of the top students in our class and a good friend. I just… can't believe she's gone. The abuse from my track mates is getting worse. Everything's heading in the wrong direction. I can't focus. I don't know what's happening. I just want it to end..." Solan paused, visibly shaken.

"Something happened at practice on Thursday. Braden Kriegg tripped me during our wind sprints and fell purposely on top of me. It knocked the wind out of me, and I couldn't breathe. He... he wouldn't get off and started yelling at me. When I looked into his eyes... I don't remember what happened next, but they had to take him to the hospital." Solan stood and walked away from the recording. It was several seconds before she returned and continued.

"I can't wait to see my sister, just one last time. I miss her now more than ever. I need to share the news about Tyberius Alexander with her before it's too late. I know now without a doubt..."

The hologram faded, and Solan never finished her sentence.

"Vernal Equinox. Semester eight, graduation day. Today I leave for home, and this will be my last entry. I'm afraid that I'm losing control. I can't stand the pressure inside my head any longer. All I want is to be free of this burden." Solan's appearance had worsened, as if she hadn't slept in days and couldn't seem to focus into the recorder. "I've been having more dreams about the painting. This time it came to me while I was in the stacks. Someone, or something, seemed to be calling my name. I followed it, but just when I got there the dream ended." Solan fidgeted with the screen, her hand shook so badly that she could barely control it. "Although Joshia is gone, she felt the same way I do about the numbers we saw. The math doesn't add up, the final painting no longer exists... and I've run out of time." She stumbled forward and ended the recording.

The transmission faded, and Jet continued to stare at the silent holopad, lost in thought. He'd forgotten about the others until Sylvant scooted her chair back and walked down one of the dark aisles. Cutter started to call after her, but Jet shook his head at him.

They all waited silently, and eventually, Sylvant returned and took a seat. Her eyes were red and puffy.

Bo cleared his throat after a second and spoke up. "So… what have we learned? Where is this profound information you mentioned?"

"I never said we'd find a cure or anything like that," Jet replied. "I only implied that this journal might shed some new light on our situation."

Vail shook her head. "I knew this was a bad idea."

"You're hell-bent on being a nuisance, aren't you?" Cutter said.

"Nice choice of words, because that's probably where we're all headed unless Stroud can come up with something better than a journal," Vail shot back. "Forgive me for being so skeptical, but pretty paintings aren't going to cut it."

"Solan seemed to believe that the paintings have something to offer, unless you think she was lying," Cord said. "It can't hurt to look into it."

Jet stood and walked around the table. "There's one more thing I should mention, and it has nothing to do with the paintings."

"We're listening," Bo said.

"I met Sylvant at a small café called the *Hydra 7* on Friday. Before we could talk, I saw that strange mirage and followed it to an abandoned factory nearby. There was a meeting taking place that I'm pretty sure I wasn't supposed to see. There were several Skylight professors in the group, and it looked like they were having one hell of an argument. The only word I could make out was from Plannar. He said, Myranda."

"That makes no sense, why wouldn't they just meet somewhere on campus?" Bo asked.

"Exactly," Jet said.

"So, they were having a secret meeting?" Vail asked. "Because it sounds like we're back to the conspiracy theories."

"What are you thinking, Jet?" Cutter asked.

"I'm thinking I could probably find my way back there," Jet answered.

"And how would you know when their next meeting is?" Bo asked. "Because it doesn't sound like something they'd advertise."

"There was a skylight eclipse at about the same time," Jet said. "Something tells me that when there's another eclipse in that area, there might be another meeting." Jet pulled out the holodisk he'd stolen and placed it on the table.

Cord took it and loaded the information onto his holopad, which showed all the skylight eclipse patterns for the next six months. "Looks like the next eclipse in that area won't occur until January 17th."

"So, we'll have to wait till then to see if you're crazy, Jet," Bo said.

Jet pulled the holopad closer. "This is odd…" He pointed at an eclipse occurrence near the university, and everyone looked.

"That's freaky," Bo said. "It's a triclipse, and right here on the campus, too."

"What's that?" Cutter asked.

"Three belts coinciding to create an extremely dense eclipse. It's a rare event," Cord said.

"But the date, Cord," Jet said. "It's on Christmas Day."

"Why is that so odd?" Cord asked. "Eclipses happen all the

time in the system. Christmas is just another day; you're being superstitious."

"I don't know," Bo said. "Maybe it's an omen?"

"Anyway, we're going to crash that meeting in January," Jet said. "We're going to find out what the hell is going on around here."

"Count me in, if I make it that long," Bo said.

"Vail, Cord?" Jet asked.

Vail shrugged. "Sure."

"You know I'm in," Cord said.

Cutter nodded agreement, and everyone looked at Sylvant and waited. She thought for a moment. "I'll think about it. But right now, you all need to focus on your next step."

"Which would be what, exactly?" Vail said.

Sylvant slid Van Saint's book over in front of her and leafed through the pages. "I think it's time for you all to take a field trip."

CHAPTER

The Realization

ΑΒΓΔΕΖΗΘΙΚΛ<u>Μ</u>
ΝΞΟΠΡΣΤΥΦΧΨΩ

EVERYONE AROUND THE room began to chatter as Professor Sylvant sat calmly with her arms crossed.

"Wait, you're assigning us homework?" Bo asked.

"I don't think that's any of your business," Vail said. "You're not my professor."

Cutter nodded agreement. "Jet and I have a lot of practice coming up."

"Guys, relax!" Jet said, motioning for the others to calm down. "Sylvant, what do you mean?"

Sylvant nodded at one of the paintings in the book. "Obviously, these meant something to my sister. You've all mentioned them in your dreams, as did Solan. Have any of you heard of Noetic Science?"

"I have," Cord said. "It's a theoretical science that was established in the late 1900s, based more on internal, or inner consciousness."

"That's right," Sylvant said. "Christian Albright was a big supporter of it. He even taught a few classes."

"Sounds like smoke and mirrors to me," Vail interrupted.

"As I was saying," Sylvant continued. "What I'm hearing from each of you fits into Noetics. You were conscious, or subconscious, of these paintings, even before you saw them in this book."

"So, what's this field trip about then, Noetic Science?" Bo asked.

"This book isn't going to tell us much," Sylvant said. "In my studies, I always find it best to see the real deal, up close and personal."

"You're suggesting we actually go see these paintings?" Vail asked. "And how do we do that if the final one was destroyed in a fire?"

"But we *can* start by looking at the other two," Cord said, dusting his slacks as he leaned against the table.

"Okay. It's a plan, at least," Jet said. "We'll just take it one painting at a time. Where do we find them?"

Sylvant shook her head. "Let's find out." She pulled the holopad close to her and logged onto the system network. Thousands of entries and blogs flooded the screen when she typed in the name of the first painting. "Here we are."

Everyone crowded around the table as Sylvant continued. "*The Realization*. Says here that it will be on display next week at the Skylight Gala. Some of the most famous works of art will be on display, in fact."

"Tickets are bound to be pricey," Jet said. "Not sure any of us can afford that."

"Don't worry about the cost, I can get tickets through the university," Sylvant said.

"Alright, that's one down. Then what?" Vail asked.

"*The Plan*," Sylvant said. A picture of the painting hovered over the table. "This one belongs to a private collector." Sylvant sat back and rubbed her delicate brow with long fingers, then shook her head. "I know this lady. Her name is Lybra, and she doesn't allow people into her gallery."

There was a disgruntled moan from Vail. "Well, if she doesn't let normal people in, then she's sure as hell not going to let us in. Euph's probably spook her as much as everyone else."

"Don't say that." Bo glared in her direction.

"She's right, though," Cord said. "We're not likely to get in. So, the trail stops there."

Sylvant held up a hand. "I have several contacts in the art department. I may be able to work some magic."

"So, Professor… I'm curious. Has hearing any of this changed your opinion of us yet?" Vail asked, seemingly determined to get an answer out of Sylvant. The glow from Vail's unblinking eyes filled the area around her cheekbones with a turquoise haze as she waited.

"I know you all want an answer," Sylvant said. "But I don't have one. All I can do is offer my assistance. If that's not good enough, then I will go."

At this, everyone except Vail stood and began talking.

"Professor," Cord said, "Ignore Vail, she's a very disturbed individual."

"Don't be ridiculous, Ledbetter," Vail said. "She's no different than anyone else."

Cutter moved in to stand between Vail and Cord while Bo stood next to Vail and placed a hand on her thin shoulder. "Vail, I think we should take her offer," Bo said. "Who cares what she thinks, if she's willing to help us."

But Vail ignored him and shrugged his hand off her shoulder.

She turned to face Cutter and glowered up at him. "What about you?" she scoffed. "Do you think we're crazy?"

"That answer should be obvious," Cutter answered coolly. "I'm here, aren't I? Besides, my concern isn't to save you."

"So why are you here, then? To make us look like a bunch of bumbling idiots?" Vail shot back.

"No, sweetheart. You're doing a good enough job on your own," Cutter said.

"Very funny," Vail replied. "Jet wants you here, but maybe we don't?"

"Give it a break, Vail," Cord said.

"Mind your own business, Ledbetter," Vail shot him a glance.

"Guys!" Sylvant said, snapping her fingers. "Let's focus on the task at hand, shall we? This squabbling isn't helping."

"She's right," Jet said. "We're going to the Gala and that's final."

"Good," Sylvant said, gathering her things. "Which means you'd all better start getting along. You boys need to find tuxedoes. And you..." Sylvant said, giving Vail a long look, "You need a nice dress. Otherwise, you're not likely to get into this hoity-toity event."

As they left the stacks, Jet reminded them all to use caution. Vail walked up the stair without a word, and Bo followed right behind her. Cord continued to wander around the stacks, looking through the old books with genuine interest, while Jet and Cutter remained at the table, looking at Professor Sylvant.

"You alright?" Jet asked.

"I just… I didn't think I'd get so involved so quickly," Sylvant replied.

"Your sister was your best friend, wasn't she?" Cutter asked, taking a seat across from her.

She nodded. "I thought I was over it until I saw her in the journal. All those memories came flooding back."

"You never really get over it," Cutter said. "You just learn ways to cope. Believe me, I know."

Sylvant looked at him for what seemed like the first time that evening. She glanced down at his tattooed arms and tilted her head. "You've been through the same thing, haven't you? How long has it been?"

"Not long enough," Cutter said.

"Perhaps you're right. But I know my sister would have wanted me to help, no matter how painful it is," Sylvant said. "It's what she would have done. I know that much."

"And my younger brother would've wanted me to do the same thing," Cutter said.

There was a moment of silence before Jet spoke. "I'm sorry… for both of you. I can only imagine what it feels like to lose a loved one. But, I'm glad you're both here. Something tells me we're going to need you two before the semester's over."

"The entries in your sister's journal were spliced," Cutter said. "Was there something your sister didn't want others to know?"

Sylvant shook her head. "Just the part about the man she believed to be our real father, Tyberius. But the section about him was left in. To be honest, I'm not sure she's the one who spliced the entries. It doesn't seem like something my sister would do."

"I'm certain it's someone else unless you believe in ghosts," Cord said. He was nearly invisible in his all-black attire and caused Sylvant to jump. "I'm sorry, Professor, I don't mean to be insensitive. But the odds of Jet stumbling onto her journal are highly unlikely, which means he was meant to find it. And, those entries weren't manipulated in a way to hide something… they were meant to direct us towards something."

"The paintings," Jet said.

"Correct," Cord replied.

· • • • • ● • • • • ·

THE CHILLY EVENING breeze bit right through Jet's tuxedo. He hunkered forward and blew into his hands to warm them. He was learning that the seasons moved quickly in the Skylight System, especially further out from the Core. But it seemed even more noticeable on that Friday evening. Despite the cold, he preferred to wait outside, alone and away from the crowds. Most people recognized him now, thanks to all the media coverage he received from the ongoing blaze season. But that didn't change the fact that everyone distrusted him.

He continued to glance anxiously at his watch. Everyone was now thirty minutes late for the Gala. The skyport was busier than normal with the holiday season approaching, and he grew concerned that the others were lost. He vowed to fly them in one of the university skiffs next time to avoid any confusion. He looked at the tickets Sylvant had finagled for them. It was the 89th Annual Skylight City Gala, which was a very *snooty* event, according to her. But snooty or not, they were on a mission to see one thing; a painting by Van Saint called *The Realization.* And he was going to make sure they saw it tonight, no matter what it took. It might be their only chance.

He watched the skiffs speed by and was about to call Cutter when he noticed a group of well-dressed students walking towards him. Jet called out, causing several bystanders to look his way.

Vail glared at him as they approached. "Thanks for making a scene."

Jet sighed and guided them towards one of the larger cabs waiting nearby. "Relax. This should be easy." He forced Cord and Vail inside. Bo and Cutter hopped in the opposite side.

"Where to?" the driver asked impatiently.

"Peripheral and Ninth," Jet replied.

The driver turned without a word and floored the accelerator. Jet ignored him and turned the privacy screen on. He looked at them, snapping for their attention. "Listen up. Sylvant says this is one of the biggest draws in the system, which means lots of people. Everyone be on your best behavior; we don't need any trouble. Hopefully, we won't draw too much attention, and we're in and out without an incident."

"And where is Sylvant?" Vail asked.

"She's not coming, so don't worry about it. Besides, she got us the tickets. These probably weren't cheap," Jet said and handed each of them a holopad ticket.

"So, what's the game plan again?" Bo asked.

"Like I said, in and out," Jet replied.

"The sooner this is over, the better," Vail said. "Probably a waste of time anyway."

Cord shook his head. "We've got free passes to one of the biggest events in the system, and you don't want to do some sightseeing?"

"And get ogled and gawked at by Skylight's finest citizens?" Vail said. "No thanks, Ledbetter."

Cord shook his head and began studying from his holopad, his fingers tapping the holographic menu deftly.

Jet brushed some lint off the tuxedo he'd borrowed from the

university's athletic wardrobe. Vail was wearing a striking black dress that accented her pale shoulders. Around her neck was a tarnished locket that drew attention to her long neck. Cutter and Bo had also borrowed tuxedos from the athletic wardrobe.

Cutter and Vail chatted softly during the cab ride, Cutter trying to explain blaze to her, which was awkward to watch. Vail obviously didn't care for the sport, and Cutter usually didn't have the patience for such people. But surprisingly, he didn't seem to mind, and neither did she. Bo tugged at the sleeves of his tuxedo, trying to stretch the cuffs to fit his long arms. He was noticeably anxious, more so than the rest of them. With everyone preoccupied, Jet took the opportunity to chat with Cord.

"Why don't you take a break from studying and enjoy the evening?" Jet said, looking at the complex equation over Cord's holopad.

"I've got to finish this for one of my professors," Cord said without looking up.

"Don't you have your own studies to do?"

"No, I've completed all of my work. This particular professor is writing a book and couldn't solve these equations."

"So, you're doing his work for him? Doesn't that seem a bit unethical on his part?"

Cord shrugged. "Probably."

"Why are you doing it then?"

"Because I want to graduate this semester." Cord finally stopped to look at Jet. "If I don't help him, he probably won't let me graduate until next semester."

"It's just odd that a Skylight professor would ask you to do his work," Jet said.

Cord rubbed his chin. "If you want something done right,

you do it yourself. That's always been my philosophy. Obviously, this professor doesn't share the same belief. I'm not saying I agree with his principles, but it's his business, not mine."

"But Cord, what you're doing right now, tonight, *isn't* on your own. We're helping each other. What do you say about that?"

"Well, that's different, I suppose. Besides, I approached you first, if you remember."

"But you just said you prefer to do things yourself." Jet chided, enjoying the moment.

"It's hard to trust others since most people have so little trust in us. You—or should I say, *we*—should understand that, of all people," Cord said evenly. "That's why I prefer to work alone."

"That may be true in some cases, but sometimes you have to trust others. Like now. We need each other."

Cord considered. "You're right. I don't deny it… there are times. But rarely for me. Old habits die hard."

"Just remember, you don't have to face this alone, not anymore," Jet said. "We have to believe in each other if we're going to have a chance."

Their taxi slowed to a stop. Jet hopped out and held the door for the others. He paid the driver and watched him speed off before turning to look at the throng of people in front of them. The sleek looking convention center projected into the night sky, which lit up the evening clouds with multicolored spotlights. They all stood curbside, momentarily speechless as they gazed upon the thousands of people littering the open plaza in front of the event center. The Gala was in full swing with a multitude of media crews hounding the highbrow guests. Jet even recognized a few of the professional players from the Skylight City blaze team.

He turned, bringing the others together into a huddle. "Let's get in and out of here without incident. Most people are focused on the celebrities," Jet said, feeling like he was directing his blaze squad. "I think it'll help if we split up, sound good?"

"Fine. Let's get this over with," Vail said.

Jet and Cord moved through the large plaza along the far-right side while Vail and Bo took the left. Cutter walked right up the middle, pushing and shoving to draw as much attention away from the others as possible. Jet and Cord kept their heads turned away from the activity and didn't make eye contact with anyone. Out of the corner of his eye, Jet watched Cutter in the middle of the hubbub but lost sight of Vail and Bo.

They were nearing the entry when someone shoved Jet from behind. He almost tumbled to the ground but quickly caught his balance and wheeled around to find the last person he'd expected to see at such an event—Korbin Daze. Beside him stood Plexus. Jet stared at them with Cord looking on curiously and muttered to himself, cursing his luck. Of all the people he could have bumped into, it had to be these two.

"Friends of yours?" Cord asked.

"Not really, just teammates," Jet said.

"How the hell did you score tickets to this event. Steal them?" Daze asked.

"I could ask you the same thing," Jet replied.

"My father is CEO of Centient Corp.," Daze said. "Complimentary tickets. I guess you're hoping to sneak in?"

"It's none of your business why I'm here, actually. See you on the field." Jet turned to leave, but Daze reached out and grabbed Jet's collar. He heard it rip when he turned around and tried to stay calm.

"Don't be stupid, Daze," Jet said in a low voice. "This is trouble neither of us need right now."

"You should choose your friends more wisely, Jet," Cord said. Daze looked at him.

"Cord Ledbetter," Daze said. "You're that smart freak. Shame, you'll be dead soon, like Stroud. You've got what… three, maybe four years? Good riddance."

"You're a pretentious fellow, aren't you?" Cord said. "Tell me what you've accomplished, besides throwing a ball around and squandering your family's wealth. Though, I suppose that counts for something. Another lackluster talent, pretending you're someone special."

"Maybe, but it's better than living like dirt. And I've got all the time I need, which is more than I can say for you two. But what say we step over to the alley and chat about it?"

Cord remained calm and didn't show any sign of intimidation as he stood his ground. Jet felt Vail and Bo step up beside him without looking, his attention still focused on Daze. Vail faced Plexus with pure hatred on her face, and Plexus returned her stare with disgust. Bo stood next to Vail, his fists taught, waiting for Daze to make the first move. Jet had a bad feeling that something was about to happen they'd all regret.

"Jet," Cord continued. "Too much time spent with lesser people dulls the wit. Shall we move on?" Then Cord did something that caught Jet off guard. He winked at Daze.

"Oh crap," Jet whispered.

Daze reached for Cord's neck in anger but didn't release Jet's collar. Plexus rushed in and grabbed for Vail. Jet whirled and gripped Daze's fist, trying to stop him from hitting Cord. But Cord was lightning quick and easily avoided Daze's fist, which landed heavily on the stone wall behind him. Daze wailed just as a massive shape moved in and pinned him to the wall. Jet turned, finally released from Daze's grip, and rolled away. The maneuver ripped the rest of his tuxedo collar off. Cutter's hulking form pinned Daze to the wall and pressed his forehead against its surface.

"Make another move like that, and you'll be missing a throwing arm," Cutter hissed. Vail froze, and Bo released Plexus as they all looked at Cutter.

"Alright, just let me go," Daze said, blood dribbling down his chin. Cutter did so just as several media crews burst upon the scene. Camera lights flooded the area and Jet's worst nightmare suddenly became a reality—they were the morning news already, and they hadn't even made it inside yet. There would be some explaining to do to Coach Plannar.

Cutter released Daze, who turned and vanished instantly with Plexus close behind. Jet grabbed Vail and Bo, dragging them towards the main entrance. "Let's go. Now!"

They handed their tickets to the usher and hurried inside where the media wasn't allowed. Once inside, he looked at Cord.

"Why'd you do that?" Jet asked. "You knew it would set him off."

"He was going to do something ill-advised anyway, I just helped him along," Cord said.

Cutter wiped some blood from a scrape on his fist. "It's alright Jet. He had that coming."

Jet shook his head. "It's not alright, because this is going to be all over the morning news. We're going to have to answer to Plannar for this."

"It's attention we didn't need. Thanks Cord," Bo said.

"Plannar won't kick us from the team, Jet," Cutter said. "We're too far into the season."

"I know. But we may be running stairs after practice for the rest of the semester, and that's time we don't have to spare right now. We'll be lucky if he lets us off with just a warning."

Vail sighed. "Are you boys done?"

Jet took a deep breath. "We can worry about it tomorrow. Let's find this painting and avoid any more trouble."

"They've got an active net system," Cord said and walked over to a nearby kiosk. He logged in and located the painting. "Here, in the far corner." A portion of the floor glowed bright, directing them where to go.

Jet led the way, following the virtual pathway. The convention center was vast, reminding him of Crux Stadium, but without the seating. They walked past several exhibits with strange paintings and bizarre sculptures. Most of the newer artwork wasn't done on canvas, but in holographic fashion, which simply projected into thin air. Immense groups of upper-class citizens browsed the artwork and paid little attention to them, which Jet was thankful for. The path finally ended at a large painting, hovering in a secluded corner of the convention center. A clear box encased it and protected it from aging and vandalism.

An elderly couple stood gazing at the painting with a young boy between them. The child was clearly bored and hopped on one foot to keep himself entertained. Jet and the others stood quietly behind them, unnoticed, and listened in on their conversation.

"The Realization," the gentleman read aloud, tugging thoughtfully at his gray mustache. "Oh, dear. This was the crazy lady, the one that was murdered while painting it. She was a euph, they say."

"Crendall!" his wife exclaimed and backhanded his arm with

a plump hand. She pretended to glance around. "You shouldn't say that."

"Dorris, please. Such silly nonsense. What's so special about it anyway? She wasn't even that good."

The child spoke up. "I like it, grandpa. The brush strokes are sparkly."

"Hmmm… You're right. It does seem to almost glow in the light, an interesting technique. But the subject matter I'm not so sure about. It's exactly what I'd expect from a euph."

Dorris cringed again at the word. Vail sighed, which caused them to turn suddenly.

"Why, we didn't realize—" the lady began, but paused, interrupted by her own gasp. Her skin turned several shades of pink from embarrassment and then went white as a sheet.

"Come dear. We should be moving along now," Crendall said promptly.

"Don't run off because of us," Vail said. "By all means, stay and enjoy the freak show."

With one last nervous tug at his mustache, the man took his wife's hand and walked away. Vail stood with her arms crossed while Cutter and Bo looked on. Cord ignored them and stared at the painting.

Jet turned to see the child staring up at him.

"I like your eyes, mister," the child said.

Jet knelt and looked into the young boy's eyes. There was no hint of fear or discrimination in his expression, just innocent curiosity. "Thank you," Jet said. "That means a lot to me."

"But… why are my grandparents so afraid?"

"What's your name?" Jet asked.

"Joseph," the child said.

"Sometimes, people are afraid of things they don't understand," Jet said. "I wish it wasn't like that. But what's important is you're not afraid, and that's a really brave thing."

The child tilted his head and thought for a moment. "I think I understand, sir."

"That's good, Joseph." Jet said and ruffled his hair. "Can I ask you a question?"

The young boy nodded and smiled.

"Can you tell me what you see in that painting?"

Joseph turned and looked at the artwork. "It's really shiny. It looks like the pretty flower is going to get hurt by that storm. It's kinda scary."

"Is that all you see? Look really hard."

Joseph squinted and held his hands over his eyes as if searching for a lost toy. "I'm sorry, mister. That's all I see."

"That's okay, Joseph. You'd better go find your grandparents now; they'll be—"

"Joseph, come now!" Crendall hollered and hurried over to snatch him away. The child smiled and waved back to them as he was dragged away.

There was a moment of silence as they watched the family leave. Jet stepped up next to Cord. "What do you think?"

Cord read the holographic narrative out loud. "*The Realization* was painted by Shiloe Van Saint at the age of twenty-three. Most of her work held a mysterious and ominous nature within the heavy brush strokes. Her style portrayed a shimmering effect and is rumored to hold hidden messages. An investigation into her work was launched, but no proof of proclaimed prophecies has ever been found. This particular work of art depicts a lone flower on a barren plain. An ominous storm cloud on the horizon threatens to strip the delicate flower from its roots. Many have speculated that the flower represents the artist's feelings of abuse and neglect. Although it was never proven that she suffered from the effects of ephebus mortem, some experts believe she was the first true case."

Cord fell silent as they stared up at the painting. The lightning in the background seemed to flicker inside the thunderhead. In the foreground, the delicate flower was bent low from the intense wind and had been stripped of everything except one black and white petal. But it wasn't the looming thunderhead, the lightning, or the last remaining petal that drew their attention.

"Do you see the numbers?" Bo asked, turning to Vail.

She nodded.

"What does it mean?" Bo asked.

Cutter walked around the back of the painting. "What are you all talking about?"

"You can't see those numbers?" Bo pointed at the painting.

Cutter gave him a look. "I don't see anything, except for the painting."

Jet shook his head. "I don't know why Cutter can't see it."

"But they're just numbers unless Brainiac here understands them," Vail added.

"Roman numerals, actually," Cord said. "Reminiscent of a clock, only there are twenty-four, instead of the typical twelve one might expect."

"Well, we already know that the final painting was destroyed," Vail said. "So, even if we do figure out what this means, what are we supposed to do next?"

Jet shook his head. "One at a time, it's all we can do for now and hope that things fall into place."

"That's a lot to hope for, especially when time isn't on our side," Vail said.

. • • • • ● • • • • .

When Jet and Cutter finally got back to their dorm, it was late. Cutter hadn't said much on the way back, other than, "Are you sure you saw what you saw?" Jet had to explain it to him several times, but Cutter remained confused and somewhat skeptical.

Jet went to his room and decided to call Sylvant with an update. He grabbed his holopad and punched in her number. There was the typical soft hum, and then Sylvant's image came into view.

"Hi, Jet. Everything okay?" she asked.

"Everything's fine," Jet said. Sylvant's study was the typical clutter of holographic notes, reminders, and schedules that blurred her image.

"You're calling late," she said, leaning back in her chair and rubbing her eyes.

"I know, sorry. But I figured you'd still be up."

"Sometimes I wonder why I ever wanted this job." She stifled a yawn. "Did you see the painting?"

"We did, and thanks for the tickets, by the way. I bet they were expensive."

"A favor from an old friend," Sylvant replied, dismissing it with a wave. "So, tell me about it."

Jet leaned back on his bed. "Well, there was something odd about it, some sort of holographic image embedded in the canvas.

It looked like Roman numerals, kind of like an old-time clock, according to Cord, except it had more numbers than typical. The strange thing was that Cutter couldn't see it, though."

"You're certain?"

"Positive," Jet replied. "We asked him several times. We even asked another person who was there."

Sylvant propped her hands in front of her face, considering. "That sounds like pretty advanced technology. I don't know that Van Saint would've had that capability back in her day."

"Can you think of what it might mean?" he asked.

Sylvant leaned back in her chair, considering. "I don't know. I can't say without seeing it," she said. "Van Saint was said to be reclusive and didn't talk to others much. So, I don't imagine there's any additional information out there beyond what we've already read. Maybe an expert would know more."

Jet nodded and continued to look at her, hoping she had more to say.

"I'm sorry, Jet. I don't have any answers tonight," She rubbed her temples and glanced at her watch.

"I understand," Jet said. "I don't mean to bother you."

"It's okay, but I really do need to get back to work. I'm barely treading water at the moment. I need to finish my next assignment before tomorrow. When are you and the others getting together again?"

"We meet as much as possible down in the stacks, but it's random because of everyone's schedule." Jet said and paused, wondering if he should ask for any more favors tonight. He tapped his knee as he considered.

"Is there something else on your mind?" Sylvant finally asked.

"You… mentioned trying to get us access to Lybra's estate," Jet said. He held his breath for a second.

"Right," Sylvant said. "I'm still working on that, but it's going to take some time. I'll let you know as soon as I hear something."

"Thanks again," Jet said. "We'll wait to hear from you."

"Can you handle the others till then?" she asked.

"I think so," Jet sighed. "We're all so different… it's going to be a challenge."

"Well, if anyone can pull this all together, it's you."

Jet raised his eyebrows. "You sure about that?"

"They look to you for guidance, not me," she said. "Whether you've noticed it or not."

Jet shook his head. "I've been so busy with everything else lately, I… don't know."

Sylvant paused and started to say something else but stopped.

"What is it?" Jet asked.

"Nothing. It's nothing… I need to get back to work, that's all."

"You don't have to do this, you know," Jet reminded her. "If it's too much—"

"I know," she interrupted. "I know. But it's what Solan would have wanted. I owe it to her."

"What's it going to take for you to believe?" Jet asked. The blatant question caught her slightly off guard.

She held his gaze through the hologram. Several seconds passed, and she opened her mouth to say something, but smiled instead and waved goodnight.

Jet watched her image fade and laid back. He'd hoped for a more enthusiastic response about the painting and was somewhat disappointed. He could see Sylvant was still struggling with her emotions, and he felt some guilt over it.

It was past midnight, but he couldn't quiet the thoughts in his head. He stood and walked out to the balcony and was surprised to see Cutter sitting in a chair, gazing down at the commons below.

"Couldn't sleep?" Cutter asked.

Jet breathed in the cool evening air and shook his head. "It's already getting cold. Amazing how quickly the seasons change here. Not like the ARC, is it?"

"Got that right," Cutter agreed. "Something's gnawing at you, what's up?"

Jet leaned against the rail. "Can't stop thinking about that painting. I hate to admit it, but Vail has a point. There really isn't much to go on."

"She's a downer. Don't let her get to you. Still... there's something about her."

Jet looked at Cutter. "What are you talking about?"

Cutter shrugged. "Just… I don't know. There's something about her that drives me up the wall. You know what I mean?"

Jet turned to face Cutter and smiled. "Is there something you want to tell me?"

"What?" Cutter said. "Come on, don't give me that look. You want to choke her too, sometimes. Am I right?"

"You like her, don't you?" Jet asked, hardly believing what he was hearing.

"Ah," Cutter shook his head. "Forget it. She's trouble I don't need right now." He leaned against the rail next to Jet. "Was that Sylvant I heard?"

"Yeah. I called to give her an update. I thought she'd be a little more interested," Jet said.

"But she wasn't?" Cutter said, almost as if he'd known she wouldn't be.

Jet shook his head. "Not so much. Which brings me to another topic."

"And what would that be?" Cutter asked.

"You."

Cutter looked at Jet. "What about me?"

"I assume you want out now, especially after tonight," Jet said. "You said you couldn't see the numbers. Now's your chance to leave, because if you stick around much longer, you'll be labeled crazy like the rest of us."

Cutter shrugged and stood up straight. "I'm not going anywhere. I already told you that, and I told you why. I don't want to hear another word about it. Besides, I have a feeling that things are about to get interesting, and I don't want to miss it."

CHAPTER

The Plan

ΑΒΓΔΕΖΗΘΙΚΛ<u>Μ</u>
ΝΞΟΠΡΣΤΥΦΧΨΩ

It was over a month before Sylvant contacted Jet. Even though he was in the front row of her Tuesday and Thursday class, they hadn't spoken.

During those weeks, the blaze season enveloped most of Jet's free time. And thanks to their scuffle with Daze and Plexus, they'd all had to run stairs after practice for those weeks. Jet had some concern the union he'd created with the others might fade away. However, he insisted they continue their meetings down in the stacks. Cord was usually the first one there each night, and surprisingly, Vail was available when the group met. Bo was there too, but remained aloof. Cutter, who was perhaps the busiest with his extra practice sessions, still managed to make time for them, though Jet wondered if Vail had something to do with that now. Sylvant remained cautious and kept her distance. She reminded them that her goal was to provide resources, and once again, she'd come through in a big way. By using her pull as a professor, she had gained them access to see the next painting called *The Plan*.

Jet climbed up to the observation deck of Apex on a blustery

Friday afternoon as the temperature plummeted towards freezing. He shivered; his hair still wet from the lightning-fast shower he'd taken after practice that day. The others huddled together on the backside of the tower to break the wind splashing over the deck like a frothy gale. Vail shielded herself behind Cutter while Cord and Bo stood opposite of them.

"Finally!" Vail huffed, blowing into her hands.

"Why are we out here?" Bo said.

Cord tried to appear suave, but Jet saw him shivering beneath his black trench coat. Cutter wore a light jacket with no sleeves and seemed oblivious to the chill.

"I wanted to share some good news, and the stacks just didn't seem like the cheeriest place to do it."

"Find a cure?" Vail chided. She leaned forward, and Jet noticed the tarnished locket again as it slipped from beneath the torn collar of her jacket. She quickly tucked it back in.

Jet shook his head. "Sylvant got us a viewing to see the next painting."

"You mean someone actually agreed to let us in?" Bo asked.

"That someone is a lady named Lybra Howling," Jet said. "Her estate is located in the wealthy Vent Quarter of Skylight City."

"Great, more snootiness," Vail said.

"I hear she's a recluse," Cord said.

"If that's true, why would she be so anxious to let us in?" Vail asked.

"Does it matter? Let's just get there before she changes her mind," Bo said.

"Well, we're scheduled for tomorrow evening," Jet said. "She wanted us there in the morning, but Cutter and I have a game."

"My track meet ends around five, so I shouldn't have a problem after that," Bo said.

"Cord, any scheduling issues?" Jet asked.

"Not on my end, no. I usually finish my work early."

"Vail?" Jet asked.

"What do you think?" she replied.

Jet sighed. "Alright then, let's meet at the university hangers at nine o'clock *sharp*."

"University hangers? The commuter skiff doesn't dock there," Bo said.

"No, it doesn't. That's why I'm flying this time," Jet said. "I don't want to take another chance on everyone being late again."

"You have a license?" Bo asked. "You know how to fly one?"

"Yes, relax."

"Those things are dangerous," Bo continued. "There's no way I'm getting in one of the tiny ones."

"What are you talking about?" Jet asked.

"Superstitions, I think," Cord chimed in.

"A lot of euphs have died in skiff accidents, Jet," Vail added.

"You too?" Cord said and gave Vail a long glance. "I didn't think you'd fall for those hoaxes."

"I didn't say that, Ledbetter," Vail said, but with some hesitation. "I only said a lot of us have died in them."

"So, none of you have a skiff license because you think they're unsafe?" Jet asked.

"I just don't want to spend my student money on a license," Cutter said.

"Easy for you to say," Bo said. "You don't have to put up with all the staring crowds on the commuter skiff. Still, I don't trust the smaller skiffs, Jet."

"Well, get over it, because I'm flying us and that's that," Jet said. "Besides, the university's skiffs are probably one of the safest forms of travel."

Bo shook his head doubtfully and left.

Cutter shrugged and gave Vail a nod. Cord wrapped himself in his trench coat and followed Cutter and Bo. Vail started to turn and leave.

"Vail, wait," Jet said.

She stopped to look at him, her lips pursed white from the cold. She blew into her worn-out mitts and pulled her jacket tighter. "What's up? You want me to talk to Bo about the skiff thing?"

"No, nothing like that. Just wanted to talk."

She sighed. "How long will this take?"

"I just wanted to hear your thoughts," he said.

"You're going to have to be a little more specific, Stroud."

"Alright. Let's start with that locket of yours," Jet said, pointing at it. "Who gave you that?"

"You always this nosey?" she asked.

"Sometimes, when I'm curious."

Vail shook her head, "Which is all the time." She frowned. "A boy gave it to me, if you must know."

Jet looked at her and raised his eyebrows. "Seriously?"

"Why? Didn't think I could ever get to know someone else?"

"No… well, yeah." Jet stammered.

"Well, I do… *did*," she said.

"And you keep the locket because it reminds you of him?" Jet asked.

"No. It's a reminder of how quickly things change."

"Are you saying he was one of us?"

Vail looked at Jet for a long moment. She pulled the locket out and held it up to the fading sun. "He was a senior when we met. I was just a freshman. His name was Stephen Brit, and he tried like hell to get my name. Of course, I played hard to get. Finally, in my second semester, I started talking to him. We spent a lot of time together, shared things that others obviously couldn't understand. Long walks, all that sappy stuff… he just seemed to understand me like no one else ever has."

Jet thought for a moment. The name, Stephen Brit, rang a bell. Then he remembered. Brit was a blaze player. In fact, he was the last one to play the sport who'd had ephebus mortem. "That's why you hate blaze, isn't it?" Jet said. "It reminds you of Brit."

"I never said I hated blaze."

"You seem to dislike it quite a bit, though."

"Let's just say that I have better things to do than watching a bunch of people knock each other silly." She paused as a few students ventured out onto the frosty observation deck. They noticed Jet and Vail and quickly moved to the other side of the platform. Vail clenched her jaw in frustration.

"What do you think about the next painting? Should we go see it?" Jet asked.

"I don't know. Why are you asking me? I'm not a scientist or a professor," she said and threw up her hands. "Speaking of professors, I'm curious to hear what Sylvant had to say about the first painting."

Jet could still hear the skepticism in her tone. "Why is it so important to have Sylvant's buy in?"

"Come on, Stroud," she said. "You feel the same way, whether you admit or not. You can't stand there and pretend that it doesn't matter."

"But what difference does it make?" Jet persisted.

"It makes all the difference. Don't you get it?" Vail shook her head and started walking towards the exit.

"I guess I don't," he said, following behind her. "Explain it to me."

"Look, I know she can get tickets for us, and help us behind the scenes, and that's great. But is it really that important?"

"Hold on," Jet pulled at her arm. "I thought that *was* all that mattered to you, finding a cure?"

"I want to find a cure," she said. "You bet I do. But that's not the most important thing to me. Maybe it used to be, but somewhere along the way… I guess I've changed."

"Does this have something to do with Brit?" Jet asked.

Vail didn't meet his gaze. He'd hit the mark.

"Seeing how other people judged Brit and me, every time we were together… I wished so badly they'd just accept us for who we were. Then he died and never got a chance to feel that acceptance, and I live with that knowledge every day." She took a deep breath before continuing. "I hate them for that, Stroud. Maybe you can accept these people for despising us, but I can't. So yeah, believing in something is important, maybe more important than living."

Jet was taken aback. He hadn't realized she harbored such feelings, but now it all made sense why Vail acted the way she did.

"I get what you're saying," Jet said. "But we can't force Sylvant to believe something she's not ready for, or anyone else for that matter. It's a decision she'll have to make on her own, if she ever does. She has her own demons, just like we do."

Vail considered it and sighed. "I just don't understand how some people work. Of all people, Sylvant should believe in us for heaven's sake! I mean, her sister and all… It frustrates me to no end when I see how controlled you are about all of this. Don't you ever just want to give up?"

"It's crossed my mind a few times," he said.

"I don't know how you do it," she said. "I wish I did, though."

"Well, to answer your original question," Jet continued. "Sylvant didn't really have much to say about the last painting."

"So, if she doesn't know anything, then who would?" Vail asked.

Jet shook his head, "Maybe Professor Keoff."

"No way," Vail said. "We don't need any more professors involved."

Jet nodded. "I agree. We're on our own. Maybe this next painting will shed some light for us."

"I doubt it," Vail sighed. "Look, Stroud, don't get too excited about this. I've been here long enough to know. Every time something good happens I always end up disappointed."

"I get the sense this is different, though," Jet said.

"How could you possibly know that? You haven't even been here for a semester. You have no idea—"

"It has nothing to do with how long I've been on Skylight," Jet interrupted. "I'm talking about that voice in my head, and you know exactly what I mean. You've heard it too. And right now, it just feels different than it has in the past."

She hesitated. "Still, I want to be cautious."

Jet chuckled. “Cautious? That doesn’t sound like the Vail I know.”

She shot him a steady glare.

“No offense, of course,” he added quickly.

“You’re too optimistic.” She took a deep breath and shook her head. “Just don’t come crying to me when I say I told you so.”

“Well,” Jet sighed and crossed his arms. “Hopefully, it won’t come to that.”

The setting sun had broken through the clouds, and Vail turned to face it. “I’m tired. I was like you when I first got here, hopeful and energetic. But this place has drained me. Now I just want it to be over, and sometimes I don’t care how it ends.”

He stood silently next to her. The sun had nearly set behind Earth, and the lamps around them were beginning to hum to life. He watched his breath slowly dissipate into long, hazy puffs and waited for Vail to leave, but she didn’t. “Do you have family here in the system?” he asked.

Her expression hardened. “I try not to think about them,” she said.

“So, you didn’t get along?”

“Not really. Why… did you?”

He shook his head. “No. I never knew my family. I was raised in an orphanage.”

Vail faced him as she listened, but seemed to stare right through him, lost in her own thoughts.

“I don’t know what it’s like to have a family, so there’s no resentment, I guess,” Jet continued. “I just got on with my life. I learned to play blaze, and it helped me focus on something else.”

“That’s how you met Cutter?”

Jet nodded. “I didn’t *really* get to know him until just recently. He’s had his fair share of tough breaks.”

“Tough breaks, huh?” Vail quipped.

“Family issues,” Jet said, not wanting to talk too much about Cutter’s past without him there. “Anyway, it’s nice having friends, don’t you think? I assume this is what a family would feel like.” He paused to look at her.

She returned his gaze. “I’m fine,” she said flatly. “With or without anyone else in my life, if that’s what you’re getting at.”

“What about Cutter?” Jet asked.

Vail hesitated before answering. “Nothing’s going on, if that’s what you’re thinking.”

Even though he could see there was more to it, he decided not to push her. “Right,” he said.

“Anything else on your mind, or can I leave now?” she said weakly.

“Why do you think we’re being followed?” he asked bluntly. The sudden change in tone caught her off guard.

“What?” she finally said.

“We’re being followed. All of us. Solan mentioned that her track coach and Professor Keoff both followed her. What if that’s true?” Jet said.

“I… don’t think there’s a connection between the professors and the student murders if that’s what you’re getting at.”

“Yeah, but what if there is?” Jet said.

“Conspiracy theories again. You just won’t let it rest, will you?”

“I’m just asking the question.” Jet raised his hands.

Vail looked back to the sunset, which was almost gone now. “Then we’ve got bigger problems,” she said.

"My thoughts exactly," Jet agreed.

. • • • ● ⬤ ● • • • .

"REMEMBER, WE'RE STUDENTS from the university's art department," Jet said. "Everyone clear on that?"

Vail and Bo stood near a fountain in the mansion's courtyard, oblivious to what he'd just said. Cutter hovered next to him with Cord looking over Jet's shoulder, his black trench coat buttoned all the way up. Well-manicured shrubs surrounded them, and the soft pitter-patter of the fountain echoed around the space. It was already dark, and Jet was tired from the day's game. They'd won again, but he had taken a beating in the process and could feel several bruised ribs under his throwing arm.

He looked at his watch and rapped the door handle for a third time.

"What's taking so long?" Vail blurted impatiently.

"Are you sure we're at the right place?" Bo asked, pulling out his holopad to check the address.

"Everyone just calm down," Jet said.

Finally, the door cracked open, and a butler peered at them through the crease. "You are to wait inside," he said and disappeared, leaving the door open for them to enter.

Vail gave the others a frown and kicked the large door open with her heavy boot. Everyone followed her inside. Cutter was the last one in and shut the door behind him with a resounding thud.

They stood in an airy rotunda. The tall space stretched up several stories, topped by a clerestory that allowed some diluted moonlight to filter in and reflect off the highly polished stone floor. Jet found a plush velvet bench and sat down. Vail continued to stand in the center of the space with Cord and Cutter, while Bo waited near the door. Several paintings hung from the walls, and Jet stood to take a closer look at one in particular. Soon, he felt the others standing next to him.

"That looks like a painting by the same lady," Bo whispered.

"That's because it is," Cord said.

The painting depicted a young girl standing in the middle of a wheat field. She was wearing a tattered dress that whipped about her ankles from the wind. The wheat stalks around her seemed to sway in the wind. But there was something else in the background of the painting that Jet couldn't quite make out. As he leaned in closer, the image began to grow clearer and more defined. Then the painting was suddenly littered with thousands of flowers in every imaginable color, tumbling through the breeze. Jet felt as if he were standing there in the wheat field with the girl.

"Stand here, look." He grabbed Vail by the arm and guided her to the same spot. "See it?"

"What, I don't see—" Vail paused mid-sentence, abruptly mesmerized.

"The Struggle Within!" a voice rang down from the top of the staircase.

They all turned to see an elderly lady standing at the top landing. She had a cup of steaming tea in one hand and leaned heavily on a steel crutch.

"That's the name of the painting," the lady continued. "Though I'm still not quite sure what it really means. I've studied it for years now and paid a hefty sum for it as well… if I remember correctly, which I probably don't. Oh well, one tends to forget these things at my age. But, enough of that, it's not the one you're here to see." She looked at them for a second longer and then hobbled down the stairs one at a time. "There we go, easy-does-it," she said, refusing to set her tea down. "Now, let me have a look at you, all of you. Hmmm, let me see," she said once she had reached the bottom.

Jet glanced at Cord, Vail, and Bo. Cutter stood a slight distance to his left. Jet turned back to look at the elderly woman. The fact that she could still walk, even with a crutch, was remarkable. She wore a long flowing multicolored scarf that seemed to shimmer in the light. Only her hands and face were visible, and it appeared that arthritis had set in long ago. Her hands rested lightly on a metal crutch, curled into a ball and twitching uncontrollably. Her face was lined with the deep crevices of age, but her eyes were bright and alive. Jet could tell that what time had taken from her physically, it hadn't taken from her mentally.

"I must apologize. I haven't properly introduced myself," the lady said. "Lybra Howling." She limped over to Jet. He smiled warily at her.

"Jet Stroud, I presume? And, blaze, is it? You're quite the passer… going to set some records, I'm sure. That is if you're around long enough."

She limped over to stand in front of Cord before Jet could reply. Her hunched form was dwarfed by Cord's tall frame. "And you must be the young Mister Ledbetter. Oh, yes… I've heard of you, too. You're quite the mathematical genius."

"And do you mind if I ask how you know so much about us?" Vail blurted.

Lybra turned and eyed her as a predator might a dangerous prey. "Vail Hart, of course. Let me just say that I have some connections at the university. I am, well, without sounding too haughty, one of the university's biggest donors."

Vail eyed the old lady suspiciously with her arms crossed but didn't respond.

Bo stood next to Vail, looking around the rotunda and avoided Lybra's gaze. She hobbled over to stand in front of him, waiting for him to acknowledge her. It was an uncomfortable moment until Cutter cleared his throat.

"We're just here to see the painting," he said.

"And who might you be?" she asked, looking at him, but still standing in front of Bo. "You have no place here, especially amongst the likes of these four."

Cutter looked at her and smirked. "If you're implying that they need permission to be my friend, then you're mistaken."

"Indeed," she said. "I would think, just the opposite."

Jet turned to Cord with a confused look. Cord returned his look and shrugged.

"Can't we just get on with it?" Vail interrupted. "Who cares what the crazy old bat thinks, Cutter. Let's get this over with."

"That's enough," Jet said calmly. He turned to Lybra. "Please, we have to be back to the university soon. A quick look at the painting is all we need for our report."

Lybra stared thoughtfully at Cutter. "This way!"

She turned and stuck one arthritis-ridden hand in the air, signaling for them to follow her. "Corsely! Drinks for our guests!" she commanded sharply and handed her empty teacup to her butler. "His family has served me for nearly two decades. I imagine his mother is turning over in her grave right now… four euphs in my home, goodness gracious. Anyway, follow me!" Lybra's mood had changed almost instantly as she hobbled off.

Vail stood rooted in the center of the rotunda glaring at the back of the retreating old lady. "Euphs! Did you hear that Stroud?" she muttered irritably.

"Drop it!" Jet hissed. "Just play along until we can get out of here." He walked quickly to catch up to Lybra. Cord followed close behind with the others bringing up the rear.

"Can I ask you something?" Jet said once he'd caught up to her.

"Of course. Ask away, dear," she chimed.

"How is it that you've come by so many of Van Saint's paintings?"

"Oh, that's easy; lots of money. They are very sought after, her paintings, some more than others."

"But why?"

"They're clandestine, of course," Lybra said, stopping in the middle of the large hallway to turn and look at him. "Oh, come now. Don't tell me you've not heard about that?"

Jet shook his head. "Sorry, no."

"Why, this is remarkable. You're a euph, just like Shiloe Van Saint, and yet you don't know?"

Jet stood looking at her with a blank expression, pretending ignorance. "I thought that was just a rumor, Shiloe having ephebus mortem?"

"Oh, never you mind… just follow me, and I'll explain in a moment," she said, turning and continuing down the hallway.

Jet looked back at the others. Corsely, the butler, followed at a safe distance with a tray of drinks and a scowl on his face. Jet dropped back from Lybra, who was humming a tune to herself and snapping.

"She's crazy," Vail whispered.

"Perhaps," Cord said. "But she is elderly, and senility isn't uncommon."

"She's freakin' me out," Bo muttered. "The sooner we get out of here, the better."

"Don't be fooled. She's clever!" Jet hissed. "We need to stay focused. This may be our only chance to see the painting. Just don't say anything else that'll get us thrown out till we see the painting, okay?"

They followed Lybra as she hobbled into another corridor with a large, grand stair at the far end.

"No vector accelerators?" Jet asked.

"Don't trust them after my accident. Besides, I need the exercise… at least, that's what I keep telling myself," Lybra said, laughing herself into a coughing fit.

They climbed the stairs slowly behind her, which seemed to take an eternity. When they reached the top landing, Jet gasped. They were standing in a large art gallery that occupied the entire upper level. The floor plate was open with no walls or columns to obstruct their view. The space was littered with sculptures and paintings that looked to span across several centuries and perhaps millennia.

"This is my private collection," Lybra explained as they followed her out into the middle. "My late husband and I, rest his soul, had been collecting for over half a century before he passed away. Many of these works date back to our earliest civilizations. I imagine your Professor Sylvant would love a glance at some of these."

"Why won't you let her, or anyone else, for that matter?" Cord asked. "A shame. It's an extraordinary collection."

"It is, my dear boy," Lybra said. "Very few are lucky enough to see my collection. But I'll be damned if any professor comes through my doors."

"Then why us?" Bo asked.

"Corsely. That will be all." Lybra dismissed the butler abruptly. Corsely set the tray of drinks down and left quickly, glad to be away from them. Lybra watched him go before continuing. "You four share something in common with one of the greatest artists known to the human race. Van Saint was more than just a painter. Tell me, what did you see in that painting downstairs?"

Jet shook his head, continuing to play dumb. The others followed his lead and kept quiet.

"So, the passive voice?" she asked, looking at Jet as if trying to read his thoughts. She turned to Cutter. "You, Cutter, is it? What did you see?"

Cutter looked at Jet and the others. He shrugged," Not much, really. Don't see what the big deal is."

"I believe him," Lybra said, pointing her crutch at Cutter. She looked at Jet. "Why do I not believe you?"

Jet shook his head. "I don't know, just telling you what I saw, which was nothing."

Lybra shrugged and turned. "Well, perhaps some people may think that Van Saint was just an ordinary person, that she didn't really have ephebus mortem. But do you know what I think?"

"Please tell," Vail said, a sarcastic edge to her voice.

Lybra fixed her with a cold stare but continued limping around the gallery. "Van Saint could see into the future—she was a prophet. I intend to discover her secret, and price is no object."

Lybra started walking again towards the far wall of the gallery and stopped in front of a painting, "This is my favorite." She pointed at a small unframed portrait of a middle-aged man.

"What's special about it?" Vail asked.

"This is perhaps the most important person to ever walk amongst us."

"Christian Albright," Jet said.

Lybra smiled. "Indeed, it is."

Jet stood directly in front of the portrait and stared at it. Something began to materialize just as it had in the other paintings. The letter 'A' became very prominent.

"What is it?" Lybra whispered eagerly, watching Jet's expression closely. "Tell me what you see." She stood next to him, and one arthritic hand reached out like a hooked talon, latching onto his shoulder.

"I… nothing," Jet lied, avoiding her gaze.

Lybra's anxious expression turned to a frown. "Well, let's try this again," she growled, leading them past several more paintings. "This is the one you requested to see. This is, *The Plan*."

Like the one at the Gala, this one too hovered in place by some sort of anti-gravitational device. Although it was titled *The Plan*, Jet didn't see any instructions or blueprints on its surface. He had seen it several times in the book, and in real life it looked much the same. The large eye in the center of the painting resembled a color wheel of sorts, the rods, and cones of the iris dividing it roughly into twenty-four equal divisions. The background was muted and dull, making everything beyond difficult to see. But the longer he stared, the more prevalent nine red streaks of paint became, which were easily the most distinctive characteristic of the painting. He'd read that they were Van Saint's final paint strokes, even as she was murdered. The streaks of paint seemed to wander aimlessly outwards from the center, carving their way across the rough canvas like a river of blood scored into a lush landscape. In fact, two of the streaks ran the entire length of the painting, top to bottom from the 12 o'clock to the 6 o'clock position, dividing the painting in half. But then other images began to float into the foreground. Inside the colorful sphere were twenty-four symbols, and outside of it was an enormous amount of random equations. The complex math was connected by thousands, perhaps millions, of tiny vibrating strings, working in symphony like an orchestra. The painting seemed to thrum to life, and Jet backed away from it with his hands over his ears as it grew louder. It reached a fevered pitch in his mind and he shut his eyes.

"You see something," Lybra whispered from behind him. "Tell me what it is!"

Jet stumbled out of his trance with a shiver, surprised to feel goosebumps on his arms, and rubbed them vigorously.

"Tell me… speak!" Lybra repeated. "If ephebus mortem holds true, you'll all be dead soon anyway, so what difference does it make? Why should any of you care?"

Shocked, Jet glanced at Vail and Bo, who both had uncertain expressions on their faces. But when he looked at Cord, there was pure ecstasy on his face. He was seeing something in the painting that held him completely mesmerized. Jet felt a sudden urge to leave. He needed to get them out of there.

"I'm sorry, Miss Howling," Jet finally said. "I'm afraid I don't see anything. It seems you were wrong about Van Saint and her paintings."

Lybra leaned heavily on her crutch, and a snarl twisted her lips till he could see her yellow teeth. She moved in closer so that he could hear her whisper. "Don't lie to me, Mister Stroud. It might be the last thing you do."

Jet had become accustomed to threats throughout his life but receiving one from an elderly lady who was perhaps four times his age seemed oddly unnerving. At first, he wasn't sure how to react.

But after a brief pause, he felt anger start to boil over. He pulled away from the rancid heat of her breath and looked down at her. She looked up into his eyes with contempt, yet something caused her to shift uncomfortably in his stare.

"What good are threats to me? I'll be dead soon anyway… right?" Jet replied calmly.

He walked towards the stair but did not turn his back on her. He gripped Cord's black trench coat and guided him towards the exit, placing himself between Lybra and the others. Cutter stared at Lybra, placing himself between her and Jet, waiting until the others were down the stair.

"Keep your distance," Cutter warned.

Lybra looked up at Cutter, hobbled closer. "You have no idea what you're getting yourself into, young sir."

"Am I supposed to be frightened by that?"

"If you are wise, then yes." Another smile twisted her upper lip, and her bright eyes lit up.

Cutter finally turned and made his way down the stair and hurried after the others.

"We'll see each other soon, Mister Stroud," Lybra called down after him as if this were just another minor setback to her.

As soon as they were out the front door, Jet turned to Cord and gripped him by the lapels of his coat. "Cord, what was it? What did you see in there?"

Cord was still in a trance and didn't answer.

"Hey, Brainiac!" Vail snapped her fingers in front of his face.

"Cord, quit messing around," Bo said, stepping in.

"Crazy old bat," Vail commented over her shoulder as she looked back at the mansion. "I knew she was mental, Stroud. Was it worth it?"

"Never mind. Come on, let's go." Jet led the way quickly out of the courtyard. "Cord, talk to us on the way back. Everyone keep your eyes open for a taxi."

There was a hint of snow in the late November air along with an unsettling stillness in the posh Vent District. They walked clumped together under the streetlamps, Cutter leading the way.

"Well?" Vail asked, looking at Cord.

"It was very advanced math. Some of it I've never seen before," Cord said. "Cutter. What did you see, if you don't mind?"

"A big, shiny eyeball."

"You didn't see the math, or the streaks of blood?" Bo asked.

Cutter looked at him with a sidelong glance as they walked. "What the hell are you talking about? There was no blood."

"When did you say that painting was composed?" Cord asked Jet.

"Over a century ago," Jet said. "I don't recall the exact date."

"Scanning back through it all, some of the math I just saw has only been around since recently. Something doesn't add up," Cord replied from underneath his coat. "Besides, she was a painter, not a mathematician."

"Wait. You remember what you saw?" Vail asked.

"Of course. I've got it all right here." Cord tapped his forehead.

"You actually remember all of that junk?" Bo asked incredulously. "How's that even possible?"

"I have a photographic memory," Cord said.

"What?" Jet said. "Why didn't you tell us?"

"Actually, that's one of my little secrets, and I'd prefer to keep it that way," Cord replied. "I've never told anyone, but I feel like I can trust you all."

"I really don't care what you call it or how you do it. Just figure it out!" Vail suddenly picked up her pace, moving ahead of Cutter.

"Already working on it, but I'm not sure how long it will take," Cord said.

"Hey," Jet said, catching up to Vail. "What's wrong?"

"It's nothing," she said. "Let's just get back to campus."

Cord and Jet exchanged glances, but Bo said nothing as they hurried along behind her. Neither Jet nor Cord noticed the shadow keeping pace with them from across the empty street.

CHAPTER

Cord's Conundrum

ΑΒΓΔΕΖΗΘΙΚΛ<u>Μ</u>
ΝΞΟΠΡΣΤΥΦΧΨΩ

On Tuesday evening, the group met down in the stacks. Only the occasional sound of the breeze crooning through the space broke the silence. A foreboding tension had settled over them. One thing was still on everyone's mind… what was next? The third painting, *The Verification*, no longer existed, having been destroyed in a fire long ago. Jet sensed that their fate—whatever that fate was—now rested in the hands of the talented senior mathematician, Cord Ledbetter. If he didn't turn up any clues, they appeared to be at a dead-end.

Vail and Bo sat quietly at the table watching Cord work while Jet tried to finish some of his homework. Cutter, bored, had left the table and was wandering around somewhere in the back.

"How hard can it be?" Vail asked, her patience wearing thin. "Thought you were smart, Ledbetter?"

Cord looked up at her. "You're more than welcome to take on the task if you think you can do this any quicker."

"Vail, come on," Jet said. "Give him a break."

"Well, is he going to take the rest of the semester, or what?" she persisted.

"It does look kinda tough, Vail," Bo said, leaning in next to Cord to get a better look.

"This math is like nothing I've ever seen before, and that is saying something," Cord said in his slow drawl and loosened the top button of his starched oxford.

"If anyone can do this, it's you," Jet tried to reassure him.

"Not to be a downer, but the end of the semester is getting closer," Bo said.

"I've noticed, thank you," Cord said. "However, I refuse to make up answers. It's… strange math. That's the best way I know to explain it."

Cutter returned with a few books. "Strange, huh? Don't think I've ever heard anyone describe math in those terms."

"Yeah, me neither. What do you mean?" Bo asked.

"Have a seat; this might take a minute." Cord kicked out a chair for Cutter to sit.

Everyone huddled around Cord's holopad while he stared at it for a long moment.

"Come on, just say it," Vail said. "What's got you so spooked?"

"It's not so simple," he said. "I just need a minute to think how best to explain it, since none of you are mathematicians."

They waited quietly for Cord to gather his thoughts. "First, I want to be clear about the discrepancies I've found. Notice how unstructured certain parts of these equations are. See the confusion here and here?" Cord pointed to a few areas of the hologram. "This is a basic mistake. Anyone who could compose such an advanced equation of this magnitude would never do this. Here's another one. I've been finding these inconsistencies all over. So, it's either incomplete or seriously flawed."

"But didn't you say that you based this all on memory?" Bo asked.

"Yes."

"And this equation, or whatever, it's like novel-length, right?" Bo continued.

"Are you implying that I made an error?"

Bo shrugged. "Well… it's a really long equation."

Cord shook his head. "I didn't make any errors. It's exactly as it was in the painting, that I assure you."

"I'm just trying to understand, that's all," Bo said.

"I'm just as bewildered," Cord said. "I'll continue to work, but at the moment I have no answers. I'm asking each of you to give me some space while I work, and I promise to solve this before the end of the semester."

The others looked uncertain. Cutter clapped Cord on the back. "I know it may not mean much, but if there's anything I can do to help, I will."

"I appreciate that," Cord said. "Just room to work is what I need right now."

Cutter stood to leave, and Vail grabbed her backpack to follow him. "Cutter, wait," she said, hurrying up the stairs after him. Cutter looked back and waited at the top landing for her.

The rest of the group sat around the table and watched as the two disappeared up the stone stairs.

"What was that?" Bo asked.

Jet looked at them and chuckled. "Your guess is as good as mine."

"You know something, I reckon," Cord said. "He's your roommate, after all."

"Yeah, well, she was asking about him the other day," Jet said. "I thought she was just curious, but apparently there's more."

"She'd better watch out, Cutter seems unpredictable," Bo said.

"Actually, I'd be more concerned for him," Jet said.

"I'll agree with that," Cord said. "Vail can handle herself, no doubt."

Cord bent back to his work. Bo made eye contact with Jet and motioned his head silently for him to follow. Bo stood to stretch and walked off.

Jet wrinkled his brow, confused, but followed Bo into the dark recesses of the stacks. After a few aisles, Bo spoke softly. "I need to talk to you."

"What's wrong?" Jet whispered back.

Bo looked back towards Cord and then shook his head. "Not around the others. The Skylight Open is our last track meet of the year. Can you be there, alone?"

"Why can't we talk here? I'm sure Cord can't hear us if that's your concern," Jet said and looked at Bo in the dark. Their eyes illuminated the shelves of books around them in a splash of turquoise and purple. Bo's voice was unsteady, and his hand shook as he gripped the shelf next to him. His eyes roved back in forth in the dark as if searching for something. The sudden change in his demeanor alarmed Jet. Bo seemed to be on the verge of a nervous breakdown.

"I can't explain it to you right now," Bo whispered. "Doesn't feel right. I don't know how else to put it. Just… promise you'll be there. Can you do me that favor?"

"Okay, Bo," Jet said. "I'll be there. You can tell me then."

• • • • • ● • • • • •

VAIL PAUSED BEHIND Cutter's large frame at the top of the stair. The others were out of earshot. "Mind if I tag along?" she asked.

Cutter looked back over his shoulder. His broad, pierced brow furrowed inquisitively. "Why not?" he shrugged. "Surely things can't get any more bizarre around here?"

Cutter peered through the bookshelf, waited for a second, and then pushed through, followed by Vail like two wraiths in the night. They walked nonchalantly, as was their character, out through the library rotunda. Even though it was late, that didn't mean the library was less occupied. With the end of the semester approaching, more students were starting to study around the clock. Cutter drew plenty of attention on his own, but with Vail in tow, everyone gawked openly at them. It made Cutter smirk, he didn't mind it one bit. Vail seemed annoyed, as though she might drop an obscene gesture at any moment.

They left the library and blended into the heavy mist. The wind had died down from earlier that day, allowing the mist to settle in. The moon was hidden from view, and the nearby lamplights dotted the sidewalks like glowing cotton balls.

"Would it be awkward if I said that I liked you?" Vail said bluntly.

Cutter chuckled. "Wow. That's one hell of a pickup line."

"I didn't mean that I *like*-like you."

"What *do* you mean then?"

"Just that you seem to be someone I'd like to know better."

"How much better?" Cutter asked.

"Start with friends and leave it at that, for now. How does that sound?"

"Like a pickup line."

"Whatever," Vail said, but with the hint of a smile.

"Why so interested in me, by the way?" Cutter said.

"What can I say? I like your style."

"There's gotta be more to it than that."

"Well, you don't take any attitude from others," she said. "You do what you want, when you want."

He shrugged. "Okay. What else?"

"You don't mind being around people like Jet and me… you're just different."

Cutter didn't say anything as they strolled.

"So, what family issues have you had?" she finally asked.

He turned on her. "Did Jet tell you that?"

"Maybe. Does that upset you?"

But Cutter wasn't fooled, knowing Jet would never tell anyone those things they'd shared, least of all to Vail. She was trying to get a reaction out of him. He shrugged and kept walking. "Did you use your special powers to get the information from him? I mean, look at you. Can you see through walls with those eyes?"

Vail flushed. Cutter watched her fist tighten and her jaw clench.

"Bit touchy, aren't we?" Cutter said. "I mean, both of us… when it comes to certain topics."

"I… guess I deserved that," she said and relaxed. "Why are you helping us, Cutter? You're just ruining your image. Don't you get it? No one wants us here."

"Does it look like I care what others think?" He paused as a few students walked by and then pulled her along into a courtyard.

She sat down on a stone bench, crossed her arms, and looked up at him.

"Yeah," Cutter finally said. "I've had family issues. It's not something you'd want to hear."

"Try me," she said. "I dare you."

Cutter hung his head and thought for a moment, but still hesitated. "This isn't a competition of who's suffered the most, Vail. That's not what I want."

"You have no idea what a real struggle feels like," she continued. "You don't know what it's like to feel rejection year after year. To have your family ripped away, your parents prosecuted… your sister jailed and shipped off. To watch your boyfriend die and know that it's all your fault. This… thing! This curse you have no control over!" Vail stared at Cutter as a tear rolled down her cheek. "It'll never end till I'm dead. How could you understand?" Vail said, her voice husky in the cool mist.

Cutter stood frozen for a moment, trying to adjust to her sudden change in mood. Then he crouched in front of her and grasped her shoulders. "My father… he murdered my younger brother because he was handicapped. I was powerless to help him, and I blamed myself for years. Maybe the same way you blame yourself. Look, I don't pretend to understand the pain you've been through… or Jet or the others. I only know that you have an opportunity every day to turn something negative into a positive. That's what I took with me… that's all I *could* take with me."

"You sound just like Jet," she said.

"Well, maybe blaze has something to do with that. It's a good outlet for frustration and anger. I think you should join the team, maybe," he chuckled. "You'd be a hell of a blaze player."

Vail looked up at him and knuckled a tear away. "No way. Besides, I'd hate to put you out of a job."

They both erupted in laughter.

"That's probably true," Cutter finally said and sat down next to her.

"So, you couldn't help your brother, but you can help Jet, is that it?" Vail said. "That's why you're here?"

"I guess so," he said.

"But it looks like Jet can take care of himself," Vail said.

Cutter nodded. "Damn right he can."

"What about me?" she asked.

Cutter looked at her. "From what I've seen so far, I'd say you can take care of yourself just fine. Do you need my help?"

She shrugged. "I wouldn't say no."

Cutter held her gaze as she leaned in, paused, then kissed him.

CHAPTER

Bo's Confession

ΑΒΓΔΕΖΗΘΙΚΛΜ
ΝΞΟΠΡΣΤΥΦΧΨΩ

November ushered in December with a flurry of activity. The university was festive with color, and decorations littered the campus in celebration of the holiday season. Students were eager about the upcoming winter break and final exams. There was a game-like atmosphere around campus since the blaze team was ranked number one in the polls. They were undefeated, something that had eluded Skylight for nearly three decades. Two more games remained on the schedule, though, and it had been a brutal season for Jet. Practice sessions lasted longer into the evening, and Plannar ran the team ragged in preparation for each weekend game.

The group continued to meet each night down in the stacks. Huddled together in the chilly basement, they tried to focus on their assignments as Cord worked through the mysterious equation. Jet was keenly aware of Bo's attitude following their conversation.

Did Bo think he was going to die soon?

Jet also noticed Cutter and Vail acting strangely. They would often sneak off into the stacks, Vail heading one direction and Cutter the opposite. They would eventually return, Vail out of breath, and Cutter's hair disheveled, which brought a smile to Jet's face each time. Though it was something he never thought he'd see, Vail seemed happy, and so did Cutter. It all made sense to Jet. They were both so similar in many ways. He tried not to think about the negative side of what might happen, though. He only wanted to see them happy and tried to burn those memorable moments into his head. However, the foreboding feeling in his stomach wouldn't leave him in peace.

Jet rolled out of bed around 6:30 on the following Saturday morning and dressed in his jeans and varsity coat. It was chilly outside with temperatures in the system dipping near freezing. He shuddered at the thought of the university's cross-country team running in it.

It was a quiet trek with most of the students still in bed enjoying their day off. After a brisk stroll he eventually saw Chroma lighting up the surrounding mist like fire. Its billboard held the day's news, weather, and information about the track meet, which included the college rankings. At the top-ranked position was Bo Blake. Jet stopped and stared at it amongst the hustle-and-bustle of the other runners. He'd had no idea Bo was the number one runner in all of college.

Jet no longer had to push his way through crowds of students; they simply stepped aside as he approached. Someone tapped him on the shoulder, and he turned to see Bo, his blonde beard tinged with frost. Bo fidgeted with his jersey, and Jet wasn't sure if it was pre-race jitters or the same anxiety he'd shown during their last conversation in the stacks.

"Well, here I am," Jet said. "Let's talk. You got butterflies or something?"

"Are you alone?" Bo asked, his head down. As usual, they drew plenty of stares, but there was nowhere to talk in private.

"Yes. The others are probably still in bed where it's nice and warm. Why did you want to talk to me here at your track meet? Why not earlier, or someplace more private?"

Bo took a deep breath and exhaled, puffing out a cloud of steam. "Because I wanted to do this my way, on my own terms."

"Okay," Jet said. "What's wrong? Why won't you look at me?"

Bo kept his head bowed and didn't look at Jet. He stammered, as if he'd been rehearsing what to say for a long time. He wrung his hands and started to talk, then faltered. Adjusted and started again. "I wanted to say that… I have something to share, and I want you to tell it to the others. Will you do that for me?"

"Sure. But why me, and why not you?" Jet asked.

"You're the one. That's how I want it… I won't be around to do it."

Jet narrowed his eyes. "What exactly do you mean by that?"

"There's no time to explain. Just listen. There's something you need to know. I should have told you already and I feel like this will be my last chance. You know that voice you get in your head sometimes?"

Jet nodded. "I know what you're talking about. It's been growing louder over the last few days."

"It's a warning bell, I think. Look at my hands…"

Jet looked down at Bo's hands. He was struggling to keep them steady.

"That voice has been ringing nonstop the last few months. Right now, it's so loud I can barely think."

"It's okay, I'm right here," Jet said, trying to calm him. "Just tell me what you need."

"I think I'm out of time," Bo said and finally looked up. Bo's eyes shone so brightly that Jet had to shield his own eyes.

"Bo, what's happening with your eyes?"

"Doesn't matter!" Bo said through clenched teeth. "Just listen. Remember the mirages we talked about, the ones you catch from the corner of your eye sometimes?"

Jet nodded and tried to focus on what Bo was saying. Runners around them started moving towards the starting line. It was difficult to listen to Bo's whispers with all the commotion.

"Jet!" Bo said. "You need to hear this."

Jet's attention snapped back. He felt alarmed now.

"There was one following us from Lybra's estate that night," Bo continued.

"Are you sure?" Jet said. "I didn't see it."

"That's because it didn't want you to," Bo hissed, showing his teeth.

"But that makes no sense. I've seen them before. Why not that night?"

"Ask Vail," Bo said. "I bet she saw it, too."

Jet shook his head and looked at the clock. Chroma had started the two-minute countdown, and an announcer asked the runners to take their positions. "Why would you and Vail see it and not me?" Jet asked.

"I don't know why…" Bo trailed off. He started talking quietly to himself. Jet stood next to him and suddenly realized Bo was having a breakdown.

Bo snapped back to attention and grabbed Jet by his coat and pulled at him. "These mirages choose who can see them. They're trying to tell us something. I never could figure out why, though. I tried—"

"Bo, let's talk later. We can sort it out after your race—"

"You don't get it. This *is* my *last* race!" Bo grabbed Jet by his shoulders. "I'm going to die!"

"During the race? How do you know?" Jet asked.

"I just know. Look at my eyes… at how bright they are. It's my turn to die. It's up to you now. You need to figure this out. I thought I could do this on my own. I was wrong. I should have been more honest with you and the others. Maybe this information will help. Tell the others I'm sorry."

There was less than a minute left on the clock, and all the runners had taken up positions along the starting line.

Jet had a sick feeling in his stomach. "Then don't run this race! Just drop out. We'll find the others and figure this out together."

"It's too late. You can't help me now," Bo mumbled, and his shoulders slumped forward. He bowed his head and knelt to the ground.

"Jet. Do you remember telling us about the night of the storm… you saw Solan's name, right? Well, I've seen a name, too. Many times."

"What? Why didn't you say so before!"

"I'm sorry," Bo said.

"Listen, Bo. Just make it through the race. Do whatever you have to and make it. I'll be at the finish line waiting for you. Got it?"

Jet didn't know what else to say. He tried to think of some words of encouragement, but nothing came to mind.

A horn blared out from above, and the runners leapt from the starting line. Bo stood and gave Jet a weak smile. He turned and bolted, easily catching the lead runner. He yelled something over his shoulder as he ran. Jet barely heard him over the stampede of feet.

"Sojahn Quark."

· • • • ● ● ● • • • ·

CORD SAT IN the stacks, legs crossed, perusing his work.

He was confused.

For the first time in his life, he was feeling something he'd never felt before—uncertainty. He'd always been first, always won, always figured out a solution. He was a savant, and he knew it. And, he had promised the others he would find a solution—he didn't plan on letting them down.

However, there was a voice in his head, babbling nonstop like a countdown timer. Cord knew that the others felt it, too. Day and night, it was there. A persistent reminder that he needed to be efficient and diligent. Another side effect of E.M.? Perhaps.

Cord scrolled through the multiple lines of complex math, trying to make sense of it again. He'd actually had a revelation of sorts, primarily because he couldn't solve the equation. That's when he knew it wasn't meant to be solved. That's also where he'd hit another dead-end.

He stood and walked around the stacks, tugging at the front of his black vest and straightening his starched collar. Now that he knew the equation was a diversion, he could start thinking outside the box. Nonetheless, he knew that wasn't his strength. He needed structure and direction. His imagination only went so far.

He found himself standing in front of the main bookshelf. There was something odd about it to him. He gripped it in his wiry hands and gave the shelf a tug. It didn't budge an inch. He picked up Van Saint's book, thumbed through it, then set it back on the shelf.

A breeze rushed past, turning his skin into goosebumps. The hair on the back of his neck stood up. Although he found the stacks foreboding atmosphere appealing, he felt suddenly spooked.

Cord popped his collar straight, strode confidently back to the candle lit table, and sat down. He began his new approach, hoping it would yield a different solution this time. There was always more than one way to solve a riddle.

· • • ● ● ⬤ ● ● • • ·

AFTER THEIR TALK, Jet waited at the finish line for Bo. Even though Bo had been projected to win the race, he never crossed the finish line. Jet wanted to believe Bo had simply twisted his ankle or dropped out of the race. But deep down he knew what had happened. Bo's grim tone before the race told Jet everything he needed to know. And, the nagging voice in his head was confirmation that Bo was dead. Jet waited as long as possible but finally had to leave. He needed to prepare for his blaze game later that day and was supposed to meet Cutter at the stadium to stretch.

Jet managed to stay focused enough to help the team to a victory. Cutter, as usual, racked up plenty of offensive and defensive stats, recovering a fumble in the end to win the game for Skylight. After the game, Jet checked his holopad to find a message from Cord. "See me right away, all of you!" Cord was vague most of the time and usually kept his emotions in check. A message like this meant he had uncovered something.

Jet showed Cutter the message, and both agreed to skip dinner at Blazers, hoping Coach Plannar wouldn't notice.

"How's Vail?" Jet asked as they left the stadium. The lights around the facility lit up the afternoon sky as they jogged briskly.

"Fine. Why?" Cutter asked.

"Just curious, that's all."

"You're not very good at small talk, you know that?" Cutter said. "What's on your mind?"

"It's Bo," Jet said.

"What about him?"

"I'll explain when we get to the stacks. The others need to hear this too."

When they arrived, Vail was already there arguing with Cord.

"How does that get us to the next step?" she asked.

Jet and Cutter walked in and sat down. Vail was ranting over Cord's shoulder as she paced with her arms crossed. Cord sat in the wing-backed chair and watched her calmly.

"What's going on?" Cutter asked. He let his backpack drop to the floor and looked at Vail.

"Brainiac here has had a revelation," Vail said. "Tell them, Ledbetter."

Vail groaned and spun Cord's holopad around to face Jet and Cutter. "Take a look at this, Stroud. Tell me how this is supposed to help!"

Jet looked at the hologram projecting from Cord's holopad. It was a jumble of numbers, some highlighted, others ghosted in the background. "What am I supposed to be looking at?" he asked.

"A solution… kind of," Cord said. "Have a seat, and I'll explain."

Cutter looked around the stacks. "So, Jet… where the hell is Bo?"

Vail and Cord paused, noticing he wasn't there.

"We… need to talk about that," Jet said.

Vail leaned against the table. "Is this bad news?"

"I think so," Jet said. "He didn't finish his race this morning when he was supposed to."

"We need to call him then, now!" Vail said. She dove into her backpack. "What if he needs us?"

Jet reached over and touched her arm. "I'll explain in just a minute. Let me say something first… It's what he asked me to do."

"You already know something's wrong?" she said. "How can you stand there like that?"

"Vail. I promised him I'd do this. Just listen to what I have to say, okay?"

Vail reluctantly set her backpack down.

Jet cleared his throat. "Bo wanted to see me this morning, alone. He asked that I share a few things with the group. But first…" he turned to face Vail. "Is there something you'd like to share with us about the night at Lybra's estate?"

Vail stared at him as if she had been expecting the question. "Okay, fine," Vail shrugged. "I saw something following us that night. I take it Bo did too, but you didn't?"

"Cord, what about you?" Jet asked.

Cord shook his head. "I didn't see anything."

"Bo seems to think that these mirages are visible only to the ones they choose," Jet said. "He didn't say why he believed that, though, and honestly, I don't know what to think of it. If you two saw something that night and Cord and I didn't, maybe there's some proof to his theory."

"Was that all he said?" Vail asked.

"No, there's more. He also mentioned a name. Remember, I've been seeing Solan's name. So, this might be the one he was seeing. He thought he could figure it out on his own, and I guess he was afraid to tell us about it."

"What was the name he saw?" Cutter asked.

"Sojahn Quark," Jet said. "I have no idea who that is... was."

"*The* Sojahn Quark?" Cord asked. "Impressive. She was another former student who had E.M. and died before graduation. But that was like fifty years ago, I think. She would have been a brilliant scientist, too."

"Vail, I think it's time to hear it," Jet said.

"I don't know, guys. This is probably not the best—"

"What's the name?" Jet asked again, cutting her off.

She took a deep breath. "It's my old boyfriend, Brit."

At that, Cutter narrowed his eyes, Jet's jaw dropped, and Cord leaned back in his chair staring at her in shock.

"I told you," Vail said. "What are you gawking at, Ledbetter? Let's hear yours. Go on!"

"Cord?" Jet said. "Who is it?"

Cord cleared his throat. "This will be as confusing to you all as it's been to me."

"Ledbetter," Vail said, lowering her voice.

Cord shrugged. "It's Solan Alexander."

Jet let his backpack drop to the floor with a thud.

"Well, you got me beat there," Vail said.

"When Jet mentioned Solan, of course I had to figure this

out," Cord said. "I wanted to understand why both of us were seeing her name. Sorry Jet, I should have said something earlier."

There was a moment before Cutter finally broke the silence. "What does the information Bo shared really tell us?"

"I'm still not sure," Jet said. "Unless one of you have some thoughts. It was the last thing he told me, so obviously, he felt it was important. The only pattern I see are former E.M. students. Whether it ties to the authorities or faculty, I don't know."

"Why are you referring to Bo in the past tense?" Vail asked.

"I'm being honest with all of you right now. Bo didn't sound well this morning. He thought today's race would be his last."

"All the more reason to find him!" Vail said.

"I tried to talk to him," Jet said. "I offered to help, but he didn't want it. I don't know what was going through his mind this morning. He wanted to be left alone. He didn't finish the race. I think it's obvious what happened."

"I'm not going to settle for that," Vail continued. "We need to contact him!"

"Vail. He's gone," Jet said.

"You don't know that! Call him!" Vail said, trying to hold her voice steady.

Jet nodded. "Okay. But let me do it alone. We don't need a committee." He turned to Cord. "Let's hear what you found. Make it quick, please."

Cutter and Jet sat down next to Vail on the opposite side of the table. Cord stood, loosened his collar, then flipped his holopad around and the hologram projected around the table.

"Take a look at this section of the riddle." Cord highlighted the problematic series of equations for them to see.

"So, it's a riddle now?" Cutter asked.

"I've changed my approach," Cord said. "Whoever wrote this was too smart to make these kinds of simple errors," Cord motioned at the highlighted area. "He, or she, was hiding something. I was just too focused on trying to solve the equation that I missed the obvious. If there's a solution, it's been tucked away deep. It would take someone well versed in math to even discover this much."

"Which you did, we know you're smart. On with it," Vail said.

Jet held up a hand. "Hold on. You're saying that someone purposely made this equation wrong to hide something?"

"That's my theory. Someone went to great lengths to cover something up."

Cutter leaned back in his chair. "But you haven't figured that part out yet?"

"Not completely. But look here." Cord selected a number with several zeros behind it.

"Is that really a number?" Vail asked.

"This is called the Planck Length," Cord said. "It keeps repeating, but in the wrong places."

"What exactly is that?" Jet asked.

"You mean the Planck Length?" Cord said.

"We're not mathematicians, remember?" Vail said.

"It's a measurement," Cord said. "It's about one hundred million billion billion times smaller than an atomic nucleus.

"Why are you telling us this, Ledbetter?" Vail replied. "We're on the clock, let's go."

Cord was about to say something when Jet interjected. "Cord, out of curiosity, did you count how many times this number occurs?"

"No, why?" Cord said.

"Maybe we should?" Jet said.

Cord sat down and typed something on his holopad. At the bottom of the hologram a number appeared.

"What does 2,412,630 tell us?" Vail said. "Is that how many light years away the cure is?" She shook her head, stood, and walked off. Cutter pushed back in his chair and followed after her.

Jet turned back to Cord. "Can you think of anything this number might represent?"

Cord stared at it. "No, and I'm not even sure we're on the right track."

"What if there's a pattern we can look in to?" Jet said.

"It's possible," Cord thought about it. "I'm at the end of my imagination; that's not my strength. I'm open to ideas."

"See what you can come up with. I'll call Bo."

Jet lifted his backpack to leave and Cord grabbed his arm. "Jet. You know he's dead. Why call?"

He stared at Cord for a moment. "I know. But I told Vail I'd do it. Maybe it's the closure we all need."

Jet decided to stop by the athletic department first, just to make certain. The race results would be posted there, and then he'd know if Bo was dead and his body somewhere in the Clipton Forest.

Jet caught the news headlines as he walked across the library's rotunda. A news crew was gathered around the forest's edge. The headlines scrolling across the bottom of the display read what Jet had known all along.

Bo was dead.

CHAPTER

Cloak and Shadow

ΑΒΓΔΕΖΗΘΙΚΛ**Μ**
ΝΞΟΠΡΣΤΥΦΧΨΩ

JET WATCHED THE news report from across the library lobby. Even though he had known Bo was dead, the sinking feeling in his stomach still hit with such force that he slumped against a kiosk and slid down to a sitting position. He tried to decide what to do next as other students walked by and ignored him. He sat with his back propped against the kiosk and lost track of time. His holopad beeped a few times from Vail, but he ignored it.

Soon, he saw the others walking toward him. Jet stood to meet them.

"We saw the news," Cutter said. His head was bowed, and he spoke softly. "What should we do now?"

"I don't know," Jet said. "What did the rest of the news report say?"

"They found a few items of clothing with his blood on them," Cutter said. "No evidence of a struggle or any witnesses, though. Apparently, he was so far ahead of everyone else in the forest that no one saw what happened."

Vail had a vacant stare. She was calm now, and her typical air of defiance was gone. "How can they make such a claim so soon? They can't possibly have enough evidence to say he was murdered."

Jet nodded. "It's similar to what happened to Myranda. There was no sign of a struggle, and they never found her body."

"I don't want this to just fade away," Vail said. "I need more information."

"From who, though? Sylvant?" Cutter said. "I doubt she could do anything."

"No, she won't have access to any of this information. We need to talk to the authorities," Jet said.

It was late, but they all agreed to go to the Skylight Authority Headquarters on the second belt. Jet signed for a skiff, and less than an hour later, they were walking into the police headquarters building. Each of them went through security before entering the lobby, which was mostly vacant at that hour. The four of them stepped to the front of the line and waited. A few attendants were on duty, and both booths quickly switched to off duty as soon as they saw Jet, Cord, and Vail.

"How typical," Cord said.

"It's pure discrimination!" Vail hissed over her shoulder.

Cord tapped Jet on the shoulder. "Detective's office over there."

Jet led the way and knocked on the door. A slender lady opened the door and took a step back before she said anything. She looked curiously at them through the steam rising from her coffee mug, which hovered unsteadily near her lips.

"We have some questions," Vail said.

"I'm… sorry, but I was just heading out for the evening," the detective said.

Jet looked down at her badge. He thought he recognized her but couldn't quite place her face. "Detective Marsh, we won't take much of your time. We're hoping to find out more about our friend."

She rubbed her forehead and craned her neck. "Come in, have a seat."

She ushered them into her office and shut the door. Vail sat down, and Cutter stood behind her. Jet stood next to Cutter while Cord leaned against the wall nearest a window.

"I'm assuming you're here about Bo Blake, the runner?" Marsh said and sat down at her desk.

"Yes," Jet said. "We just found out."

"What do you need to know?" she said.

Vail stood to face her. "Everything."

Marsh crossed her arms and shrugged. "I'm afraid I can't share much about the case if that's what you're after."

"How can you possibly determine if he was murdered? It's only been half a day, and you don't have all the evidence," Vail said.

"Detective," Cord said, "Shouldn't you be searching for him instead of claiming he's dead?"

"You don't know what we know," Marsh said.

"Is there more evidence that hasn't been released?" Jet asked. "If there is, why withhold it?"

"We need answers; we *deserve* answers!" Vail raised her voice. "I'm tired of this. I… we've been putting up with this coverup long enough!"

"Take it easy, Vail," Jet said, and Cutter placed a hand on her shoulder.

Vail glared at Jet and shrugged Cutter away. "Are either of you hearing this? She's lying, and you know it!"

"You need to calm down, alright?" Detective Marsh said. "Look, I was there. I collected some of the evidence, but I can't share anything with you. I wish I could, but this case is under the Agency's jurisdiction now. They handle these high-profile cases, and they're very strict. I'm not authorized to speak about your friend. I'm sorry, my hands are tied here."

Cord was silent, and Vail stood with her arms crossed.

Jet nodded. "Is there anyone else we can talk to?"

"I'm afraid not right now. Here's my contact information. If there's any other questions not involving Bo, you can call me." Marsh held her holopad next to Jet's. "I'm sorry about your friend. I wish I had better news."

· • • ● ● ● ● • • · ·

JET CALLED SYLVANT the next day. He knew she'd be busy and hated to bother her on a Sunday. It was apparent that she was becoming more and more distant from the group. She was harder to get a hold of, and when they did talk, she was brief and to the point.

Sylvant barely looked at him when she answered his call. She seemed uptight, and her hair was disheveled. "Jet, sorry… I'm just trying to find… something," she said, hurrying around her study.

"You want out now, don't you?" Jet said. "It's okay if you do. I understand."

In the hologram, Sylvant stopped and leaned against her desk. "Jet, no. That's not true. I'm… just so busy with finals coming up and everything else. It's been really difficult to stay in touch, as you're probably aware. I don't mean to sound insensitive with the news about Bo. I heard that, and my heart just sank. I don't know what to say."

"Sylvant," Jet began and stopped. "Look, I don't want to try and convince you of anything, and I don't expect you to believe there's some conspiracy or coverup behind this. In fact, *I* don't even know what to think anymore. I'm just not sure what to do next. I guess I thought we'd have more to go on at this point."

Sylvant finally gave up on what she was looking for and sat down behind her desk. She took a deep breath and seemed to zone out.

"You're thinking about your sister, aren't you?" Jet asked. "I didn't mean to upset you like this."

"Jet," Sylvant said, leaning forward with her head in her hands. "I think you have bigger concerns than hurting my feelings. I don't know what to tell you or what advice to give. You're a unique person, that much shows by the way the others trust you. You've managed to pull everyone together and get them working as a team. That's a special thing. I'm not sure anyone else could have accomplished that."

Jet nodded with a half-smile.

"You're right, though," she continued. "I thought I could do this and face those feelings again. I assumed that a decade of suffering was in my past, and maybe I could help you all to end this… whatever *this* is. But when I heard about Bo, it hit me. I'm watching this all over again, just like with Solan. I built a wall around myself using different excuses. It's starting to crumble right in front of my eyes now. But, I'm not giving up. I want to be here for you and the others."

A wave of guilt suddenly hit Jet as he looked at her. He was so concerned about his own situation that he hadn't noticed the pain she was going through. He had dragged her into this, and now she was suffering through the same traumatic feelings she'd felt for her sister all those years ago. "I'm so sorry, Sylvant. I didn't mean for this to happen to you again."

Sylvant's eyes welled with tears. She cleared her throat and turned away from the hologram to regain her composure. "You're a good person. You don't deserve this, Jet."

He knew in that instant what he had to do. "Professor," Jet said. "Just one more thing..."

Sylvant waited. She looked worn, reminiscent of how Solan looked in her journal. He didn't want to be responsible for anyone else's suffering, least of all hers. It was time he let her go.

"Thanks for helping us when no one else would," Jet said. "Please, don't contact me again."

"Jet," she said and sat forward quickly. "Wait! Please don't do this—"

He ended the call before she could finish.

· • • • ● ● ● • • • ·

THE FOLLOWING SATURDAY was the final game of the regular blaze season. Jet sat alone in front of his locker, trying to clear his thoughts. A thousand random voices tumbled through his head like tumbleweeds in the wind. The group was starting to collapse, even though no one wanted to admit it. Cord seemed more isolated as he worked relentlessly on the mysterious equation. But his progress had practically slowed to a halt that week. He oftentimes grew frustrated, even throwing a book across the stacks on one occasion, which was completely out of character for him. So far, all they had was a number, which added more mystery to the strange equation but led them no closer to their next step. Cord had even suggested bringing it to Keoff again, as a last resort. But that idea was once again rejected by the group.

Jet went through his normal pre-game routine. He dressed, went to the field for warm-ups, and then waited in the tunnel for the announcer to bring the team onto the field. He found Cutter in the tunnel.

"How's Vail holding up?" Jet asked.

"She's fine. I'm just trying to keep her mind off Bo," Cutter said.

"I've been wanting to talk to you about her, actually."

"Yeah, why's that?" Cutter said.

"Do you think you two should be getting so involved?"

Cutter looked at Jet for a long moment. "What the hell do you mean by that?"

"What if something happens to her?" Jet asked. "Have you thought about that?"

Cutter crossed his arms and tilted his head. "I can't believe I'm hearing this. What's wrong with you?"

"I just think you should be more realistic about this whole thing," Jet said. "I mean, we lost Bo, and I just told Professor Sylvant to leave us alone."

"What!" Cutter said, raising his voice. "Why'd you do that?"

"Does it matter?" Jet said. "She knows what's coming, and now she's gone."

"Are you trying to get rid of me? Because that's what it sounds like."

Jet stood next to Cutter but didn't look at him. He was concerned about his friend but realized his choice of words were all wrong. The conversation had turned sour quickly. But maybe the best thing he could do for Cutter was what he had just done for Sylvant?

"Man, Jet. I gotta say I'm disappointed," Cutter said. "Never thought you'd give up like this."

"I never said I was giving up. I just want you to really think about it. Vail could be gone tomorrow—"

"You need to mind your own business, alright?" Cutter interrupted. "I think I can handle myself and anyone else that comes along. That's all you need to know."

"You really think you can protect her?" Jet shot back.

"I can and I will," Cutter said. "She'll be fine."

"You can't protect everyone, especially from this," Jet said, raising his voice. "Maybe I'm just starting to realize it, and I'm sorry if that sounds negative. Maybe what happened to Bo shook something up inside of me, I don't know."

Cutter shook his head and clenched his jaw but kept quiet.

"Look, I know you like her," Jet continued. "And Vail seems happy for once—I'm happy for you both. But how's this going to end? Are you being honest with yourself or are you being selfish and pretending that everything's just fine?"

"You need to back off!" Cutter growled.

"You can't help us anymore, Cutter," Jet said. "Whatever this is, it's beyond any of us."

Cutter moved in close to Jet. "I'll decide when I go, on my terms."

"No," Jet said. "Not this time."

"You can't do this," Cutter said evenly. "It's not up to you."

Jet had made up his mind, though. He didn't need to put Cutter in harm's way anymore than he wanted Sylvant there. But, he knew he'd have to provoke Cutter to get him out of the way. He grabbed Cutter by the shoulder pads and pulled him in close. "It's my life, Cutter. I decide."

Cutter shoved Jet hard, and he fell against the player next to him, which happened to be Korbin Daze.

Daze took one look at Jet and rammed his elbow into Jet's mouth. Jet felt his lip split open and blood gushed down onto his jersey. Daze grabbed Jet by his shoulder pads and pushed him into a group of upper classmen. One of them slammed a fist into Jet's stomach, and he felt the air escape from his lungs. Cutter took two steps and hauled the upper classman off his feet and threw him against the wall. Daze swung a fist at Jet, but he dodged it easily. Daze's punch landed squarely on another player's jaw, who bellowed loudly. The noise caused several nearby players to move in and join the fight. Daze grabbed Jet again, as three other players pinned Cutter against the wall and pummeled him. Jet headbutted the next player and brought his knee into someone's stomach.

Daze rushed over and grabbed Jet again and stared directly into his eyes, his face inches away. "You're dead, prep," Daze hissed. "You started this, and now Plannar'll kick you off the team. But before he does, I'm sending you away with a painful gift."

Jet stared into Daze's eyes and felt his mood change suddenly. Daze's eyes went wide with shock as the ruckus around them faded away to silence. It was as if Jet could see into his soul, like peeking through a foggy window on a cold day. A thick greenish color swirled around an illuminated sphere. He held that sphere in his hand and felt it pulsating in rhythm with Daze's heartbeat. He knew that all he had to do was squeeze it, and he would extinguish that life force. It would be so easy. He held it for a second with confused emotions. In the back of his mind hate circled in his thoughts, tempting him to squeeze the sphere. He'd felt so much pain because of people like Daze… he deserved this!

So, why not rid the world of him? He heard Vail's voice hissing at him.

Then, something in his soul prevailed. A calming voice spoke to him.

LET GO.

Jet blinked… and let go.

Seconds later, he was standing over Daze with Coach Plannar holding two of the upper classmen against the wall. He glared at Jet. Just then the announcer's voice echoed down the tunnel. All the players stared at Plannar and waited for him to say something.

"All of you up to the field, now!"

Jet started moving, but Plannar grabbed him by the shoulder pads. "Not you, Strud."

Jet stopped and waited. Plannar reached down and touched Daze's forehead. Daze sat bolt upright as if waking from a dream. He looked at Jet, his face pale.

"Go on," Plannar told him. They watched as Daze meandered awkwardly up the tunnel and out onto the field.

Plannar turned his gaze back to Jet. "What happened?"

Jet shook his head, trying to remember the chain of events. "I don't know. There was a fight. I looked at Daze and… the next thing I know he's lying on the ground."

"You start this fight?" Plannar asked.

"No, coach," Jet said. "I know it looks that way, but I didn't."

"You know what the other players will say, don't you?" Plannar said.

Jet could see where Plannar was headed. The only player that might back him was Cutter, assuming he wasn't too upset about the comments he'd made.

"I'm afraid this isn't going to look good, Strud," Plannar said. "That's two fights you've been involved in this season alone. As much as I hate to do it, you know why I have to."

Jet was still in shock about what had just happened. And now Plannar was about to make his semester even worse.

"You're off the team, Strud. This'll be your last game here. I'd make the move right now, but since it's our last game of the season, I won't. I'll have to find a replacement for the playoffs. I'm sorry, son." Plannar placed a hand on Jet's shoulder and turned and walked up the tunnel.

Jet watched him leave and felt despair set in. First Bo then Sylvant, and now Cutter. And to top it all off, he was off the team. He threw his helmet against the wall and cracked his visor. He pounded his fist into the wall and slumped down against it. He sat that way for a while before gathering his wits and walking up to the field.

Jet played through that day's game in a haze, and his cracked visor made reading his holocypher almost impossible. But he knew that was an excuse. He kept seeing blurry apparitions from the corner of his eye, but when he looked, nothing was there. His focus was bad, and his passes sailed over his receivers. Plexus yelled at him during the huddle to get his act together. In the end, he managed to start completing his passes, and they won the game. Even though Korbin was still too stunned to play that day, Skylight had finished the season undefeated. They were headed to the playoffs as the top seed, but Jet wouldn't be with the team.

Despite the celebration and all the students rushing the field, Jet heard the voice in his head with alarming clarity. Something was wrong, and he immediately thought about Cord. With his helmet in his hand, he fought through the crowded field and found Cutter standing next to Plexus, signing autographs. Neither of them noticed him and he decided not to stay any longer. He'd upset Cutter on purpose to try and push him away and he wanted to keep it that way for the moment.

He bolted from the stadium, running at full speed through the front gates and didn't stop until he reached the library. Students stared at him in his full uniform with dried blood on his jersey. He ignored them and walked directly towards the stacks. Once he reached the bookshelf, he made certain he was alone before opening the panel. He hurried down the staircase to the bottom and stopped.

The candles were lit. He walked over to the table and pushed a chair back. Resting on the plush velvet seat was Cord's black satchel. On top of it was his holopad and folded neatly over the chair's arm was his black trench coat.

"Cord!" Jet yelled. His voice echoed around the chamber and died off. He hurried into the stacks. "Cord! Where are you?"

He searched the dark, his eyes giving off enough illumination to see by. Jet walked past the main bookshelf and stopped suddenly. Lying on the ground was a book. Jet bent down and noticed a fresh pool of blood on the floor. He picked the book up carefully and saw it was the biography about Van Saint. Blood was smeared across the page about the final painting, *The Verification*.

Jet's shock was replaced by anger, and he threw the book towards the table. It flapped and skidded to a stop near one of the chairs. He fought back tears, which surprised him. He'd only known Cord for a brief period but, for some reason, felt a closer bond with him than the others. But it was more than that. The disappointment of that semester hit him, and he sat heavily on the floor. He wiped his eyes with the back of his hand. If he'd felt this, then Vail would have too. She would've known something had happened to Cord as well.

Jet walked over to the table and picked up Cord's holopad. He called Vail, but she didn't answer. He tried again, wondering where she might be. Then it hit him. He knew exactly where he would find her. He took Cord's holopad and stashed it between a few books on the main shelf, then bolted up the staircase.

Jet sprinted across the frozen campus grounds, not bothering to stay on the sidewalks. Twenty minutes later, he hurried through Observation Station and up to Apex. Leaping three steps at a time, he opened the portal door and braced himself against the rush of wind that slammed into him. He climbed the tower's ladder and called for Vail, but the husky wind stifled his voice. He walked the perimeter and looked for her, then stopped. He heard a sob and looked over the edge of the platform. He saw the silhouette of someone sitting beyond the safety rail and dangerously close to the edge.

"Vail!" Jet called. She didn't move, her back facing him. "I know you can hear me, Vail. I'm coming out—"

"No!" she yelled back and looked his way. The intense glow of her eyes made him pause.

This can't be happening! he thought to himself. *Not Vail too!*

Her cheeks were rosy red and wet, her glowing eyes reflecting her tears. Ice had formed along her eyelashes. "Don't you dare come out here, Stroud!"

"What's the matter with you?" Jet said, stopping at the guardrail. "It's just me."

"I know about Cord," she said. "I found his things. He's dead, just like Bo. Just like we'll be soon."

"Don't say that," Jet said. "We can work together and finish this."

Vail laughed, a hysterical tone in her voice. "Don't lie. You're no good at it."

"So, what are you going to do, jump?" Jet said. "What does that prove?"

Vail looked down. "It proves that I have control. I'll decide when it's time, not them!"

"I understand what you're going through. But Cutter won't. He'd never forgive himself, and you know it. Think about it."

Vail paused at that and began to cry again. "Tell him I'm sorry. I shouldn't have involved him in this, not the way I did."

"He's involved because he wants to be. Besides, it's too late to worry about that now. You have to finish this the right way, Vail. Don't let them win like this!"

Vail pulled her knees up to her chest and began to rock back-and-forth. Her body convulsed with cries as she released a lifetime of pain and anger. Jet watched as her protective walls finally caved in.

He climbed over the rail, took Vail's hand, and led her back to the platform. They sat on the bench together. Jet waited for her to calm down.

"This may not mean much, but whatever's going to happen, we'll face it together," Jet said.

She managed a weak smile and wrapped her arms around him. "I hate that you saw me like that."

"Don't worry, your secret's safe," Jet said and nudged her.

"Sure," she smirked. "What the hell happened to you, by the way?" she said.

Jet looked down at his blood-stained jersey. "It's a long story, and it's been a long night."

"That's not from Cord… is it?" she said and turned away to hide her face as she tried to regain control again.

"No… a fight I was in before the game," Jet said. "Look, we don't need to talk about Cord right now."

"But he was in the stacks," Vail said.

"Right," Jet said, suddenly realizing that no witnesses would have been there.

Vail pulled her holopad from her backpack and logged into the system network. In the headlines was a picture of Cord and the tickertape below read: *Mathematical Savant, murdered at the Skylight University MathWorks Laboratory this evening.*

"That's not possible," Jet said. "He wasn't at the math lab. No one should know about that but us."

"Stroud, I'm starting to freak out. I think the authorities are in on this, along with Skylight faculty. Didn't you see them that night at the factory?"

"Yeah," Jet said. "A bunch of them. But now we have proof to show Detective Marsh. Cord's items and blood are still in the stacks. That should prove he wasn't in the lab."

"Really?" Vail said. "What would they think if two other euphs were the only ones to know about Cord's murder?"

"So, you think they'd pin this on us?" Jet said. "Come on."

"Detective Marsh is in on this whole thing, Stroud!"

"You don't know that, Vail."

"She was clearly lying to us that night," Vail shook her head. "You may not be able to tell when someone's lying, but I can."

Jet thought for a few seconds. "I think we need to go back to the stacks. I want to take another look around before we do anything else."

Vail pursed her lips. "I don't know if I can go back there right now. I'm cold and tired. There's also something wrong with my eyes."

Jet hadn't mentioned anything to the others about Bo's eyes the day he disappeared. Now, he was afraid to admit to himself what it might mean. But, he didn't want to talk to Vail about it in her current state.

"Alright. Let's get you back to your dorm," Jet said.

"If you're going to the stacks tonight, you should call Cutter," Vail said. "It'd make me feel better if he's with you."

"Well, I don't think Cutter's very happy with me at the moment," Jet said.

"What did you do this time?" Vail asked.

"I said something I shouldn't have, but I don't want to talk about it right now. I just need some time to fix it. Maybe after that, we can all regroup."

Vail narrowed her eyes. "There's something you're not telling me."

Jet shook his head. "Come on, let's get out of here. You're freezing."

"Not until you tell me what you said to him."

"Forget it, Vail. I already said I didn't want to talk about it—"

"Stroud," Vail said. The sharp tone in her voice startled him.

"Alright, fine," he said. "I'll tell you on the way." He didn't want to witness another breakdown. He just wanted to get her down from Apex and back to her dorm room. He'd worry about everything else after that.

They made their way down to the campus grounds and walked briskly towards the dorms. The campus was silent, since most of the students were still at the stadium, celebrating.

"Alright," Vail said. "Let's hear it."

"You're not gonna be happy with me either," Jet said.

"Just say it already," Vail said through clenched teeth and blew into her mittens.

"I was concerned about Cutter's safety, and I didn't want him around anymore," Jet said and braced himself for an onslaught of profanities, but Vail didn't say anything.

"I'm sorry," Jet continued. "I know that you two are—"

"Shut up," Vail hissed. She stopped walking and held a trembling hand to her forehead.

"What's wrong?" Jet asked. "You alright?"

"Can't you feel that?" she said and let out a gasp of pain.

Then he felt a dull sensation creep up the base of his spine and into his forehead like the onset of a migraine. His stomach knotted up like he was about to be sick.

Jet grabbed her hand, and they both started running. The pressure in his head eased slightly as they moved. He saw something move in the shadows of the buildings. He knew what was following them, and he knew they couldn't outrun it.

"In here," he whispered and pulled Vail into the recess of a covered porch. The door to the building was locked. They huddled close together in the cold shadows and waited quietly.

Something that resembled smoke seemed to filter into the courtyard, and Jet caught his breath. He felt Vail stiffen next to him.

"What is it?" she whispered.

"Be quiet," Jet warned.

The shadow seemed to know exactly where they were hiding. There was nothing they could do but watch and wait. Jet could see through it, but the light around its profile was altered as if it bent light to conceal itself.

Jet tensed and prepared to fight but realized he couldn't move. The shadow had somehow managed to paralyze his muscles. He struggled with all his strength but couldn't lift his arms. All he could do was watch as it approached. The apparition ignored him and went straight to Vail.

It stopped directly in front of her. She moaned with discomfort, and Jet sensed the shadow was exerting some sort of psychic pressure to keep both of them immobilized. Most of its focus was on Vail, and it was causing her a great deal of pain. Her face was contorted in fear and anguish. The thing lifted what looked to be its hand, and Vail's arm did the same. That's when Jet noticed its eyes for the first time. They seemed to be disguised at first, but he could see them clearly now, and they glowed with an intense blue color.

Then it did something that both surprised and terrified him. It spoke. Only it wasn't in a normal voice, but through his thoughts with the words forming in his mind.

Now is the time! it said.

It was strange, like someone yelling to him from the opposite end of a tunnel covered in blankets that muffled the sound. The sensation made him want to scratch his forehead, but his arms were still frozen in place.

It slipped a needle-like device from the folds of its mantle and slid the tip through her left palm. The thing yanked the device back and dropped the remnants of her flesh to the ground. Blood spilled from the wound, but it began to cauterize almost immediately. Light flooded from the opening in her hand, flashing and flickering like an old fluorescent bulb trying to warm up. The light from the wound matched Vail's burning eyes perfectly and pulsated to her heartbeat. A symbol emerged, one that Jet thought he'd seen before.

Vail screamed and convulsed, then collapsed to the ground. Her eyes grew dim, and the light in them flickered out. She lay on the cold ground, her lifeless form unmoving. Jet waited to see her take a breath, waited for her eyelids to close, all the while trying to convince himself that she was really just asleep and would awake at any moment. But nothing happened. He had just witnessed her murder and had little doubt he was next.

When it finally turned to face him, an excruciating pain erupted inside his head. He winced and let out a cry. The pain continued to increase like a vice clamping down on his brain. He was on the verge of passing out when the pain subsided and then vanished. He collapsed to the ground breathing heavily.

The thing looked around uncertainly. Something or someone had distracted it. It gathered Vail's body, and Jet watched her magically disappear within it. Then it left the courtyard. As it did, something dropped to the ground.

Jet eventually struggled to his hands and knees and felt around in the dark for the item she had dropped. A few seconds later, he found it and held up Vail's tarnished locket.

He stared at it in the moonlight through rapid puffs of his breath. He was exhausted and disoriented, and he had just witness Vail's murder. But he was hopelessly outmatched and couldn't possibly stop the thing even if he could catch up to it. Something inside of him was screaming to get up, though. He owed it to Myranda, Bo, Cord, and Vail. He could at least follow it and hope to find out more, maybe see where it was taking her body.

Jet stood and sprinted in the same direction as the shadow.

Somehow, he could sense it was headed for the university hangers. It meant to flee.

He ran the entire way and took a few short cuts to make up some time. The campus was still vacant, and there were no crowds to slow him down.

He arrived just as the shadow was loading Vail's body onto a skiff. The skiff was different than any craft he'd ever seen before. It was black and slightly camouflaged in the same way as the shadow. It hovered silently, ready for takeoff. In his haste he'd thrown caution to the wind and stepped too far into the hanger. The shadow sensed his presence and turned to face him.

It jumped forward, and the pressure in his head returned with a greater intensity this time. However, the pressure only lasted a few seconds as something else entered the hanger. The shadow sensed it too and paused.

The cloak-like mirage that had been following him that semester barreled into the shadow and toppled it. Suddenly Jet had control of his mind and body again. He rolled to his stomach but was too exhausted to stand and run.

What he witnessed next was difficult to comprehend. The cloak stood in front of him as the shadow picked itself up from the floor. It dove at the cloak, but the cloak shifted and spun so quickly that Jet could barely follow its movements. A flurry of blows and parries followed. It kicked the shadow against the skiff then lunged forward with a blow that just missed and crumpled a portion of the skiff's hull. The shadow, sensing it was outmatched, leapt into the waiting skiff. The engines roared to life and the craft shot from the hanger bay.

Jet felt himself start to lose consciousness. The pressure exerted from the shadow had taken a toll, and he was on the verge of passing out.

The cloak stood, looking after the skiff for a second, and then turned to face him. No more than a blur in Jet's fading vision, the cloak bent and lifted him. The last thing he remembered before losing consciousness was staring up into the glowing eyes of Solan Alexander.

CHAPTER

The Triclipse

ΑΒΓΔΕΖΗΘΙΚΛ**M**
ΝΞΟΠΡΣΤΥΦΧΨΩ

THE NEXT MORNING Jet awoke with a splitting headache. He rolled over and looked at his bedside clock. It was half-past eight on Sunday morning. He laid there on his back, staring at the soft sunlight filtering into his room and tried to stop his head from spinning. He remembered Vail saying something to him last night and then…

He sat upright and leapt from his bed, steadied himself, then hastily logged on to the system network. In the headlines was a picture of Vail. The reporter stated she'd been killed on campus at the top of Apex, where she'd been a regular visitor. The reporter cut away to a field crew at Vail's home on Skylight City. Her father, who happened to be a wealthy banker, was being followed by the news crew. He hopped into an expensive-looking skiff and waved the news crew away, declining to comment.

Jet sat down at the kitchen island and held his head in his hands. He ran his fingers through his matted hair while trying to piece the events from last night together. He recalled discovering Cord's items in the library and then rushing to find Vail atop

Apex. After he'd talked her down, the shadow had killed her and taken her body. He had followed it to the university hangers, and that's where things got fuzzy. The cloak had defended him from the shadow and the last thing he remembered was looking into the eyes of Solan Alexander before passing out. And somehow… he'd ended up in his dorm room.

He stood and paced around the small kitchen. He felt suddenly trapped, and he had no one left to talk to. He was starting to regret his decision to push Cutter away.

He walked over to Cutter's room to knock on the door, but it swung open when he tapped it. The room was empty except for the furniture. There were a couple of fist-sized holes in one wall. On Cutter's bed was a holopad. It blinked, indicating there was a message on it. Jet picked it up and walked over to the kitchen island. He stared at the holopad for what seemed like hours. Eventually, he sat down and played the message.

The hologram appeared with Cutter sitting on his bed, a timestamp in the corner read 4:15 a.m. that same morning. His clothes and belongings were packed in the corner as if he were getting ready to leave. He stared into the hologram, fidgeting with the strap on his backpack. His eyes were red, and dark circles clung beneath them. "Jet, I guess you were right," Cutter said. "Cord, now Vail. Just like that, they're both gone. I don't even know what to say or where to start. That detective called me after the game…" Cutter faltered, stood, and walked around his room before sitting down again.

"I heard you come in last night," Cutter continued. "I didn't want to argue with you, so I'm leaving this message instead. I know that's crappy, but… maybe it's better. I don't know what to think. I've never felt this uncertain in my life. I thought losing Vail would hurt the worst but turns out it isn't. I was angry at you, now I realize you were just looking out for me, trying to save me instead of yourself. If your wish is that I leave you alone, then… I will." Cutter bowed his head and sat silently for a moment. "I'm going away for a while, maybe travel the system. I don't know if I'll be back to school next year. I don't even know if I want to play blaze anymore." Cutter stood. "I'm sorry, Jet. Sorry things ended like this." Cutter shut the hologram off.

One by one, they were all gone. Even though Sylvant and Cutter had left because of his choosing, he still could barely believe it. A thousand questions swirled through his head. He stood, kicked the barstool, and threw the holopad across the room. It hit the wall and shattered to pieces with a thud that echoed around the room. He expected his next-door neighbor to come rushing over, but when no one knocked on his door, he suddenly realized that it was Christmas Eve. All the students and faculty were gone for the holiday break. He'd completely lost track of time.

Jet started to pace the room again, trying to fend off the flood of emotions that rushed through his head. There was one last option he could think of.

He pulled his holopad from his backpack and dialed Detective Marsh's number and waited. A few rings later, she answered. Jet was caught off-guard, halfway expecting she wouldn't take his call.

"Mr. Stroud," she said, "To what do I owe the pleasure?" Her hair was pulled back in a ponytail, and a light sheen of sweat glistened on her brow. She pedaled on an exercise bike but didn't stop or slow down.

"Are you serious?" Jet asked.

"You're wanting to know more about your friends, I take it?" she said. "And I've already told you that information is classified. Simple as that."

"Let me guess," Jet said. "You've collected evidence on Cord and Vail, but it's under the Agency's jurisdiction, just like it was with Bo? Am I right?"

"You got it," she said.

"So, Cord at the MathWorks Lab, and Vail at Apex?" Jet asked.

"Yes. They were alone, which they shouldn't have been."

Jet sat back and crossed his arms. "I know you're lying."

"How's that?" Marsh said.

"Cord was in the library last night," Jet said.

"Is that a fact?"

"Yes. And Vail was with me."

Detective Marsh finally stopped pedaling and cleared her throat. "Where's your proof?"

"Why can't you just answer the question!" Jet felt his heart pounding in his chest, his fists clenched. "What are you covering up? This Agency, or whatever they are, what are they hiding? Why aren't you doing more about these student murders?"

"Mr. Stroud," Marsh said and toweled sweat from her brow. "Strange things are happening that you don't understand, so I get why you're confused. I don't pretend to understand how you feel right now—"

"You're right," he cut her off. "I saw something last night when I was with Vail that I can't explain. It was a shadow, almost invisible. It stunned us, then killed her."

"You're delusional," she said. "That's what I've heard from other students like you over and over again."

"But what if I'm not? And how come all the others like me say the same thing? How do you explain that?"

"I'm not a psychologist, Mr. Stroud. All I can tell you is what I've read from the experts."

"I recognize you now," Jet said.

Marsh paused with the towel pressed to her brow. "What do you mean?"

"You were in that meeting with the professors and other members of the authorities. I saw you talking to Professor Keoff. It was at an old factory building near The Hydra 7."

Marsh took a deep breath and let it out. "I'm not going to have this conversation right now."

"Can I meet you somewhere then?" Jet asked. He felt like his last hope was tied to this detective who he barely knew. "Please, anything you can offer would help."

She hesitated, and her shoulders relaxed. "I'm afraid I can't do that." She reached up to disconnect the call.

"Hold on," Jet said.

She paused and looked at him.

"What did you say to Cutter?" Jet asked. "I hope you didn't threaten him or—"

"Or what?" she said.

Jet realized there was nothing he could do. No one would believe him, and he had no real proof anyway.

"Listen," she said. "What I said to him was for his benefit and yours, and maybe that's best for everyone, in the end."

"You had no right to do that," Jet said.

"So, you'd prefer him to suffer your fate as well?" she asked.

"No, of course not. But I can handle my friends and myself. I don't need you."

"Then why are you calling me?" she said. "Look, everything happens for a reason. Things always work out the way they are meant to. Remember that." She switched off the transmission so abruptly that Jet didn't have a chance to say anything else.

He leaned against the kitchen island for support, feeling like he'd just lost his last link to reality. He was weak, tired, and mentally drained. There was no fire left in his soul. He felt cold inside. He'd never felt more alone.

· • • • ● ⬤ ● • • • ·

It was Christmas Eve, and nearly every student had left for the holiday break, heading home to different parts of the Skylight System. The blaze game had been the culminating event to end the semester. Even though the campus was mostly empty, Jet had nowhere to go and no one to spend the break with. So, he spent most of that day lying in bed, listening to the wind howl outside his patio door. The typical sound of students having dinner in the commons below was missing, and all was silent now. At some point that day, the weather turned blustery and billowing clouds rolled in. Jet heard small pellets of ice tapping his window as sleet began to fall. But it wasn't the weather he was worried about—it was the familiar voice in his mind.

He sat up and looked at his bedside clock. It was 5:37 p.m., and the voice urged him to get up and do something. He grabbed his coat and an extra sweater, stuffed it into his backpack, and left his dorm room. He ran all the way to the library and pushed through the front doors. There was only one attendant on duty when he arrived, and no students to be seen.

He didn't bother to check for people when he reached the bookshelf and walked straight down the staircase. He flung his items into one of the chairs, lit a few candles, and stood there, wondering why he'd chosen to come to the stacks. It was probably the one place he shouldn't be. But he knew why he was there—the voice had led him there. If he was going to make a final stand, this is where he'd do it, not cowering in his dorm room.

"Well, here I am!" he yelled. "What now?"

The cold draft answered with a low drone. Jet put the extra sweater on, walked over to the main bookshelf, and stood in front of it. The pool of Cord's blood had been removed and scrubbed clean. He looked up to find the book about Van Saint sitting on the shelf. He remembered throwing it at the table in anger. Someone had replaced it.

Jet reeled around. "Where the hell are you!" he yelled. "What do you want from me!" His voice echoed through the chamber, only the books there as a witness.

Jet took the book and sulked back to the table. He set it down, letting it fall open. The entire middle section of the book was gone and it had been replaced with another document. Jet pulled it closer and read the opening text out loud. "Vishmu," he whispered. "What's this?"

There was no author's name or any other identifying mark on the opening page of the text. The edges were rough and serrated as if someone had torn them out of another book and stuffed them into this one. He leafed through the pages, which depicted bizarre diagrams, outlandish math, and several foreign languages. Cord might have understood the math, but it was beyond Jet's comprehension. According to the text, Vishmu had originated more than two thousand years ago, but there was no exact date. It was thought to be a psychic state of mind and had continued to evolve into an eclectic patchwork of theories and beliefs over the ages.

Occasionally, Jet would stop reading and practice some of the techniques, at least the parts he could understand. By relaxing, he found that he could achieve a near trance-like state of mind while still maintaining conscious awareness. It was an odd, out-of-body experience that seemed to heighten his senses. He continued reading for what seemed like hours until seeing something that made him pause.

Only those of rightful Heliographi heritage may practice Vishmu. Those who are not shall be placed in mortal peril. One who comes into possession of this book should halt any further quest for knowledge contained within and return this manuscript to its rightful owners.

Jet reread the warning again before cautiously setting the book aside. Heliographi was a term Albright had created, but in this text, it sounded like some sort of clan. Alarmed, he wondered if he'd crossed some forbidden line.

He glanced down at his watch, noting that it was already past five o'clock in the afternoon on Christmas Day. He'd spent the last twenty-four hours down in the stacks reading through the book.

He sat back and rubbed his eyes, shivering in the cold breeze that threatened to extinguish the candles. He shook off a sudden cold chill and took a quick stroll around to stretch his legs. He eventually found himself standing in front of the main bookshelf and thought about Cord. If only he had been there. But what could he have done to protect him?

Absolutely nothing.

Jet knelt to look for the pool of dried blood. It had been thoroughly scrubbed away, and there was virtually no sign of it. As he knelt, he noticed a small drop of blood on the lowest shelf, though. Then another on the second and third shelf. In what should have been a struggle, the blood seemed too well placed. Jet stood on his tip-toes and looked at the next shelf, then the next. There was a single drop on each one. Jet recalled the smeared blood across the page showing the final painting called, *The Verification*. Was it possible that Cord's last act might have been a final clue? He'd sworn to give them a solution, after all.

Jet felt his pulse quicken as he began to pull books down from the shelf, his hands trembling. He piled them on the floor around him, trying not to stir up any dust. Finally, waist deep in books, Jet took his holopad and shined a light onto the masonry wall.

"This can't be..." he whispered.

True to his word, Cord had somehow found the final painting. It was a shame the others weren't there to see it. Hanging about two meters off the floor and a meter to the left of the main shelf was the final painting rumored to have been destroyed by fire. It had been right beneath their noses the entire time. Down in the basement was the perfect place to protect it, too. Here, it had gone unnoticed amongst the sea of forgotten books. He felt the hair on the back of his neck stand up as he stared at it. He was seeing something not many people had ever set eyes on. Jet took a few steps back to get a better look at it, nearly tripping over the books surrounding him. He guessed this painting's worth was more than the entire library and every book in it, and Lybra would probably kill to get her hands on it.

The scene depicted what appeared to be a heated debate. Two dozen people sat or stood around a wooden table in dramatic poses. To one side stood a group of people, hunched and withered, cowering from the light. The Greek symbols and roman numerals carved into the edge of the table matched the first two paintings. Jet stepped in closer, trying to read the holographic text that appeared to be written in some sort of mathematical language. Perhaps it was a story or prophecy, as Lybra believed.

Then, with growing clarity, something drew his attention. Dark shadows began to appear from the canvas like thickening smoke. They seemed to perch on the edge of the table, hovering menacingly between the men and women. But, rising up between them were twelve cloaks, similar to the one he'd seen throughout the semester. They appeared stalwart and defiant, unlike the skulking shadowy figures. He could almost hear their argument, an ancient war that had raged between them. The scene erupted in his mind as if he were there amongst them. Then his eyes began to burn.

Jet pulled himself away and staggered around the books. He knew his eyes were changing, even without looking in a mirror. He couldn't catch his breath—he needed to get out of the stacks. Crashing his way through the books, he grabbed the pages of Vishmu and stuffed them into his pocket. He shot up the stairs two at a time, sprinted across the library rotunda and out into the cold December evening.

The sleet had turned to snow, and the ground was covered with a light dusting of it. Jet tried to ignore the chill wind that seemed to bite right through his sweater as he sprinted aimlessly. His vision seemed hazy, like he was seeing the world through a negative lens. He wondered if this was how Myranda, Bo, Cord and Vail had seen things before the end. He knew that his time had finally come.

He stopped at Revelations Plaza and sat down at one of the benches. He wrung his hands, trying to get warmth to flow through them as he weighed his situation. He was still trying to decide what to do when the moonlight fluttered and then dimmed noticeably. Jet looked up.

"The triclipse," he muttered. With all the recent events, he'd completely forgotten about it. Three of the outer belts were slowly crisscrossing the moon, simultaneously casting a profound shadow onto the campus grounds. Jet watched as the rare event unfolded.

The leading edge of the triclipse crept over the landscape of the university, seeping into the snow like black ink spilled across a fine white linen. Then the snow began to fall in heavy sheets.

The lamp posts around him flickered and went out. Jet didn't wait for them to power back up and stumbled off through the thickening snow. The wind-whipped snow blew in dizzying sheets, and he was soon disoriented. He reached for his holopad to light the way and realized he'd left it in the stacks. With the snow beginning to accumulate he had no idea where he was, but felt the urge to keep moving and began to jog.

Before long, his shoes were soaked through, and he could only see a few feet in front of him. He no longer needed to see where he was going, though. Something else was guiding him now; the familiar voice in his head was stronger than before. It was telling him exactly where to go.

Alpha.

The blizzard continued to gather intensity, along with mounting pressure in his head. The white puffs of his breath started to come in quicker gasps as he ran faster. His palms and knees bled from where he'd slipped and fallen to the frozen pavement, but he couldn't feel his extremities anymore and barely noticed. He could sense the shadow stalking him, lurking somewhere beyond in the snow. He picked up his pace, wincing at the burning in his lungs.

To his left, he saw something move and looked in time to see the shadow near a cluster of trees. Just ahead, he could see his destination and mustered his strength for a final dash. Within seconds the pressure in his head intensified, and the shadow approached. It seemed to know where he was headed and doubled the pressure inside his head. White spots danced in Jet's vision, and he stopped in agony. Panic set in, and he almost collapsed.

Vishmu. Prepare.

He focused and relaxed his mind, willing his remaining effort on the technique. Gradually the pressure eased, reversed, and then faded. When Jet opened his eyes, the spots were gone, and he could see again. He stood and nearly fell over, then slowly started running.

Through the haze of snow, he noticed the silhouette of Alpha Hall looming in the distance. He was less than one hundred meters away, but his strength suddenly faded, and he nearly collapsed. *Even if he did make it, what was he to do next?* He was simply trusting the voice in his head now and made a last dash. But with less than twenty yards, exhaustion finally took him, and he collapsed to the snow.

He could visualize his friends standing at the end of a long hallway, calling to him. Vail and Cutter yelled encouragement, and Cord and Bo pleaded for him to stand. The snow was soft and comfortable, though, and he felt like he could sleep there forever. *Let the cold white blanket wash away all my pain and suffering*, he thought. *Let it end my misery forever*. His entire life, full of insults and ridicule and discrimination, seemed to slip away like water from a faucet.

STAND.

It took every bit of strength he possessed, but he stood and began to move again. One step at a time, he was thankful for his athletic conditioning. He took wavering steps, each one pushing him through the knee-deep snow and closer to Alpha Hall.

Despite his best effort, though, he had come to the end of the road. Standing directly between him and Alpha Hall was the shadow. Jet halted, his breathing heavy and arms hanging limply at his sides. He was a stone's throw from Alpha Hall, but his chances of making it were gone.

He felt his blood run cold as the apparition solidified in front of him. It seemed to float effortlessly over the snow toward him. Then, with a slow deliberate movement, it raised its shapeless head and looked directly at him.

Jet yelled so loud that his vocal cords seared with pain. His soul felt like it was being ripped from the inside out. His body went limp as he continued to scream into the howling wind.

RESIST.

Jet clenched his fists and focused, concentrating every fiber of strength left in him. He gazed into the shadow's glowing eyes. He remembered the sorrow at losing Cord… the grief at seeing Vail's lifeless body. Rage began to build inside of him.

Stay... calm.

Jet heard the voice and he relaxed, subdued his anger. Once again, the pressure in his head dissipated.

For the first time, he sensed the shadow's confusion. He felt its rage emanate from its glowing red eyes.

It leapt at him, intent on using physical force to kill him this time. Jet stumbled backward, knowing he didn't stand a chance in a hand-to-hand fight, but steadied himself and stood his ground. He would go down fighting, at least.

The shadow struck him across the face before he could even raise his hands. He fell into the snow and struggled quickly to his feet. Fresh adrenaline coursed through his veins, and some of the fatigue left him. But the shadow was gone, blending into the falling snow.

Why resist when it's easier to give in?

Jet felt goosebumps erupt at the thing's voice in his head. He ignored its taunt and continued to back towards Alpha Hall, cautiously scanning the snow. In his thoughts, he heard the shadow mocking him, trying to tempt him into anger. It mimicked the sound of Vail's voice in a desperate plea for help. It berated him for being too weak to protect her.

His searching hands finally brushed the cold stone of Alpha Hall. In the mottled moonlight of the triclipse, the barren thicket around its base cast skeletal shadows across the stone's surface, and he tried to blend in. Relief coursed through him, and he leaned against the building momentarily. He worked his way around the building towards the far end.

The shadow struck him with such ferocity this time the blow hoisted him off his feet. It straddled him and gripped his throat, squeezing with super-human strength. Jet grappled at its hands, but the grip was hard as rock. He gasped for breath and felt his windpipe being slowly crushed. He was on the verge of passing out when the familiar voice came to him again.

RESIST.

The shadow heard it too and released its grip. It stood and backed away from the building.

A flash of light erupted, and two shimmering cloaks appeared from an opening in the side of Alpha Hall. One of them grasped the shadow and cast it against the stone wall with such force the stone cracked. Jet rolled out of the way, gasping for air.

He lay in the falling snow and listened to the voice in his head, which seemed to be coming from the tallest cloak.

You won't get away with murder, not this time, it said.

The other cloak positioned itself on the opposite side of the shadow.

You'll all be dead, once we find the memoirs. What difference does it make if this one dies? the shadow replied.

Both cloaks shot forward without warning. Jet tried to follow the frenzied pace, but the sparring moved too quickly in the dim light.

The fight didn't last long, though. The shadow was outnumbered and knew it. It feigned an attack and then turned and fled. The shorter cloak moved to pursue it.

Wait! the taller cloak commanded.

It stared at Jet through glowing iridescent eyes in the falling snow. Jet stood his ground but then relaxed. If the cloaks had wanted him dead, they would've done it already.

The tall cloak removed its scarf and hood and magically materialized before him. Jet was face-to-face with Solan Alexander. She hadn't aged a day and still resembled her younger sister, Professor Sylvant. She was beautiful… and deadly.

"Follow me," she said bluntly. "No questions."

Without another word, Solan replaced her scarf and hood, blending magically into the surroundings. She stepped through the opening in the side of Alpha Hall and disappeared. The other cloak waited for him to follow. Jet turned and walked into the opening. A dull grinding noise rattled the ground as a stone door swung closed behind them. An ominous thud echoed down the tunnel and plunged them into complete darkness.

CHAPTER

Flotsam

ΑΒΓΔΕΖΗΘΙΚΛ<u>Μ</u>
ΝΞΟΠΡΣΤΥΦΧΨΩ

THEY MOVED RAPIDLY through a network of underground passages. The steel walls reflected the only light source, a bright greenish glow coming from Solan's right hand. A dank, musty smell filled the tunnels reminding Jet of the cave system he'd grown up in. He was so exhausted that he practically tripped over his own feet to keep up with Solan.

"What is this place?" he whispered, the sound of his voice echoing off the walls.

"Lyrinthum," Solan answered over her shoulder.

"What?" Jet asked. It was easier to talk to her, now that she'd removed her hood and scarf. But the other cloak remained hidden behind them, like a wraith in the darkness.

"It's a secret network of tunnels buried deep below the campus. These passages were covertly built at the same time as the university, nearly a century ago by order of Christian Albright himself," she explained without turning or slowing. "We're probably near the library now."

Jet's suspicions had been correct. It explained how Solan was able to move around the campus discretely.

The small group continued through the tunnels at a brisk pace. Jet had a good sense of direction and had a feeling they were headed for the university hangers. There was a flood of questions he wanted to ask her, but he refrained for the moment.

The tunnel started to gradually rise when they came to a sudden halt.

"Wait here and keep quiet!" Solan whispered. She climbed up a ladder and paused at the top, listening. She turned a lever and disappeared through the portal. The other cloak stayed behind with Jet. A second later, Solan poked her head back in and waved for them to follow.

The hanger bay was dark and silent. Off to one side were two skiffs. Solan directed him to accompany her while the other cloak boarded the adjacent skiff. They fired up the engines and within minutes, were airborne and zooming away from Skylight University.

As they ascended, Jet looked down at the snow-covered university, thinking about the chain of events that had led him to that moment in time. But he quickly turned his attention to the mysterious person sitting next to him. At the beginning of the semester, Jet thought he'd been seeing a ghost—a mere side effect of ephebus mortem. But Solan Alexander had been alive all along, and she was sitting less than a meter from him. Jet finally had her one-on-one.

"Where are you taking me?" he began, settling into his seat. They were cruising faster than any skiff he'd ridden in before.

"Headquarters. Some refer to it as Flotsam."

Jet frowned at her. "Flotsam? As in debris? I didn't know there was any in the Skylight System."

Solan didn't answer right away, as if considering something. "Then wait and see," she said.

"You've been following me all semester, haven't you?"

"Perhaps," she answered without turning to face him. "Then again, maybe you were seeing things."

Jet ignored the sarcasm. "Why?"

"It was my responsibility to protect you."

"Protect?" Jet waited to see if she had anything more to offer, but she didn't respond. Unlike Sylvant, Solan didn't seem very talkative, and he assumed getting answers from her would be a challenge. Nonetheless, he pressed forward. "What can you tell me about the abandoned factory? I know you led me there, but why?"

She considered it again before answering. "Yes. I led you there on purpose. As far as why, I won't say right now. You'll have to wait."

"So, you *were* the voice guiding me?"

"At times, yes," she agreed. "The pages you found tonight were ones that I left for you to help strengthen that connection, or voice, as you call it. I planted the seed, though the premonitions you've felt weren't solely because of me. With practice, we can even communicate with normal people, but that can be dangerous."

Jet shook his head. "We? Who are you referring to? I still don't understand," he said, trying to piece everything together.

"Jet, most of what's happened this semester has been without the Agency's approval—"

"Hold on," Jet stopped her. "Who is the Agency? And why didn't you just approach me to begin with?" He felt his skin flush.

"What about the others, why weren't they protected? Are you saying they could have been saved, too?"

"Relax," Solan said in a calm but stern voice that made him settle back into his seat again. "I'll let someone else explain who the Agency is. As for why you were never approached, it's because our organization is forbidden to do so, at least until the time is right. It was one of our main directives. However, that doesn't mean we couldn't watch over you. We protect the students we feel need our protection, which is something we've been doing for a long time. We are invisible to most, and those being watched never even notice us, if we choose. I was assigned to you but was instructed to have no contact. I was supposed to remain hidden, though I allowed you to see me on several occasions."

"Yet you stood idly by and watched while that shadow thing killed the others? You could have saved them!"

"That is not my place!" Solan said, raising her voice. She took a deep breath before continuing. "We're fighting a losing battle, despite our best efforts. The Agency is in uncharted territory right now. The fact that we're even talking is strictly forbidden. But we could no longer protect you at Skylight University, and we couldn't afford to lose you. We had one option, and regretfully, we had to use it."

Jet didn't like the sound of what she was saying. "Why am I really here?"

"Be patient," she said. "Answers are coming, I promise."

Jet eased back and gave his head a rest. All he wanted right now was a warm bed and a few answers. After a silent moment, he asked another question. "So, why were you assigned to me?"

"As I said, the responsibility fell to me," Solan said. "Your warden is not ready yet, and I was the next in line."

"My warden?" Jet asked. "You mean my family? I have no family. They left me when I was—"

"I'm referring to a different type of family," Solan said, with a bit of frustration in her voice. Jet could tell she was tired, too. "I know this is difficult to understand. I was overwhelmed, too, when I first learned about all of this. Trust me and be patient."

Jet was still struggling to understand her, though. So, Solan was the next in line to protect him? Yet it seemed quite a coincidence that he'd been in touch with her sister over most of the semester. He wondered if Solan was using him for something else.

"You've been trying to connect with your sister through me, haven't you?" he said. "You know she still misses you."

Solan winced and gripped the controls tighter but didn't look at him. He sensed he was treading on thin ice and refrained from saying anything else about Sylvant, for the moment.

Jet stared back out the window, lost in thought. According to Solan, this organization, the Agency, had been providing protection for special students for a long time. But they were also forbidden to have any contact with the ones they protected. Yet, they had broken their own rules by speaking to him, something they had never done before.

"Who started the Agency?" Jet blurted.

"Who do you think?" she said.

Jet knew the answer. After all, Christian Albright had either created or been involved in everything else, so why not a secret organization as well? Jet smiled sarcastically. He wasn't buying any of it, just yet.

"But you will," Solan said.

"What?" he asked.

She reached over and tapped his forehead, “Better keep those thoughts buried deep, especially where we’re going.”

Jet blushed, wondering what else she had heard. “And when are we going to get to this place?” he asked, changing the subject.

“We’re here.” Solan nodded towards the horizon.

Materializing through the mist were the shattered remnants of the ninth belt. Large chunks of it floated at awkward angles, orbiting independently of one another. It gaped at them like a grinning set of shattered teeth, gradually solidifying as they approached.

“Headquarters,” Solan said, pulling up the skiff’s holographic console. It plotted a course for her, and she leaned back in her seat. Jet watched the white flush away from her knuckles as she relaxed her grip, now that they’d arrived.

“So, this is Flotsam?” Jet asked, looking skeptically at a large free-floating hunk of the belt.

“That’s just a nickname for our headquarters,” she said as the skiff’s speed slowed.

“I thought that was Memorial Park?” Jet said, noticing all the traffic in and around the topside bunker of the belt. He remembered hearing about it during orientation. After a large meteor storm had destroyed the entire ninth belt, it had been converted into a public park and dedicated to the citizens of the Skylight System. Since that fateful day of the storm, most people no longer considered it a belt.

“Things are not always as they appear. You of all people should know that.”

Solan was right. As their skiff maneuvered beneath the massive, wrecked hull, a large hanger door opened. Any observers from the park above would’ve assumed their skiff was a maintenance vehicle. Solan took over the controls and eased the skiff inside, landing it gently onto one of the docking bays.

"Right under everyone's nose," Jet commented.

"Most people are so preoccupied with their surroundings they can't see what's right in front of them," she said.

Jet thought about the painting he'd searched for all semester long, only to realize that it had literally been right in front of him the entire time.

After they docked, Solan climbed out of the cockpit, and Jet followed her. Several workers hooked the skiff up to a power supply system. Solan spoke to one of them, who then hurried off. He returned with a transport vehicle, and she motioned for Jet to join her. Soon they were cruising along a main thoroughfare.

He gazed around in astonishment at the sheer size and internal operations of the facility. He began to wonder if the park above was merely there to provide a diversion for this secret complex below. All of the visitors and public air traffic actually helped disguise the underground portion better. It was clever.

They traversed up through several large causeways until finally arriving at a series of offices. Solan got out of the transport and directed him to follow her. They entered one of the offices, and she offered him a seat.

The office felt more like a study, its exterior wall reminiscent of a ship's hull. Exposed steel beams ringed the room vertically, leading his eyes to the ceiling high above. The steel hull creaked and groaned, probably still unstable from the structural damage it had sustained nearly a century ago. Off to one side was a fireplace, which seemed out of place amongst the steel and glass. Dotting the exterior wall were several portal-like windows revealing clouds floating in the moonlight. A large seal was set into the center of the floor, which portrayed the Heliographi symbol and torch.

Jet noticed the torch was actually a lower-case letter *i*, similar to the ones he'd seen around campus. The symbol was surrounded by twelve stars and twelve symbols. Around the outside of it was a phrase he'd become familiar with: *For the Greater Unity of Humankind.*

"What does it mean?" he asked, glancing down at the seal.

Solan continued to stand near the door, apparently preferring not to sit. "This is the seal for the Lucem, or *the Light.*"

"Do you mean the Agency?" Jet asked.

"No, the Agency has nothing to do with us, they weren't around back then—"

The door to the office opened, and Solan stopped midsentence. A tall man, probably in his early sixties, walked into the room. His dark-skinned face contrasted with a silver beard and a scar ran from cheek to forehead. His long pencil-like nose reminded him of Professor Sylvant. He also wore a cloak with his hood pulled back and a multi-hued scarf hanging loosely around his neck. Beneath one of his sleeves, Jet noticed a reddish-orange light. His eyes glowed the same color.

"Jet Stroud," the man said, and held out his hand.

Jet nodded and shook his hand, not sure what to say.

"As you can see, Jet, I have E.M. and I'm well beyond the age of twenty-four. Yet, I'm very much alive, at least I think so," he said, smiling broadly. "We have a lot to discuss." He motioned for Jet to have a seat while he sat down behind the large desk.

"I must apologize, I've not introduced myself," the man said, settling into his chair. "My name is Tyberius Alexander, and I run this operation, or at least this small branch of it. Sterllar might have mentioned my name."

Jet nodded. "Sort of."

"I thought she might have," Tyberius said, giving Solan a stern look. "Can we get you anything? A drink or food perhaps?"

"I'll take some answers and then a warm bed," Jet said.

A smile creased the man's weathered face. "You can rest soon. My apologies for delaying that for the moment. First, we need to talk. I'll try to be quick. Then I promise you can rest."

"That would be nice," Jet said.

"Good, why don't you follow me," Tyberius stood, turned, and left the office, followed closely by Solan. Jet stood there for a moment, confused by their sudden departure. Then he hurried to catch up.

"Where are we going?" he asked.

"To a special place. I believe it will help you understand what we do and why you're here."

They walked down a large corridor and past several workers wearing uniforms, all of whom stepped to the opposite side of the passageway.

"They're also part of the Agency?" Jet asked once they were out of earshot.

Tyberius nodded. "The Agency is a large organization with many departments, each specifically designed to ensure the continued existence of the human race. After the Unbalance, Albright wanted to make sure a second catastrophe wouldn't happen." Tyberius stopped walking and turned to Jet as he scanned the vacant corridor. "Although not everyone is to be trusted, even here," he continued in a lower voice. "The Agency has many facets, and our group is just one small branch in the greater scheme."

"But an important one, right?" Jet asked, noticing that Solan had said very little since Tyberius had arrived.

"Perhaps," Tyberius said. "Though some might say otherwise. Regardless, we need to be cautious. Not everything is as it appears, as you're aware." Tyberius straightened his cloak and continued down the corridor.

Jet followed, wanting to ask more questions about ephebus mortem, his friends, and the Agency. But he waited, hoping the place they were headed would answer those questions for him. He continued to take in his surroundings as he went over what he'd heard so far. The Agency—a secret organization established by the late Christian Albright to protect the human race—was based inside the wrecked hull of the largest section of the ninth belt. Above it was Memorial Park, a tourist attraction used to distract and disguise the Agency's location below.

It appeared that the Agency was mobilizing for something big. Training operations were taking place, and supplies were being loaded onto large freighters across several hanger bays.

"What's going on here?" Jet whispered.

"Later," Solan hissed, "No talking right now."

Finally, they arrived at the end of a corridor. A pair of massive steel doors stood in front of them.

"After you," Tyberius said, watching Jet closely.

Jet glanced at Solan, who had no expression on her face. He opened the doors and walked apprehensively into the room beyond.

CHAPTER

The Hall of Prisms

ΑΒΓΔΕΖΗΘΙΚΛ<u>Μ</u>
ΝΞΟΠΡΣΤΥΦΧΨΩ

NEITHER TYBERIUS NOR Solan followed Jet inside as the doors closed behind him with a soft thump. It took several seconds for his eyes to adjust to the dim lighting inside the room. In the center of the circular hall stood a large round table that immediately captured his attention. A circular skylight refracted the moonlight like a large prism and doused the table with the colors of the light spectrum. Jet walked around the room and counted twenty-four empty chairs. The wooden table looked ancient, and it was checked and cracked around the edges like an old log exposed to the elements for too long. There was a massive split right down the middle, which Jet assumed was from the stress of time, and it was held together by some invisible anti-gravitational force. Roughly carved symbols and numerals aligned directly in front of each chair.

Jet took a quick step backward when he finally realized what he was looking at. It was an exact match to the painting called *The Plan*. It was also the same table he'd seen in the painting called *The Verification*.

After a second stroll around it, he began to notice the walls of the space. There were several paintings highlighted by the dim light. He recognized the iridescent brushstrokes immediately as Shiloe Van Saint's work. He moved closer to one in particular, which depicted a red sky with thunderclouds rolling across an open plain. Lightning flashed ominously in the background. In the foreground, a disembodied hand held a torch that sputtered in the wind. Chills ran down his spine as the scene came to life, immersing him into the fury of the storm.

"I imagine Lybra would love to get her hands on these paintings."

Jet turned to see Tyberius and Solan finally enter the chamber. "You know Lybra?" he asked.

"I know of her," Solan said. "She's well connected, but more of an annoyance than anything."

"You don't need to worry about her anymore," Tyberius added. He touched the back of each empty chair with his fingertips as he walked around the room.

The door opened again, and a lady walked in and stood next to Solan. Jet recognized her glowing eyes as the other cloak who'd accompanied Solan and rescued him. With her hood pulled down and scarf lowered, he thought he knew her face, but had trouble placing it.

"You still look a bit confused," the lady said.

Jet knew her voice, and a look of wonder crossed his face. "Detective Marsh?"

"That's right. My real name is Jinnie Dinn, but my friends call me DiJinn," she said with a grin and chuckle. "I'm sorry I couldn't be more direct with you earlier. But, I think you'll understand why in a moment."

Her facial features were different than what he remembered, but somehow it was still her.

"How's it possible?" Jet asked. "You have E.M., but how do you disguise your eyes… and your face?"

"We can discuss that later," DiJinn said. "There are more important issues right now."

"Can you at least tell me what you said to Cutter?" Jet asked.

DiJinn looked at Tyberius and Solan. Tyberius gave her a nod. "I told him not to worry, you'd be alright," she said.

"So, you lied to him?" Jet said.

"Did I?" DiJinn smirked. "Here you are, safe and sound."

Jet shook his head. "Does that mean I get to go back and finish college?"

DiJinn crossed her arms and bowed her head. "I'm afraid it doesn't work like that. I know this is confusing. It took time for all of us to accept it, too. Hopefully, it'll all make sense once we've explained."

"Alright, I'm listening," Jet said. "Let's get to the point. I'm guessing we're in this room for a reason?"

"This is known as the Hall of Prisms," Tyberius said. "As you can see, it gets very little use these days. Christian Albright built this table."

"But this table must be centuries old," Jet said. "Is this a joke?"

Solan sat down at one of the chairs and leaned back. "No, it's not a joke."

"This table is much older than a few centuries," Tyberius said. "It was built by Albright, only that wasn't his name back then. But names aren't important right now." Tyberius motioned to the empty chairs around the table. "Albright was different—we're all different, including you. That much is evident. What I'm about to tell you will be difficult to understand, but it's time you learn the truth." Tyberius paused and motioned to a seat near the far end of the table. "Why don't you take a seat… that one over there will do."

Jet looked at the chair Tyberius pointed out. Etched into the table and directly in front of the chair was a large symbol that resembled the letter M. Jet eyed it curiously and sat down. As he settled in, he felt as if his soul was being ripped from his body, and he lost all sense of consciousness.

He floated over his person in an out-of-body experience. He stood on an immense field, the tall grass beaten down and trampled around him. The ground was littered with the gore of battle… bodies, blood, and broken weapons. In his left hand was a large golden shield and in his other hand was a spear. Whatever had just happened, he'd been a part of it.

Jet released the spear and shield and let them fall to the ground. There were others nearby, sifting through the dead for survivors. Somehow, he knew these people, like they were his family. Like sensing the presence of a loved one in a dream, he felt connected to them through an unbreakable bond.

Jet's vision grew hazy, and the dream ended just as quickly as it had materialized. He was back, sitting in the chair and gasping for breath. "What just happened?" he asked.

Tyberius watched Jet closely for a second and then nodded to Solan and DiJinn as if he had known something all along. "That was a glimpse of a memory from your past. It's something you'll become more familiar with over time." Tyberius took a seat at the opposite end of the large table. "Every seat in this room was once occupied. This chair is mine, that one belongs to you. It was Albright's greatest hope that we might all continue to work together in peace. Sadly, that vision never came to be."

"Who exactly are we?" Jet asked.

Tyberius stood and pushed in his chair. "Look at my eyes. They're similar to yours but different in color, are they not?"

Jet remembered the color wheel in the painting called *The Plan* and its correlation to the symbols. Tyberius's chair was near the one o'clock position of the table. The colored wheel coincided with the color of his eyes and his chair's location, just like in the painting. "These symbols, they match the color spectrum."

"The color spectrum correlates with us," Tyberius corrected him. "These symbols, which most people refer to as the Greek alphabet, are, in reality, our given names. That system was developed and modified somewhere around 800 B.C. by Albright—again, that wasn't his name at that time. Eventually, mankind adopted the symbols as a form of communication, and its real meaning was soon forgotten. That was over three thousand years ago."

Jet glanced at Solan, who sat statuesque just a few chairs down and seemed to be meditating. DiJinn stood quietly behind a chair at the three o'clock position with a vacant stare.

Jet looked at the table again. "This looks like a time dial, but with twenty-four hours."

"It was never meant to be a functional clock, at least not in the way a sun or moon dial works," Tyberius said, placing his hands behind his back and strolling around the table. "Albright was asked many times why he designed it this way, of which he claimed to have no recollection. So, it remains a mystery. We are an ancient race known as the Heliographi, twenty-four entities who have traveled through time. Each spirit seeks out a specific type of persona that fits its preference and then resides within that person's soul. This table, or color spectrum, as you call it, is a key element in our history and perhaps one of the oldest pieces of our lineage."

Tyberius paused to gather his thoughts. "There are said to be many links to our past, and this table is just one of them. The *Book of Vishmu* is another, although there are several copies of it floating around. It's hard to say what Albright's true intentions were when he built this particular artifact."

Jet stood and walked around to stand in front of a triangle-shaped symbol. "This represents you?" he asked, pointing at it.

Tyberius nodded from across the room. "Try to understand that we are physical beings, just like anyone else. But there is a part of us that has been around for much longer than any language or alphabet. We know which symbol represents each of us because of the color spectrum." Tyberius motioned to the individual symbols etched into the table's perimeter. He paused momentarily before glancing at Solan in what seemed to be a nervous expression. Solan quickly looked away.

"The light of day," Tyberius continued, directing Jet's attention back to the table, "And the dark of night. These have been around since the beginning of time. There has always been a delicate balance in the universe. Most people don't realize how important this balance really is. Without it, we would not exist. Look where your symbol falls in relation to the others."

Jet's symbol was on the cusp of what Tyberius referred to as the 'light' and the 'dark.' The top and the bottom of the chart seemed to be the dividing line, the major split in the table running roughly from the 12 o'clock position to the 6 o'clock position. Jet assumed that the twelve symbols on the left side made up the evening hours, and the twelve symbols on the right side represented the daylight hours. His symbol, the M, was just on the right cusp of the division. Next to it was Vail's symbol, the N. But hers was on the left side. So was Bo's, based on their eye color.

He suddenly grasped what Tyberius was trying to tell him. The thought hit him like a thunderbolt, and he leaned forward to rest his head on the table. "Vail… and Bo, too?" he whispered.

Solan stood and turned away. "Joshia… she was also a close friend of mine—I know what it feels like."

Tyberius bowed his head, giving Jet a moment before speaking. "Balance is sometimes difficult, and we have all suffered because of it. You are not alone."

It felt as if the life had been sucked from him. So much had happened to him over the course of the semester, and now this. He had already lost his friends once, only to learn that briefly, they were still alive. His hopes had soared momentarily but plummeted again. He wondered if this was perhaps a fate worse than death for Bo and Vail.

Jet stood and walked over to one of the windows. He stood there, staring out at the clouds and moonlight beyond. The others remained silent, giving him time.

His hands were shaking. He couldn't stop thinking about his friends. Vail, with her non-apologetic attitude and in-your-face personality, had just seemed to turn the corner in their last conversation. He had felt more connected to her than ever before. And although he'd not really had the chance to get to know Bo better, he felt there was a bond between them he couldn't explain.

"What will happen to them?" he asked, sitting down at the table again and tracing the etched form of the letter N next to him. Splinters from the table pricked his finger, causing it to bleed. He welcomed the pain.

"They have very little choice," Tyberius said bluntly, perhaps realizing that being direct was the best approach. Solan clenched her fists.

"Very little choice?" Jet asked.

"They can convert or die," Tyberius said, leaning on the table for support. "They can fight it, but it would likely kill them."

Jet pounded the table with his fist. The thud echoed around the rotunda room. The others waited silently, pensively. "That's not fair. They didn't ask for this! And now you're saying they have no choice?"

"I never said any of this was fair. It's just the way things are and always have been," Tyberius said firmly. "None of this is easy, for any of us. We've all known others who ended up on the other side of the spectrum."

"You said they don't have a choice, Bo and Vail," Jet said. "But what about us? What choice do we have?"

"We have the freedom to choose," Tyberius said, his head still bowed. "But know that if you don't go through the conversion ritual before the age of twenty-four, the spirit inside of you will leave. Then you would likely die."

Jet shook his head and chuckled. "Well, that doesn't sound like much of a choice either."

"At least you get to make that decision, unlike our colleagues," DiJinn said.

"How are you still alive?" Jet asked Tyberius. "You're older than twenty-four."

"I was a Heliographi long before the Prism Affect was set into motion. Things are different now, since our eyes began to glow. If I were to pass away, the same would be true for me the next time. I would have to go through the conversion ritual before I turned twenty-four years old or die."

Jet stood again and shook his head, trying to understand everything he'd just heard. He took a deep breath and decided to move on from thinking about Bo and Vail. "What caused this table to split?" he asked. "It doesn't look natural."

"We are part of a dispute," Tyberius said. "One that's been going on for a very long time—"

"A dispute?" Solan interrupted. "Is that what you call it, father?" She had been mostly quiet throughout the conversation, but Jet could see this was a sore point with her.

"Solan, not now," Tyberius said, holding up a hand for silence. She looked defiantly back at the table.

"We haven't always been at odds with the Atrum," Tyberius continued. "In fact, there was a time when we were at peace with each other, working as one to discover our origins. But a little over two thousand years ago, something happened that caused us to go our separate ways. We made a pact and have had very little contact with the Atrum until recently, when the pact was broken."

Solan spoke up again. "Remember that I told you it wasn't my place to interfere when Vail was taken?" she said. "That was a part of the pact. We've held true to our word and not interfered in their affairs, but the Atrum haven't." A look of anger flashed in her eyes, but she quickly subdued it. "The murder of Van Saint and Albright, not to mention the outright attack on you, proves that our suspicions were correct all along."

Jet kept glancing over at the symbols next to him. *Vail and Bo were his sworn enemies?* He could hardly believe it. As odd as it sounded, Tyberius, DiJinn, and Solan believed that some sort of entity was living inside of their physical being—inside of everyone who had ephebus mortem, in fact. He felt numb as he looked at the empty chairs.

"Over the course of time, bonds are developed," Tyberius said, seeming to read Jet's thoughts. "The shadows that took Vail and

Bo have a special bond with them, similar to the one you possess with your warden, which I'm sure Solan has already mentioned to you—"

"But why?" Jet asked. "Why would the Atrum want to murder me when I haven't done anything to them?"

"As far as we know, the spirit of a Heliographi cannot be destroyed, only slowed down," Solan explained. "But it takes time for us to realize, develop, and utilize our abilities. Imagine if all the mature Lucem were gone or missing. Who would be left to oppose the Atrum?"

"So, you believe that the Atrum are trying to kill us off in order to slow us down?" Jet asked, hearing the sarcasm in his own voice.

"We believe that is only part of their scheme," Solan said.

"The second painting you saw called, *The Plan,* is a bit of a mystery," Tyberius said. "The red streaks of blood were no accident. We believe they are actually clues. Everything about that painting was done intentionally, planned out well before Van Saint's murder."

Jet closed his eyes, trying to visualize the painting again. It matched the table exactly, from what he could tell, even the fractures and cracks.

"No one fully understands what the painting means," Tyberius continued. "We only know that it involves the Atrum and the Lucem. Right now, the Atrum probably know as much as we do."

"Whatever Van Saint was trying to tell us through that painting, it frightens the Atrum," Solan continued. "Sybold, their leader, came after you personally tonight in order to eliminate what they perceived as a threat."

"The pact was broken the instant Van Saint was murdered,"

Tyberius said. “The table was sundered in half as you can see. That’s what set the Prism Affect into motion.”

“What exactly is the Prism Affect?” Jet said. “I’ve heard that term before, but not in that way.”

“That’s just the name Albright gave it,” Tyberius said. “Our physical appearance wasn’t always like this, at least not our eyes. This key event was set in motion by several smaller ones, and we have only witnessed the beginning of it, I’m afraid. Van Saint willingly acted as the martyr. Next, the final brushstroke was from Albright’s own blood. And finally, Sybold was the murderer. But, we’re still not certain what the true purpose of the Prism Affect is. Only that it has affected us all in a way that we don’t understand. Perhaps Albright and Van Saint knew the true reason. And, it’s said that a Heliographi—one who is a skylight fallout—would set the second phase of the Prism Affect into motion. We’d assumed that was you. But since nearly all of us are skylight fallouts, we don’t know for certain who it is. That’s the big question now—who is the skylight fallout?”

“So, there’s a next phase to this whole thing?” Jet asked.

“It’s rumored there are to be four phases. The first act has already taken place… Van Saint’s murder. But when or how the next phase will occur, Albright wouldn’t say,” Tyberius said. “Perhaps he remains in hiding to keep that secret intact. Perhaps he didn’t know. Who can say?”

Jet sat in silence. A large portion of the mystery had been revealed to him. Tyberius, DiJinn, and Solan said nothing, allowing the weight of it to settle in.

“If I’m a part of this, then why did you wait until the last minute to come get me?” Jet finally asked. “You could’ve pulled me out at any time.”

At this Tyberius began pacing the room again. “We realized

some time ago that you were in danger, so we've been watching over you throughout the semester. The Atrum have become increasingly aggressive, something you've witnessed. We waited as long as we could, hoping to avoid making a move. We sent Solan and DiJinn out for you, but they were thrown off by the storm and almost didn't reach you in time. Thankfully, Solan was able to slip you some help that probably saved your life."

"The Book of Vishmu?" Jet asked.

"Do us a favor and keep quiet about that, won't you?" Tyberius said with a wink.

Jet nodded.

"Some people in the Agency disagree with what we did by pulling you out of the Academy so soon. There was quite an uproar over it," Tyberius said.

Jet remembered the argument he'd witnessed at the abandoned factory. At the time, he had no idea it was because of him.

"Remember, we were only supposed to protect you," Solan said. "Instead, we went against one of our directives and pulled you in very early, something that's been in place for nearly a century. Never has a student on the Lucem side been pulled in so soon."

"I thought ephebus mortem finally had me," Jet admitted.

"Jet, ephebus mortem is a made-up term to help protect our secret," DiJinn said. "It was a ploy developed by Albright after Van Saint was murdered. Its sole purpose is to help hide us. When it's time to bring in a Heliographi, fabricated stories are leaked by the Agency in order to carry on the myth of ephebus mortem," Solan said. "Regardless of whether it is the Lucem or the Atrum."

"Sounds like the Agency is pretty good at fabricating stories," Jet said. "Why doesn't the Atrum just expose us?"

"Why would they?" Solan replied in a matter-of-fact tone. "It would only expose them, too. Besides, they aren't concerned about such petty things."

"So how long have these cover-ups been taking place?"

"Well over a century," Tyberius said, leaning against the table and crossing his arms. His hands disappeared into the folds of his cloak as he spoke. "And I've been helping with them since the very beginning."

Jet gave Tyberius a puzzled look and then glanced at Solan. "Exactly how old are you, sir?"

"Older than I appear," Tyberius said with a wink. "But not nearly as old as Albright was."

"Not as old?" Jet asked, his eyes narrowing. "How old was he?" Once again Jet noticed the slight hesitation on Tyberius's weathered face.

"Albright lived much longer than you know, but under many different aliases. Everyone was led to believe he lived a normal life. When the conversion ritual takes place, at whatever age that person is, their aging ceases from that point on."

"How old?" Jet asked again, feeling as though he deserved to know, especially after everything he'd been through that semester.

"Three millennia… perhaps longer," Tyberius answered. "Though, no one knew exactly how old, not even him. But after his assassination ten years ago, he is now physically starting over in a new host."

Jet shook his head in disbelief. "He was a Heliographi, which means he's still alive, right?"

"His spirit is, yes," Solan said.

"What help is a child against the Atrum?" Jet said.

"Don't underestimate him," Tyberius said, "The Atrum won't,

you can be sure of that. Albright has the unique ability to remember his past with greater clarity than most other Heliographi, which makes him a dangerous adversary, no matter what his age."

"But you said he couldn't even remember why he built this table."

"Yes, that's true," Tyberius agreed. "When a Heliographi passes away, their memory is conveyed through glimpses, like the one you just experienced. Somehow Albright, and Sybold, have discovered a way to recall their past with much greater clarity. They are the only two that we know of who can see far into their past. But even they are limited."

Jet sat in silence for a while, almost forgetting the others were there. His fatigue had come and gone, and he was beyond exhausted now. His head started spinning suddenly, and it lulled forward onto the table. Then, he felt someone shaking him gently and speaking his name. He opened his eyes to see Tyberius, DiJinn, and Solan standing over him.

"Well," Tyberius said, giving his shoulder a squeeze. "I think that will do for tonight. We can finish the rest of our discussion tomorrow."

"Tomorrow..." Jet mumbled, trying to think through his grogginess. "What am I supposed to do now? I can't go back to the university. I assume I no longer exist?"

"As for what we're going to do next," Solan said. "We need to start your practice sessions. I'll be handling that. You have a lot to learn."

"I've taken care of the news reports," DiJinn said. "You won't be able to go out into public now without your alias."

"Remember, there are spies everywhere, even here within the Agency," Tyberius said. "The Lucem must trust each other now, and you have to be careful what you say and do. Keep what you know close to your heart and close your mind to others. There is no compromising on this, Jet. You must take an oath if you remain with us."

"Alright," Jet said. He rubbed his eyes and stood. Then something else occurred to him. "What exactly is Vishmu?"

Tyberius stopped in front of the door. "The oath first, then the conversion. It must be sealed before we go through this door. This won't be pleasant."

Jet nodded. "Okay, fine. Nothing's been pleasant lately. Just tell me what to do."

"Just read my thoughts," Tyberius said.

Jet chuckled. "You're joking, right?"

"You've been practicing, haven't you?"

"To save my life!" Jet said. "So, it was more like a crash course. I haven't quite got the hang of it yet."

"Come, stand here," Tyberius said in a serious tone.

Jet had been hoping for a warm bed and some sleep, but apparently, it wasn't meant to be just yet. "What should I say?" he asked, standing in front of Tyberius.

"I want you to *say* nothing. I want you to *think* everything. Remember what you've learned," Tyberius said encouragingly, lowering his voice to a whisper until it was barely audible. His voice continued to resonate inside Jet's mind.

Jet stood straight, letting his breath slow and his pulse relax, the way the manuscript had instructed. He felt his body start to float and his mind lengthen out.

Tyberius waited patiently with his eyes closed.

Jet focused his thoughts toward the end of the tunnel in front of him.

You realize that meeting Sterllar was no accident, Tyberius began the conversation.

Father, Solan pleaded, *she deserves to know. She's your daughter.*

And you should know better! It was the first time that Tyberius had raised his tone. Jet sensed that he was in the middle of a family dispute, the awkward feeling made him uncomfortable.

Solan was about to retort but stopped and closed her mind defiantly. Jet could no longer feel her presence, and only Tyberius's thoughts were open to him now.

After a moment, Tyberius continued. *Although Sterllar was valuable in helping you, she should not be involved any further in this. Hopefully, the journal and the location of the stacks will not bring her into harm's way.*

I have the journal. Jet had to focus to make the psychic speech work, and he imagined that it sounded broken.

Good, it should be destroyed. Now, to answer your question. Tyberius relaxed slightly and turned away from the door. He took a moment, rubbing his chin before continuing. *Vishmu is a complicated practice and one that ties in with what we have already discussed. It is a state of mind that allows us to realize our deepest potential.*

And what about the Heliographi Memoirs? Jet asked.

The memoirs are said to be based more on science and technology, not psionics. Albright recorded them onto parchment and then hid them away. Some people question whether he actually finished them.

He wrote his memoirs on paper? Jet didn't understand this. Paper could be ruined easily.

Albright had his own reasons. But, if the Atrum ever found those documents, I fear it would not be a good sign for us.

Then it's a race to locate them? Jet thought.

I suppose so. He obviously went to great lengths to keep such knowledge out of the wrong hands.

What was in the Memoirs that's so important? Jet said.

"Some people believe that it's a weapon," Tyberius said, talking openly now. "But of course, everything is speculative, since Albright never talked about it, even to me."

"It is a race, one that the Agency should have no part in," Solan commented, joining the conversation again. "No doubt you've noticed all the activity around here, though they have other ventures going on too."

Jet nodded, remembering the military preparations he had seen taking place.

"Several groups are seeking the lost pages of the Memoirs and their secrets," Solan said. "Some are rogue outfits, splinter cells from the Agency, lone wolves… they have no idea what they're involved in."

"Does that include Lybra?" Jet asked.

"Of course," Solan said. "She has the money to fund some of these outfits. These people understand nothing!"

"That's enough, Solan," Tyberius said in a tired voice as if he had dealt with this issue before. Solan quieted, leaning back against the table and crossing her arms.

"Does this have anything to do with the painting down in the stacks?" Jet asked.

Tyberius looked at him and raised his eyebrows. "I'm not aware of any paintings down there," he said.

Jet glanced at Solan. She had her head bowed and was shuffling her feet nervously. "I… found a painting down there. I'm pretty sure Van Saint did it. In fact, this table was in it." Jet said, nodding at the sundered wooden table.

*"The Verification!"*Tyberius stood to attention and leapt toward Jet. "Are you certain? It was said to have been destroyed."

Jet paused, glancing at Solan again. She gave him a quick pleading look and shook her head imperceptibly. "I… just happened to stumble onto it while studying one day. Luck, I suppose," Jet said.

"Hmm… an ingenious place to hide it, actually," Tyberius said. "Van Saint was a prophet, and many of her paintings hold secrets that have yet to be discovered. It would be unfortunate if it fell into the wrong hands."

"I didn't stick around long enough to see much of it," Jet said. "There was more math and other symbols, though. Cord discovered a numerical pattern in the painting called, *The Plan*."

"Did he?" Tyberius asked.

"Yes," Jet said. "He worked through what he called a 'math riddle' and came up with a number."

"Which was?" Solan asked with her arms crossed.

"It was 2,412,630," Jet replied, hoping that it would make sense to them.

Tyberius leaned back and rubbed his chin thoughtfully before shaking his head. "Perhaps Albright might have known, but that number means very little to me."

"Lybra sure wanted that information badly," Jet said. "She seemed to think it had something to do with the future of the human race."

"Well, I guess we'll just have to ask Cord ourselves then." Solan said.

The doors to the chamber swung open, and Jet turned and look directly into Cord's glowing greenish-yellow eyes.

CHAPTER

Lights of the Soul

ΑΒΓΔΕΖΗΘΙΚΛ<u>Μ</u>
ΝΞΟΠΡΣΤΥΦΧΨΩ

"YOU LOOK LIKE you've just seen a ghost, my friend," Cord said with a hint of sarcasm. But he smiled his crooked smile and held out his hand.

Jet rushed over and picked Cord up in a huge bear hug. He tackled him to the ground and couldn't stop smiling. "Cord! You're here!"

"Easy, Jet," Cord chuckled. "What did you expect?" Cord's right hand stole Jet's attention when he shook it. A gaping hole opened in the middle of his palm, clean through and cauterized. But the most shocking thing was the light pouring from the recent wound.

Jet set Cord down and clapped him on the back. Then his smile faded as he pointed at the light flooding from Cord's palm. "Someone had better explain to me what's going on."

"Relax, it's all part of the process," Cord said. "You barely even feel it."

"I was wondering when the unpleasant part was supposed to kick in," Jet said.

"Well, it does sting a bit," Cord agreed.

Jet was beginning to reconsider, though. "You said we have a choice? Is this the conversion ritual you mentioned?"

Tyberius nodded. "Yes, you do have the choice. Make it now."

"Jet, this is remarkable, actually. You should consider it. Besides, I could use a friend." Cord looked and sounded more enthusiastic than Jet remembered.

"What exactly is this process?" Jet asked. "This seems a bit archaic, don't you think?"

"We all have an inner light, or more specifically, our soul has a light. That is to say, every being in the universe does," Tyberius explained.

"But a Heliographi's light is different," Solan said. "It burns much brighter, more so just before conversion."

"Lights of the soul?" Jet asked.

"Yes, well, the ritual is actually the Lighting of the Soul," Tyberius said.

"And what does that thing do, release the soul?" Jet pointed at the metallic device Tyberius was holding. "Is it another one of Albright's inventions?"

Tyberius nodded. "Yes, ever since the Prism Affect occurred. Back in the old days, it was much more painful. Still, this is what some consider the unpleasant part."

Cord, Solan, DiJinn, and Tyberius stood looking at Jet, the moonlight from the table behind them creating a halo effect in the background. Jet was tired, hungry, and nursing a headache now. He no longer cared about what happened—he would worry about it tomorrow.

"Let's just get it over with," he said and held out his right hand. In the next instant, there was a burning sensation in his palm.

He gritted his teeth from the pain and experienced something Tyberius had called a glimpse. A flood of memories shot through his mind at light speed. It was too fast for him to stop and rewind or pause. He felt as if eons had passed in the blink of an eye. He knew certain things—secrets that people shouldn't know. He felt stronger, more agile, more aware of his surroundings. If this was Vishmu, he wanted more.

A few minutes later, he was lying on his back, the others standing over him. Cord fanned Jet with his hands, Tyberius held his arm, Solan slapped his cheek, and DiJinn stood behind them, laughing her head off.

"Alright, already. I'm okay," Jet mumbled.

"And just like that, he's back," Cord said.

· • • • • ● • • • • ·

Jet slept better that night than he had the entire semester. He spent most of the next morning simply gawking at the hole in his right hand. Light streamed through it as if someone had left a light on behind a cracked door. A brilliant, turquoise light that matched his eyes pulsed when he held his hand to his heart, though there was no warmth or heat. If he looked closely, he could see a faint letter M through the haze. He had no idea how he was supposed to conceal it, but the others seemed to have found a way. He made a note to ask Solan or DiJinn.

The following evening, Jet and Cord were allowed to go back to the university, but only with Solan and DiJinn. "You still have a lot to learn, and we can't afford to lose anyone at this point," Tyberius told them. "You need to say goodbye to your old life. It may be nothing more than a symbolic gesture, but it will help you move on to the next stage of your new life."

The next morning, they prepared to board Solan's skiff. Tyberius pulled Jet aside to explain a few last-minute details.

"You must keep our conversation a secret, as well as these items." Tyberius held out a ring and a cloak. "These are rightfully yours. Take care of them, and they will take care of you."

Jet examined them. The ring was plain with a copper hue, and a holographic 'M' floating above it. When he put the ring on, the hole in his hand disappeared, and his flesh appeared to mend. Then the most amazing thing happened—his eyes were normal, and his appearance changed. Jet assumed this was the alias DiJinn had mentioned, and it explained how she'd been able to work as a detective. When he put the ring on his left hand, however, the effect no longer worked. The cloak and scarf were way more interesting, though, and matched the ones the others wore. Its fabric was unlike anything he'd ever seen. It had a weathered feel, as though it were centuries old, and hundreds of glowing glyphs formed a tapestry in some ancient language around it. Jet didn't understand its meaning, but he intended to learn it.

Solan urged them into the waiting skiff, and soon they were on their way back to Skylight University.

"How do you both feel?" Solan asked, maneuvering the skiff out of the hangar bay. Her tone portrayed very little sense of emotion in it, which Jet was already getting used to.

"Better, thanks," Jet replied, looking out the window of the skiff as they accelerated to cruising speed. Cord sat in the back, legs crossed and long spidery fingertips rubbing his upper lip. DiJinn sat next to him, lost in thought.

"Can I ask you something?" Jet said.

She nodded but didn't look at him.

"Why was your father so upset about Albright?"

"Everyone was upset," Solan said flatly.

"I know, but it seemed…" Jet trailed off, tapping his leg and trying to think of the right words. "Almost like there was more to it."

"You're perceptive," she commented and turned to look intently at him. "Perhaps Vishmu has already heightened your awareness."

"What does Vishmu have to do with it?" Jet asked.

"The practice of Vishmu has many side effects; a heightened sense of awareness is just one of them," Solan answered. "In fact, some can even detect when others are lying."

"And what are the other side effects?"

"Haven't you wondered how I move so quickly?"

Jet sat forward abruptly. "So, that's why?"

"Strength, dexterity, longevity—our entire physical being improves the more we train with Vishmu."

Jet considered this. Apparently, the practice of Vishmu was more potent than he had realized.

"To answer your question, my father was Albright's warden." Solan's eyes flashed dangerously as she spoke. "The night Albright was assassinated, Tyberius was away on assignment and still hasn't forgiven himself. He's made it his personal crusade to locate Albright before the Atrum do."

"The Atrum would kill Albright if they found him?" Jet asked.

"Most certainly," Solan said. "Even though he's a child, it would take some effort, though."

"How did the assassination happen?" Jet asked, curious how a man who had lived for millennia and practiced Vishmu for so long could have been so careless.

"He wasn't careless," Solan said.

Jet flushed with embarrassment and closed off his thoughts.

"Someone inside the Agency betrayed us," Solan continued and pounded the skiff's console. "He was in his study that night. There was more than one person involved, and they were in and out before anyone knew what happened."

"That explains your father's mistrust of the Agency," Jet said.

"Mistrust is a strong word," Solan said. "We haven't completely given up hope on the Agency, though. Maybe they're compromised, but there are still good people involved. Vigilance is what we need now."

He tried to remember everything they had discussed in the Hall of Prisms, but it was difficult, and parts of their long conversation felt like a dream. "Your father seemed surprised to hear about the painting in the stacks. Why didn't you tell him about it?"

Solan sighed. "Ever since I found that painting my senior year, I've kept it a secret. I didn't even record it in my journal. For ten years I've tried to decipher it. Every chance I get, I'm down in the stacks. It's personal, I suppose," Solan said. "But the math is too advanced, even for me. We'll have Cord look at it when he's ready." Solan glanced back at Cord, who had his eyes closed and was in deep meditation.

"So, you told Cord where it was, and he left me the clue?" Jet said.

Solan nodded.

"Does that mean you're leaving it in the stacks?" Jet asked.

"I had a talk with my father last night about that, and he agrees, bringing it to the Agency right now might be a mistake.

It's well hidden for now, and no one knows its location but us. Perhaps it's best to leave it undisturbed."

"These paintings that have holographic messages in them," Jet asked. "How is it that Heliographi can see them when no one else can?"

"It was developed by Albright and infused with Van Saint's special brand of painting. That's about all we really know since Albright never talked about it. Our cloaks, however, work differently. The fabric bends light, something Albright developed long ago, and the Atrum have managed to replicate it."

Jet listened half-heartedly as Solan explained, but his thoughts were on Vail, Bo, and most of all Cutter.

"You worry too much about him," Solan said.

Jet turned to look at her. "Could you please stop reading my thoughts?"

"We'll have to work on that, won't we," Solan said in a serious tone. "Relax, Cutter is fine. No harm will come to him."

"I'm sure he can handle himself," Jet said. "I just feel bad for him, I guess."

"Why?"

Jet looked at Solan. "He's like you, I think. He lost a sibling a long time ago and has never really gotten past it. With me around, I think it gave him a purpose. He had feelings for Vail, and I don't know how he'll handle that either."

Solan nodded as if it were a minor setback. "As I said, the Lucem will keep an eye on him. That may become one of your responsibilities when you're ready."

"I've been wondering about something," he asked. "What does the term Heliographi mean?"

"A heliograph is an instrument that reflects sunlight to send signals, typically Morse code. It was invented in the nineteenth century, though some claim that the Ancient Greeks—that would've been us—used their shields to send signals during battle. In truth, Albright coined the term heliograph long before the nineteenth century."

"My glimpse was about that," Jet said.

"Glimpses can go back a very long time," Solan agreed. "Anyway, as the story goes, we won a decisive battle because of our ability to communicate. Others believed that it was because we used our shields to send signals. But in truth, we were using Vishmu. We were decreed the *Heliograph*, which Albright later appended with a lowercase letter *i*. So nearly four centuries after Albright had devised the Greek alphabet, we were finally given a name—The Heliographi. To most people, we are a legend, a myth. Only a few people know the real truth about us."

"People like Lybra?" Jet mumbled.

"Not surprisingly," Solan said with a look of distaste. "Some find it a fascinating fairytale, and ephebus mortem would be right up her alley."

Soon they were entering the university's airspace and hovering over a clearing called Clipton Point. Solan landed the craft gently on the blanket of snow. Cord finally stirred from his meditation and leapt out deftly, followed by DiJinn. Jet clambered out of the cockpit after him.

"Remember what my father told both of you," she said. "I'll be around, just in case you need me. So will DiJinn."

"Thank you," Jet said, "Thanks for saving my life, Solan."

"When the time comes, I expect you to do the same for others." She reached inside of her cloak and pulled out a bundle. "This was recovered from your warden, Kamber. You'll need it very soon. Guard it with your life."

Jet took the bundle and placed it inside his cloak as Solan powered up the engines. The skiff roared, kicking up eddies of snow, and then disappeared into the gray sky.

Cord and Jet watched the skiff until it was gone.

"Well, I suppose you have your own affairs to see to," Cord said, drawing his cloak around him. He pulled the scarf up and the hood over his face, disappearing from sight. "Stay safe, Jet."

· • • ● ● ● ● ● • • ·

A COLD, BONE-CHILLING mist soaked the campus that day. Jet was practically invisible, wearing the cloak and the scarf. But the campus was crowded again, now that the students were back from the holiday break, and Jet had to be careful not to bump into anyone. Tyberius had only given Cord and Jet a few hours, so he had to be quick.

Even though there was still a considerable amount of snow on the ground, the maintenance crews had cleared the walkways. On his way to Alpha Hall, Jet stopped in front of a towering oak tree, which was completely bare of all its leaves, save one. He looked up at it, noticing how the brown leaf seemed to cling stubbornly to the branch, unwilling to let go even though all the others had. A strong gust of wind howled through the branches, and the leaf finally let go, coming to rest just a few feet in front of him. Jet glanced around, knowing that Solan and DiJinn were watching him closely. He bent down, slipped the leaf inside his cloak, and left.

CHAPTER

Through Cutter's Eyes

ΑΒΓΔΕΖΗΘΙΚΛΜ
ΝΞΟΠΡΣΤΥΦΧΨΩ

CUTTER STOOD ALONE near the front as President Starr spoke from a makeshift podium. It was a small group, and most of the people who'd known Jet hadn't come, afraid of what others might say, perhaps. Even though Jet's body had not been recovered, Plannar was adamant about having a proper funeral for the young point-blazer. When he'd asked for Cutter's help setting it up, he had agreed without hesitation.

For some unknown reason, Jet had taken a university skiff on Christmas night to Skylight City. According to the news report, the skiff had malfunctioned near the outskirts of *The Hydra 7* café and gone down in a field. *Maybe he had been trying to locate that old factory complex again?* Cutter shook his head. He'd gone over their last meeting a thousand times in his head, and how he could've handled it better. Then, out of the blue, Detective Marsh had contacted him right after the game that night. She had asked him to give Jet some time alone. Cutter had been furious with Jet anyway, even though he knew he shouldn't. After some consideration though, he realized Jet was only concerned about him. Cutter had misinterpreted his intent, and felt ashamed now.

Jet shouldn't have had to worry about others when his own life was on the line.

Out of guilt, Cutter had left the holographic message instead of facing Jet. Another impulsive decision... another regretful mistake. After seeing the news report about the crash the next day, everything changed. He didn't know if he could forgive himself. His misdirected anger, his decision to leave when he should've stayed by Jet's side. He had failed his younger brother, Vail, and now Jet.

He had taken time to think, and to grieve. But he couldn't quit, no matter how much he wanted to, though. Jet would never forgive him if he did. His friend's perpetual drive to succeed and bring others together had always inspired Cutter. He wouldn't allow that light to fade. He would carry the torch now.

And now that Jet was gone, he struggled with what to do next. *Should I leave and start over someplace else?* His brief memories of Skylight already seemed cold and foreign. This place would forever be a constant reminder of his failure. But where else would he go? Could he outrun his regrets?

The funeral ended, and President Starr dismissed the handful of people. Gray mist fell softly on the black umbrellas, the light pitter-patter of rain washed down around them, and Cutter felt alone.

He stepped off the platform and shook Plannar's hand. As he left, the clouds broke, the mist dissipated and something caught his eye. A brief flash from atop Alpha Hall made him look up. Then a sunlit prism effect rained down, lasting only a few seconds before it disappeared. Cutter kicked at a few stray leaves blowing across the walkway, and a brief smile eased across his broad face. If Jet was up there, maybe this was his way of saying goodbye.

CHAPTER

A New Leaf

ΑΒΓΔΕΖΗΘΙΚΛ<u>Μ</u>
ΝΞΟΠΡΣΤΥΦΧΨΩ

JET STOOD IN the shadows atop Alpha Hall and watched the funeral. It was New Year's Day, and he was just a footnote in the archives of Skylight University now. He was officially a skylight fallout. It seemed fitting, actually, and it was exactly how he preferred it to end.

He felt his life changing, even at that instant. A transformation was coming, one that would be difficult and almost certainly dangerous. Jet looked at his hand, and the light flowing from the hole in it. He pondered what would become of Bo and Vail and wondered again what would happen if their paths ever crossed. But what he really wanted to do was talk to Cutter and explain everything to him. Console him... *tell him I'm alive and well.*

But he couldn't.

And the more he thought about it, the more he felt that Cutter was better off not knowing. Cutter didn't need any more drama in his life. He'd dealt with enough of it already. Still, maybe someday they would meet again. Jet held on to that hope and swore an oath to protect Cutter, if that time ever came.

He pushed the thought out of his head and reached into the folds of his cloak. He pulled out the leaf and held it in his palm, letting his glowing eyes linger on it. The light from his palm bathed it, shining through the holes in its dead, brown surface.

In a sense, the leaf resembled his old life. He felt fear and uncertainty. He was reluctant to let go, though he would never admit it aloud. There was a new life awaiting him, and he had to be brave enough to accept it. *This was his path now, whether he liked it or not.*

He let the leaf drop and watched it flutter in the breeze. The clouds broke and the sun lit a thousand tiny rain droplets, immersing him in a prism effect. A strong wind swept the leaf away towards the campus below and eventually out of view. Jet pulled his scarf and hood over his head and melded into the background, disappearing from the history books of Skylight University forever. He had taken his first step by letting go. He had turned over his new leaf. What adventures awaited him now were up to fate.

EPILOGUE

An Assassin – 10 Years Prior

<u>A</u>ΒΓΔΕΖΗΘΙΚΛΜ
ΝΞΟΠΡΣΤΥΦΧΨ<u>Ω</u>

Christian Albright sat at his desk, diligently reviewing the work on perhaps his greatest invention. His silver hair had grown long, and he hadn't shaved in several weeks, but none of that mattered anymore. He knew that his time was short, and he needed to hurry to get everything in order. He had been working on this particular project for nearly ninety years; his vow to Shiloe since the day she had been murdered. He was so close to being finished.

But he had known for quite some time now that he wasn't going to finish, so he had taken the necessary steps to ensure that "things" didn't fall into the wrong hands. If he were being honest with himself… he was tired. *Beyond tired.* So many years he'd worked. And now that his beloved Shiloe had been taken from him he no longer had the fire in him to go on. This project had fueled him though, a poor substitute for her warm embrace.

There was only one person who might be able to crack the code he had created. Christian only prayed to God that this person was on the Lucem side. The Atrum had been up to more than just murder over the last century, toying with things much more diabolical. His arch nemesis, Sybold, should know better. But nothing seemed sacred to the Atrum anymore, and Christian would receive no sympathy or mercy.

Albright adjusted his glasses and stood distractedly to look out of his large study window. It was getting late in the day, and he was tired from the painstaking preparations he'd taken over the course of that week. Through the heavy clouds outside of his window, he could see the shattered remnants of the ninth belt gaping at him like steel daggers. Their headquarters, Flotsam, had already passed through the unprotected part of the Skylight System's atmosphere and into the direct sunlight, causing the outside bulkheads of the hull to heat up and expand. Now they were back inside the atmosphere, and the metal hull was contracting back to its normal size with ominous creaks and groans.

He turned and looked at his work one last time before rolling the paper up and tossing it into the fireplace. He had already destroyed the rest of the copies as well and hidden the original memoirs. He smiled when he thought about how furious it would make Sybold. *Oh, to see her face... it was worth the sacrifice. It was all part of the plan.*

Another loud bang issued from the contracting hull and echoed through his study. Christian didn't flinch and continued to stare into the roaring fire. It reflected off his bifocals as he lost himself in thought. He was reminded of that night, over a century ago, when he had said goodbye to Shiloe. At that point, they had been preparing her final painting, *The Plan*. Hidden in it, and two other paintings, was the secret that would prove to be the Lucem's saving grace, assuming he had calculated everything properly. He had needed Shiloe's help to accomplish this and had spent years trying to find her. That had been over one hundred years ago. But finally, he had tracked her to the tiny subterranean settlement of Tuxson Burrough, an area beneath what used to be the great plains of North America. Together they had worked to incorporate his technical magic into the thick brush strokes of her artwork. Their combined collaboration had resulted in the hidden holographic messages, purposely left behind for the other Lucem as a guide. He, of course, didn't need such reminders, but the others would. If their physical form died, their glimpses would be hard to interpret. At first, Albright wasn't sure if the plan would work, but Shiloe's talent was greater than he had realized—she had always been beautiful in that way. He had never possessed such artistic talent, and it was one of the things that had drawn him to her, century after century. But Shiloe had been missing for over one hundred years. He'd felt certain he would have found her by now, especially after they'd set the first phase of the Prism Affect into motion. Even after scouring the entire system, he still hadn't found her and feared for the worst.

Christian placed his hands behind his back and looked at the clock. It was time. He glanced around his study before walking over to stand in front of the massive iron doors.

The study doors nudged open without a sound. Through the opening, four shadows wafted into the room like smoke through a crack. They materialized in front of Christian as he waited calmly. The door closed behind the last one and the latch clicked, locking the five of them in his study.

One of the intruders stepped to the forefront and lowered the hood of its flowing mantle, solidifying as if by magic. The rest did the same. He knew their names by the color of their eyes, even without seeing their symbols.

Silence followed, interrupted by another loud groan from the contracting hull. Christian stared down at the short Atrum in front of him. He reached up slowly and removed his glasses, revealing his glowing red eyes. As if looking into a mirror, Sybold's glowing red eyes looked back at him steadily.

It's been a long time, Albright. Sybold used her thoughts to speak to him.

Indeed, it has. Up to your old ways, I see? he replied in the same way.

Are you prepared? she asked.

As always, he said.

Their telepathic conversation was accompanied by mocking images, but he had blocked his mind off from them. Breaking through his defenses would prove impossible. Only Sybold could match his power in Vishmu, but he knew she wasn't there to mock him.

The first shadow shot forward and struck at Christian's temple for the killing blow. But the old man seemed to dissolve and swept the legs out from beneath the Atrum before it could regain its bearings. The attacker hit the floor with a thud that likely cracked a few ribs. Christian's fist shot down and struck the fallen Atrum, knocking it unconscious, but he didn't kill it. He wanted no blood on his hands tonight—that was not his intent.

The next attack came swiftly as the other two Atrum sprang forward, stepping past their fallen comrade. He was outnumbered but could stand his ground against any Heliographi, and it would take them all to defeat him. Fighting fair wasn't the Atrum's mantra, and Christian knew it. He could have had an army of Lucem with him tonight, but he had a different plan in mind. Tyberius would be angry with himself, but this is how it had to be. He knew what Sybold wanted, and right now, he was the only one capable of foiling her plan, which he had managed to do for thousands of years. He had always been one step ahead of Sybold, something that infuriated her time and time again.

This time though, he would allow her to think she had outfoxed him. He knew the Atrum's inside informant had cleared this entire sector. Deep inside the bowels of the broken ninth belt, no one would witness the event that was about to go down in Heliographi history. The Alpha—the grandfather of the Lucem for the last three thousand years—was about to fall.

Christian leaned against the bulkhead, his breath heavy from fighting the other Atrum. Sybold had only been using them to wear down his strength, knowing he wouldn't kill them. The last Atrum slumped unconsciously from his grasp and dropped to the floor. Christian stood upright as Sybold stepped forward.

He winced, coughing up a bit of blood. "You're here for the memoirs, I take it?"

Sybold's face twisted with rage, suddenly realizing that he had already guessed her plan.

Christian wiped a stray rivulet of blood from his mouth. "There is something I forgot to mention. When you kill me, there will be some very valuable information going with me."

She continued to look at him and considered. "Tell me where the memoirs are, and I'll spare you."

Christian shook his head. "If you agree to undo the damage you've done, then I'll talk." He knew this wasn't possible, though, and she knew it too.

Sybold's hand shot out.

Christian didn't try to parry the deathblow, as if he had already accepted the final outcome. A long second seemed to pass as he stood motionlessly in place. There was one final groan from the hull that echoed around the study as Christian struck the floor in a heap.

Sybold stepped unceremoniously over his body as the other three Atrum began to stir.

"Search the place," she said irritably, knowing they would find nothing. She knew that Albright had been working on his memoirs for more than a century now. She couldn't believe the old man would build a weapon capable of killing other Heliographi. Yet, that's what the fool was attempting to do. If he succeeded, it would mean the end of the Atrum. She would never allow that to happen. A weapon of such magnitude seemed contrary to everything Albright stood for. Perhaps seeing his beloved Shiloe murdered had finally pushed him over the edge.

Her goal was to obtain the memoirs and finish the weapon. Even though no Atrum possessed Albright's ability, there were several of them with the basic knowledge to finish what he'd started. Bofisto, or perhaps Sojahn could do it, and hopefully, they would have a chance very soon. Attaining the memoirs and building the weapon would be the turning point in their long war. Albright hadn't even trusted the other Lucem enough to share his knowledge. That mistake was going to cost him now.

"Over here!" An Atrum held a partially burned piece of paper.

Sybold strode over and took the document from him. Her glowing eyes glinted as she looked at the architectural plans. It was one of the missing pages of the Heliographi Memoirs.

It was the Ion Motivator.

LUCEM
M

CPSIA information can be obtained
at www.ICGtesting.com
Printed in the USA
BVHW030208200322
631458BV00005B/11/J

9 781736 302903